The Guardians of the Sun-Star and Moon-Star

Book Two

The Battle Begins

By

Sylvie Gionet

Sylvie Gionet

Canadian Intellectual Property Office-Certificates of Registration of Copyright Category-literary

Certification Date July 2015–Present License 1123321 (Title) The Guardians of the Sun-Star and Moon-Star (Book I)

Certification Date May 2016–Present License 1130603 (Title) The Guardians of the Sun-Star and Moon-Star–The Battle Begins (Book II)

©The Guardians of the Sun-Star and Moon-Star Part II: The Battle Begins.

Rider-Waite tarot deck public domain 1966

Creativeness by Sylvie Gionet

www.sgionet.com

"ESA/Hubble" Object names/text/content

Special thanks to Laurence O'Bryan and Tanja from BooksGoSocial

Cover Design: By Mirna-BooksGoSocial

Editor: Jacqui Corn-Uys-BooksGoSocial

ISBN: 978-0-9948553-4-3

Character Index and the Story so far...

It began at the Texas observatory, in the department of Astronomy & Astrophysics.

Featuring: Astrophysicist, Gabrielle Gibbor and Astrophysicist, Michael Abba.

Both scientists had made a miraculous discovery in the Texas observatory. Luminous lights shone down from the Orion constellation and guided them to two locations. In Egypt, Gabrielle found a bronze and silver pyramid and inside was The Golden Door. This portal transported Gabrielle to the northern side of a new planet named Varco-XVI. Michael went to South Africa to the Bakoni Ruins and found another portal that transported him to the southern side of a new planet named Varco-XVI. Gabrielle Gibbor and Michael Abba were humans when they arrived, but their lives are now changing. Mighty forces have placed our heroes on a new planet, where a fight for their survival will now begin.

With the discovery of the new planet, a new solar system came to light. This discovery put Project Solar Escape to work with eleven countries around the world joining observatories and scientists to study this new phenomenon. Dr. Knight, head of the project, needed to find a way to reach his two leading scientists who had gone missing on this new planet.

Countries & Messengers

1) Earth: Texas observatory: owner Dr. Knight.

Home base for Project Solar Escape.

Orion Constellation, Lota Orionis, linked to a new purple planet named Varco-XVI.

XXI-World: Ten of crossed Swords: Uriel, and Ariel.

Scientists on board at the Texas Observatory: Astrophysicists Betty Grant, Linda Stevens, and Frank Connors.

Associates to the Texas observatory: Planetary Geologist Dean Briggs and Astro Meteorologist Zach Torn.

2) Egyptian observatory scientist: Ammon Daher.

Orion Constellation, Meissa.

A mysterious planet connected to the bronze and silver pyramid in Egypt and The Golden Door, wherein lay a group of heavenly individuals.

XVI-Tower: Royal Ruler Samuel Raiphualas II.

King of Swords: Metatron & Sandalphon.

XIV-Temperance.

Seven and Eight of Pentacles: III-Empress.

Ace of Cups: Dax.

Osahar and Mira.

Pharaoh and a Queen.

Two dark soldiers.

Taxi driver: Tadeas Almasi.

Dr. Knight's colleagues from the Texas observatory:

Astrophysicists Sandra Collins.

Cosmologist Jimmy Black.

Astronomer George Snider.

3) South African observatory scientist: Andricia Pillay.

The Orion Nebula connected to the Bakoni Ruins and the new planet.

The South African observatory linked up with the bronze and silver pyramid and The Golden Door.

Brigadier General Dineo Davids, and Major General Azille Jansen.

X-Wheel of Fortune: Raziel, bearer of the Fountain of Enlightenment.

IV-Emperor: Hamuel.

Associate: Professor Isaki Lourens.

Nine painted stones in the Bakoni Ruins.

4) Italy observatory scientist: Marco Abelli. Pluto.

Orion Constellation, Mintaka.

XVI-Tower: Royal Ruler Samuel Raiphualas II.

XI-Justice: Ramiel.

5) Canada observatory scientist: Liam Adams.

Orion Constellation, Rigel.

Set of connections, Mercury, and a duplicate in the new solar system.

XX-Judgment: Chamuelle.

VIII-Strength: Raphael.

6) Turkey observatory scientist: Adlet Sezer.

Orion Constellation, Alnitak.

Set of connections, Jupiter, and a duplicate in the new solar system.

V-Hierophant: Sachiel.

XVII-Star: Jophielle.

7) China observatory scientist: Bing Cheng.

Orion Constellation, Alnilam.

Set of connections, Saturn, and a duplicate in the new solar system.

VII-Chariot: Cassiel, bearer of the Tree of Life.

8) Australia observatory scientist: Jacob Jones.

Orion Constellation, Sigma Orionis.

Set of connections, Uranus, and a duplicate in the new solar system.

Queen of Swords: Raguelle.

9) Mexico observatory scientist: Juan Beltre.

Orion Constellation, Betelgeuse.

Set of connections, Neptune, and a duplicate in the new solar system.

Queen of Pentacles: Saffron.

King of Pentacles: Efren.

XIII-Death: Sariel.

10) England observatory scientist: Angela Jones.

Orion Constellation, Bellatrix.

Set of connections, Venus, and a duplicate in the new solar system.

Queen of cups: Anaelle.

11) Austria observatory scientist: Adalard Dorn.

Orion Constellation, Saiph.

Set of connections, Mars, and a duplicate in the new solar system.

XVI-Tower: Royal Ruler Samuel Raiphualas II.

Nestled inside the Triangulum Galaxy on Planet Eugleston:

Dark room: XVI-Tower: Royal Ruler, Samuel Raiphualas II.

Bright room: Ace of Pentacles: Highborn Leader, Galasus Pagasusesia.

The heavenly messengers, and the Imperial Council.

She was Known to the Creator as (II) the High Priestess. Her Divine cards will power a life force to transform the messengers and Guardians into Godly leaders. She holds a crystal ball in one hand, her spirited book and Divine cards remain in the other. Her Divine cards represent Primary cards and her channeling cards are, Cups, Swords, Pentacles, and Wands. In the Triangulum Galaxy on planet Eugleston, inside the great Coliseum and the theater, sit the spectral tapestries. At the beginning of creation, she attached images from her Divine deck of cards to the shadows of all the tapestries.

Her cards have been dealt:

On Varco-XVI: Northern side.

VI-Lovers: Three of crossed Wands: Waxing, waning crescent moon:

Lady Gabrielle.

Queen of Wands: XVIII-Moon: Three of crossed Wands: Solar eclipse: Queen Moon-Star.

The High Priestess.

Superior Spiritual Pagan. Queen of Pentacles: Three of crossed Wands. Saffron.

Female celestial warriors: Seven of crossed Wands.

Followers.

XXI-Hanged Man: Wizards Valda, and Vance.

Queen of Scepters.

III-Empress.

Silver gate, Queen.

On Varco-XVI: Northern and Southern side.

XXI-World: Ten of crossed Swords: Ariel, sacred native spirit animals.

XXI-World: Ten of crossed Swords: Uriel.

On Varco-XVI: Southern side.

VI-Lovers: Three of crossed Swords: Sun symbol: Lord Michael.

King of Wands: XIX-Sun: Three of crossed Swords: Lunar eclipse:
King Sun-Star.

Superior Spiritual Pagan. King of Pentacles: Three of crossed Swords:
Efren.

Seven of crossed Swords: Male celestial warriors.

Followers.

Bronze gate, Pharaoh.

0-Fool: Dante. Four of Pentacles. Six chalices.

Heavenly leader, Paul, and his family.

Grand Temple.

On Varco-XVI: Eastern side.

Associates to the Texas Observatory:

Astrophysicists Josh Knight and Archaeologist Blake Knight.

VII-Chariot: Cassiel.

Celestial warriors.

Followers.

III-Empress.

On Varco-XVI: Western side.

King of Swords: Sandalphon.

Bronze serpent.

Dark tomb two dark entities.

White tomb.

Cloaks and Robes

Rainbow cloak.

Jophielle, shape shifter, double side.

Black cloaks. Heavenly warriors.

Lord Michael, King Sun-Star, Efren, supernatural Pagan,

celestial army, Samuel, Sariel, Raguelle, Hamuel, Sachiel.

Blue robes. Guidance, wisdom, and protection.

Ariel, lion of the heavens. Cassiel, traveler in space time.

White robes. Purity.

Uriel, divine influence, protector. Anaelle, air grounded.

Chamuelle unconditional love.

White and ivory cloaks. Heavenly warriors.

Lady Gabrielle, Queen Moon-Star, Ivory-Saffron, supernatural Pagan.

Raziel, shields the mysteries of the Creator. Ramiel, resurrects,

double-sided Raphael, heals.

White cloaked wizard.

       Valda has an entitlement over the bright side in the book of magic and spells.

Black cloaked wizard

       Vance has an entitlement over the dark side in the book of magic and spells.

       The wizards are double sided.

Are we alone or are we a replicated world power driven by the Gods in the vast universe?

Contents

Chapter One
The Fate of the Realms. When it Began…

Secret superpowers had previously been able to safeguard the celestial realms, but now peace in the universe was no more.

Billions of years ago, the universe developed and advanced beyond the Creator's master plan. Celestial infernos kindled asteroids to quake in outer space, and this was where creation sparked a superior way of life inside the spiraling Triangulum Galaxy. It took place on a planet called Eugleston, where the Creator had placed a series of important seeds to prosper. This spellbinding place delighted the Aristocrats, where they colonized and eventually worshipped their everlasting paradises.

Expansion in the universe ultimately brought to life a bright solar system. Nestled inside the Milky Way Galaxy was a new sun and moon, and it hosted a new planet known as Varco-XVI. Two supreme beings, what we might call Gods, put this new creation into place in the cosmos.

But in the earlier stages, the new solar system orbited a magnificent sun. The value of Varco-XVI became apparent in Royal Ruler Samuel Raiphualas II's thoughts. A Godly man named Sachiel from the paradises became aware of the dealings of Samuel who was one of the highest-ranked Gods alongside of the Creator. Sachiel found Samuel's spirit hovering over Varco-XVI and watched him uncover the dark star hidden inside of him. Sachiel, knowing the importance of this discovery, announced this to Highborn Leader, Galasus Pagasusesia, and the Imperial Council's Emissaries at a meeting. The impressive world and unique solar system that Samuel set up along with of the Creator, now sported life.

Samuel caused pandemonium in the universe.

To understand where this all began, we need to know that in the beginning, on planet Eugleston, the Creator asked two Nobles, in secret, to go to a sheltered place in the heavens. They were to return with two Godly life forms to serve alongside him. So, Samuel and Galasus were born and delivered. The Royals each had control of two tiny but most powerful internal stars. One bright star and one dark star. The Creator kept the children in the privacy

1

of his spacious royal chamber, where the attendants taught the children to grow up in the Creator's likeness.

***

It was time. Their personal assistants placed new clothing on their large, canopied beds. The young men dressed in flowing bronze and silver garments, then put on their rawhide sandals. They were now both old enough to learn the marvels of formation, so the Creator led them to the majestic library. Their eyes widened when they entered a spacious chamber and shone as they noticed the myriad lit sconces lining the stone walls. The lingering fragrance of incense also added to their alertness. They could hear water falling softly near them where it cascaded with a tranquil gentleness on the tall stone wall. Samuel and Galasus stared at the jam-packed room displaying a vast range of wares, predominantly tinted in bronze and silver. High-backed black velvet cushioned chairs surrounded a broad marble table.

"This is where you will study the customs of the Gods," the Creator said and pointed to the ancient scrolls. They both accepted the missive and gazed at the vast stone wall filled with openings stuffed with scrolls. He left them alone so they could both get started.

***

As they matured, Galasus and Samuel studied day and night in the library. The lore of the great Gods and the balancing of the universe prepared the sixteen-year-old boys for their upcoming tasks. This room and the scrolls therein existed solely to them and they were thus able to focus their attention on the ancient scrolls with no interruptions. A feeling of spirited energy filled the room with a desire for wisdom of succeeding alongside the Creator.

***

Samuel and Galasus had both grown into knowledgeable men and flourished into devout examples of their Monarchy and were once again in the room with the scrolls.

Galasus arrived at the last opening in the stone wall. He picked up what he expected to be the final scroll. When he reached the table, he sat to read through it. Then he examined a part of the scripture. It outlined how a bright and dark star can work together and evolve magnificently in the universe to

2

set up evolution. He handed the scroll over to Samuel. They both understood it would be them working closely alongside the Creator.

Samuel got up and stretched his arms and legs. He spotted something flickering inside the last carved-out space on the stone wall. "Galasus, there's another scroll in there, it's at the back."

"Oh, I didn't see it," he replied.

Surrounded by a faint light from a beam shimmering through the window, Samuel walked across the room. He reached into the back section and brought the final scroll back to the table.

"This one is unique," he said, and turned to Galasus. "There's a bronze and silver seal on it, should we break it open?" he asked.

Galasus considered the scroll and the shining seal. "How did I miss that one?" Galasus' eyes grew bigger. "I say yes, crack that seal open."

Samuel cracked the seal, and used both hands to roll out the final scroll. He tugged on Galasus' sleeve to get his attention. "There is no Highborn Leader for the Imperial Council." Samuel watched Galasus as he read aloud and lifted an eyebrow. "The Emissaries have been under the Creator's rule since the beginning of time."

"Well, that explains everything about those Emissaries. They have no leader for their council. They are all over the place and disorganized—here, there, everywhere. Half the time the Creator cannot even locate them. But they are a loyal group and chatty when you can find them standing still." Galasus paused and thought about this position for a moment. Then he listened to Samuel as he went on.

"When new stars are born into Royalty, only one can be a Highborn Leader. Or to go on by the Creator's side of evolution in the universe. I wonder how many made that decision? I have seen no Royals or even a Highborn Leader, have you Galasus?" he asked.

Galasus rolled his eyes, considering he knew as much as Samuel did. "No, I haven't, and I suppose the Imperial Council's obligations are tiresome. They need a leader. The Creator has taken care of us for most of our upbringing. I understand he doesn't want anybody to change us, so perhaps in time we might see other Royals." Galasus leaned over to listen to more.

"Look at this." Samuel flipped over the scroll. "This ancient scroll bears a seal that symbolizes a crest. It's written right here," Samuel said and

3

pointed his finger. "It appears to be a crest for Royal rulers." He touched the script and rubbed it with both hands. He felt the imagery embedded within the scroll as it came into view. "It's our coat of arms and is the same as the mark on our necks. Who would have thought?" Samuel glanced up at Galasus who was deep in thought. So, he recited and listed more. "There is a rule here, Galasus, and it states you must not alter your bright star. Now this is fascinating. You can tailor your dark star to work alongside the Creator or to be a Highborn Leader. I can't find anything else about this, so let us be cautious."

Galasus examined the epitaphs. "We have both read every scroll in this library that rewards us with wisdom, and by now we're both ready for our crowns." Galasus had an inherent aura about him and an understanding passed over him, allowing him to envisage the complete picture. When he looked at it holistically, it was an instant choice. "I need to be the Highborn Leader for the Imperial Council." Galasus knew it must be him. "The Emissaries, in their haste, don't create the best geographical settings on the new planets. The planets don't have any color and they're featureless." Galasus' concern could be heard in his deep voice.

"How do you know that?" Samuel asked.

"Well, I have eavesdropped a few times in the room that is set up for them. One day I noticed nine Emissaries exiting the room. They were rushing through the corridor. So, I snuck in and looked at their final designs for some new planets. It was a huge painting on the wall for the Creator to observe." He stood and flung his arms in the air, then settled his palms on his hips. "They are an unsystematic crowd, and the painting is just too dull." Galasus wrinkled his nose. "The Creator grumbles about them all the time. The council requires proper leadership," he recommended.

"Yes, I have heard the Creator mention the planets have no flora or fauna." Samuel shrugged his shoulders and leaned back into the chair. "And I know where this is going. How can we convert our dark stars?" Samuel gazed at him. "Can you give me some of yours?" he asked.

"Yes, right here." Galasus pointed it out on the scroll. "Your bright and dark star can work alongside my dark star. This sequence can serve as one alongside the Creator and as a Highborn Leader. Then I can solely rule the Imperial Council. Read this."

"Sure," Samuel said. "It refers to you moving in silence to balance your dark stars. But we must secure a double dark star after a new creation. Nearing the billionth-year epoch, all internal dark stars will require refurbishing. The Imperial Council's Emissaries abide by creation, they are the watchers over the stars in the universe and thus the final designers for the new planets. So, if you become the Highborn Leader, you will have an influence over the planets and the stars, Galasus. The Emissaries will be your watchful eyes, and you would be the final designer." His contemplative eyes gleamed.

"We are the Monarchs who will build up the universe. To harness and refurbish a dark star in its billionth epoch when called for." Galasus gazed directly at Samuel and flung his arms up. "We're Gods," he declared. "These two positions are extremely important, Samuel. The Creator prepared us both to be Divine beings in the paradises." Galasus proceeded to honor him. "I want you to be the Majesty in the universe alongside the Creator. I see a noble ruler alongside him," he said sincerely.

Galasus was a short, stout man. His wide green eyes shone as he said, "You can have a fragment of my dark star, Samuel." He kept his head high. "You are a skilled Royal who will unveil new and exciting elements in the universe. When you team up with the Creator, the events will take place from both of your hands, and they will be superb."

Samuel responded to his emotional phrases. "Are you certain you wish to go on with this, Galasus?"

"Yes, I need to achieve this title," he said. "Since we now know what the possibilities are for the Royal rulers."

"Well, you have a gift for decorating, as it shows in the royal chambers, and you even worked your style into our kitchen. Even the countless garden flowers you plant all over are nice but overpowering with the scent," Samuel stated and laughed. "Sure, why not, let us try this. I bet you can give the new planets the dazzle they need, and your Royal guidance to the council."

"Thank you, Samuel, your words mean a great deal to me. We are one with the Creator and the greatest Gods in the universe." Galasus felt uplifted by Samuel's encouragement. "My involvement in the future definitely leans heavily towards the council. There is a need for a title, and I feel it rising inside of me. Look at this, Samuel, there is more information to consider on the opposite side of this scroll."

"Wow," Samuel said. "It's another scroll fastened on the back, and I bet it encloses restricted information." Samuel unfastened it and rolled it open with both hands. "Only a Highborn Leader can use this knowledge if needed for impending actions," he said and looked further. "See here, there's a vague motif hiding something in a large Coliseum and a theater. I wonder who this marker belongs to?" He pointed it out and raised his head. "When you solve this mystery, please update me."

"I will, Samuel, since we are both Divine beings alongside of the Creator. It's written right here: our rights as Monarchs will develop when we embrace our future. We can continue divided. The Creator requests the intensity of two dark stars, and they must be the architects for the entire universe. If we join our dark stars, it will embrace a radiance that will prevail with evolution. I am sure you will be a driving force alongside the Creator," he remarked.

"So, let us get on with this adventurous journey the Creator prepared us for. When we immerse ourselves into the universe, I can become accustomed to the glorious surroundings," Samuel suggested.

Galasus turned and his expression was serious. "We both know of a place the Creator calls heaven—that's where the sacred seeds lie in wait of resurrection for his purpose," he said. "We all live and die by the Creator's hand, but our Grace situated us here as his Divine beings. We are both set to reign in the paradises," he said and stood steadily as if ready to go. "Together we have followed the alarming asteroids zipping through the cosmos and watched trails of dense dust piece together to uphold creation." Galasus took a breath and raised an eyebrow. "Space time and evolution is a hidden power in the universe. Gravity holds everything together. Oh, let us not forget that black holes warp space time and the early eclipses have indicated the starting of a new phase in the universe." His eyes were dancing with a sparkle. "I love following the frozen comets as they whizz by, and seeing the speedy quasars oscillating infernos of light. My favorite scene in the universe is the spinning pulsar; it is amazing how forceful this neutron star can be. A fabulous star is born within the remnants from a supernova explosion."

Samuel nodded in appreciation of Galasus' enthusiasm.

"I know the last two are some of your favorites too." He knew Samuel respected that it would now be him commanding the shockwaves traveling across the universe for evolution's sake. "The unblemished suns and the

6

radiant moons are magnificent in their existence. This passage of our journey has been long light years for us, but it sure has been enjoyable times. We're hemmed in by the most remarkable galaxy in the universe, and we live on an amazing planet. The time has arrived for us to proceed with honor," Galasus said.

Samuel too felt a sense of breathlessness when he pictured the start of the next part of their journey. "It states here we can have a wife when we complete a final cycle, if we choose to," Samuel noted and smiled at the notion. "But I expect our time in power will keep us from love for millenniums. Because the final decree shows this cycle must be perfect. So, let us work hard alongside of the Creator. Upon completion, we can unite with a Goddess," he concluded.

"That sounds magnificent, so come on, we need to get on with this," Galasus said and led the way.

Wooden doors with climbing ivy opened, and marble slabs led out to a balcony. This was where they would immerse themselves into the universe. Samuel then took most of Galasus' dark star away from him in the privacy of their royal chambers.

It took them months to wrap up the transformation. In doing so, Samuel's bright and dark star grew to be extremely powerful. The Creator knew what the two Divine beings' decisions were. They were mature Royals and ready to accept their crowns as Godly rulers for the paradises.

***

In the privacy of the Creator's Imperial Chamber, Samuel's crown was that of a God. The Creator dubbed him Royal Ruler Samuel Raiphualas II. His coat of arms rested near his heart. A bronze and silver triskelion spun his double star, and the third star stayed as one with the Creator. Samuel would serve at the Creator's side, and jointly build up the universe. The Creator dubbed Galasus Pagasusesia the Highborn Leader and placed a crown on his head. His coat of arms rested by his heart. A bronze and silver triskelion spun his double star, and the third star stayed as one with the Creator. Galasus would be the leading light for the Imperial Council. The special Monarchs amended their dark stars, and they both remained equal Royals at the side of the Creator.

***

Galasus' bright star grew wise in the ancient lore. His newly crowned head placed him at the top level. He now ruled over the Imperial Council and led them for millenniums. This was what he wished for and received.

Then good news reached Galasus via the Creator, and he summoned him to go to the set-up room.

"Samuel has worked systematically in the universe alongside of me. We have achieved a finished cycle, and it is perfect," he said. These words delighted Galasus. "The flora and fauna are magnificent, Galasus. Your guidance aided the Imperial Council, and you did an amazing job. Now the life I set on the planet will reign and the messengers will place additional items for their survival."

The animated painting glowed on the massive wall and sparkled in Galasus' eyes. Varco-XVI was prepared and now exhibited a selected life by the Creator's hand. This was in readiness for two special beings on Earth who did not yet know they were selected to fulfil an important destiny.

"Thank you, your Grace." Galasus nodded and bolted out of his chamber. He knew the moment was suitable to choose a wife. Thoughts lingered in his mind about how proud he was of Samuel, and he could not wait to reveal this to him. A celebration was in order, and Galasus wanted to set up something personal for Samuel.

But just when everything seemed to be under control, Samuel poked his dark star in the wrong place at the wrong time. This caused a dangerous situation which remained outside of the council's control. Galasus was the only one who could harness the power of Samuel's dark star. He set up the Imperial Council's Emissaries to watch over him as he needed them to monitor Samuel's brightness. If his dark star became lively, Galasus could suppress it as he had done for millenniums.

But somehow his dark star had gone astray without detection. Galasus needed guidance from the Creator. Without violating a sworn oath, which was that the Imperial Council would follow Samuel, it was now Galasus' responsibility. He must account for this misfortune and present it to the Creator.

It was a threatening arc revolving around Samuel, which meant using a new approach to solving the problem with his dark star. Determined to set things right, Galasus searched desperately in the library archives for something they might have overlooked.

When Galasus entered the Imperial Chamber, he met the Creator standing by an open window where he observed a bizarre rise and fall of lurking energy in the universe. The Creator turned and awaited his report. Galasus bowed and then raised his head. "Samuel Raiphualas II and I arranged the Emissaries to wrap up the final designs for the new solar system. Varco-XVI developed into an integral part of the Imperial Council's mission. This brought them to focus on the life you had placed there." He was motionless and dreaded a dark star's freedom. This could point to anarchy in the universe. He clutched his hands and continued. "There was something undetected by the Emissaries, your Grace—Samuel uncovered his dark star before his epoch. Unfortunately only Sachiel can identify the Godly spirits in the universe, and even he missed this notice when Samuel's dark star became too bright. When Sachiel eventually saw this, he reported it to me and the Imperial Council, but it was too late. I cannot confine his dark star," he said and nodded his head in heartache.

"Move forward with an investigation to solve this problem with Samuel. We must restrict his dark star, and if you cannot do this, he must go to trial for the violation of his dark star's uncovering," commanded the Creator.

***

The Imperial Council set the trial on the spiraling Triangulum Galaxy on planet Eugleston. Hydrogen hurled in from the universe and dripped vapors, where it transformed the columns into ice. Vast glacial bridges led the paradises' frontrunners to a packed theater. Marble statues of Gods lined the entrance, and shadowy tapestries adorned the granite walls. Swirling in midair were torches lit by a soaring flame. Nine patterned murals led to the stands filled with sovereigns from every corner of the Galaxy.

Galasus was set to discuss a concern with Samuel, who was now a great God in the paradises and his equal.

He entered Samuel's royal chamber and stood in front of him. His gaze burned into him as he searched for a shift in his stars. But he was not clear about what he was seeing.

"Samuel, we are in trouble," Galasus said. "Sachiel said he caught your spirit hovering over Varco-XVI, unmasking your dark star. What is going on with you?" He kept steady eye contact with him, and was hoping to accept that everything would be all right. "You achieved a perfect cycle and my guidance with the flora and fauna pleased the Creator. Now the messengers will bring the creations to life on this wondrous planet. You know what that means. But let's focus on you now," he said and clutched his hands together.

"How do you know it was my dark star and not yours?" Samuel asked and raised an eyebrow with a questioning gaze.

"I don't know." He flung his arms up in dismay. "We must play this mishap out as a judgement now. I have harnessed your dark stars for millenniums. How could I have missed this?" Galasus' tone was unsettled, and he rubbed his flushed face.

"I knew it," Samuel recalled. "I did say there was no more information about the joining of dark stars, so let us be cautious. Now we know it was a bad idea, and you missed the last scroll too. But I found it and brought it to you," Samuel said and shook his head from side to side. "We were two Nobles experimenting with our Godly force." He set off a dark spark from his torso and a resentment settled in him. "Where were your Imperial Council members when you needed them? This is their weakness, not yours." Samuel's eyes seemed to darken.

"Besides that, I have been feeling somewhat odd lately," he added. A solidly built man with bronzed skin, he had a noticeable birthmark on his neck. "Haven't you noticed anything unusual about me?" he enquired and closed his eyes while he took a calming breath.

"Let me look at you." Galasus paced around him. "Well, your veins are protruding more in your neck and your birthmark looks bigger." He placed his own hand on his chin. Then he slid his hand down to touch his own birthmark, but it felt the same. "*Mmm* . . . your arms are much larger, and your eyes look somewhat peculiar. Nope, I don't see anything physically wrong with you, just different."

Samuel sat on the edge of his bed and reminisced. "In the earlier stages of creation, the Creator placed my spirit in a bronze and silver pyramid in Egypt, and my spirit remains on a Golden Door. The Creator's knowledgeable influence led me to situate two portals—one is unseen on the gilded door in Egypt, the other one is hidden on the landscape in the Bakoni Ruins. I witnessed his hand ascend from the heavens. He set up a selected life on Varco-XVI for two Monarchs to reign. There were also brilliant stars glistening in the universe; a sequence of stars poured out sacred seeds to flourish on the new planet." Samuel understood life would multiply on the new planet.

He clutched his hands and continued. "Our dark stars are as one and my bright star concerns me." He rubbed his face. "My spirit reigns on The Golden Door," he noted. "Something wasn't right with me; it was like I was unsettled and slightly impatient. I wanted to go somewhere to do something, but I have no idea if I did. But this notion was short-lived, and it went away, so I thought it was nothing." He gazed up at Galasus. "Sorry, when I buried my thoughts alongside of the Creator, it was to complete a perfect cycle. But, when I felt this way, I went to find you," he said and stared at him with his mystified eyes. "And as always, you were unavailable and busy with the council. So, I didn't want to disrupt anything." Samuel eventually realized he had a loss of focus and should have gone back to find Galasus. "I don't know if my dark star did anything in the earlier stages of the final cycle." Samuel stood and watched Galasus for a reaction.

"Oh, really, Samuel, now this just adds to the setback. You thought you may have gone somewhere, but you do not remember. All I know is you were hovering over Varco-XVI and you revealed your spirit along with your dark star. It hasn't come to my attention if you did anything else." Galasus' eyes widened with this thought. "Sachiel mentioned nothing about the earlier stages. Even the Council didn't. I detected nothing unusual about you either, and you know I would have reined in your dark star before it got too bright," he said and swayed his head. "We all recognize your placements and the Creator's in the universe; thank goodness your spirit is still on The Golden Door in Egypt. No one detected if your spirit was absent. You might have done something in the earlier stages of creation without notice; now I must consider that." Galasus looked concerned. He brushed his hands across his face. "We must go to trial. I promise you I will work this out. Nobody can end your Divine entitlement. You are an important God alongside of the Creator."

Samuel regarded his tireless friend. "You have always had a great sense of timing through epochs of change with my dark star, Galasus. And you recognize what others have missed. So, let's get this over with. Now I am sure this double darkness inside of me will force me to become a considerable burden," he expressed. "I don't know what I am capable of. My internal dark star is acting up inside of me and I'm not sure if it's my dark

11

star or if it's yours." Samuel had a troubled look and wondered if he would get through this.

Galasus rolled his eyes and patted both hands to his side. He realized this trial would be tough on both of them. He left the chamber with a worried look on his face.

Samuel Raiphualas II outfitted himself in his dark red Royal clothing; he was wearing gold armor made of studded leather with black rivets. A grand sword rested by his left side as he put on his cloak. Now the kindness he had been feeling was weakening, and he felt unsettled. His dark star was stirring inside of him.

As he entered the theater, Samuel went straight to the podium. His black cloak swirled at the center of a fierce wind coursing around him. When he removed his cloak, he spotted a scorch mark on his coat of arms. Samuel embraced an understanding with his bright star, and his and Galasus' dark star were now present as one. When his bright star faded, he showed his dark lustrous star. A swift glimpse over at the Emissaries brought a glint to his dark eyes.

They went ahead with the trial. Highborn Leader, Galasus Pagasusesia, wandered to the middle of the floor and stood on a circular marble slab. He addressed Samuel. "Your Majesty, there has been a misinterpretation regarding your dark star, and I cannot harness it. The council believes something has impaired our view of your dark star and we do not know why this happened." Now Galasus recognized a change in Samuel's appearance, and it concerned him. But he had to go ahead. "What are your plans for Varco-XVI?" he asked and stared at him. Samuel did not answer Galasus. "The Imperial Council believes you're contemplating destruction; we can't let this happen. Human life inhabits Varco-XVI and portals have been installed to facilitate movement between the planets. The final arrangement of humans has crossed over into a safe environment on Varco-XVI." He paused for a moment and rubbed his sweaty palms. "Your dark star should not reveal itself." His pained look brought him to bow his head to Samuel.

Samuel's glossy eyes clouded over with a darkness. His fist pounded on the podium. "Imperial Council, watch the power you portray. I am one of the untouchable essences who rule the entire universe." His voice echoed throughout the theater. "What I wish to do is of no concern to you, so step aside." His rage lashed out without regard for anyone's judgment.

When Galasus lifted his head, he saw Samuel's dark star was overriding his bright star. Now he blamed himself. It was an authority he wanted as the Highborn Leader, but giving Samuel a portion of his dark star drew him into a serious plight.

He wrung his damp palms and dreaded the inevitable outcome, but he had to continue. "The Council cannot go by your entitlement when you uncover your dark star," he said and had a notion . . . *This might be my dark star acting strangely.*

Clutching his hands together, Galasus reflected on how special Samuel was to the Monarchy. "You exist as a cosmic architect for the paradises and you regulate the protected elements enclosed by the universe." He flung his hands in the air in despair and stared over at him. "You're a great God situated alongside of the Creator," Galasus began.

Samuel took no notice of him as his focus was on the Emissaries.

"The Council wishes to restrain your essence temporarily. I have safeguarded your dark star for millenniums. But this time it arose without warning, and now it's too late." Galasus' hands were trembling. He took a breath and regained his composure. "The Imperial Council ruled to put your unharnessed dark star in a safe place. Your Majesty, humankind will remain on Varco-XVI," he proclaimed and bowed his head to Samuel and walked away.

The Creator had Galasus and the council decide Samuel's fate, because he knew the young Royals had chosen a different path and now, they must resolve their own situation. Without warning, the Creator stripped Samuel of his Royal attire and forced him into a vortex. He then put Samuel inside a black hole and sealed it tight.

The Imperial Council was not sure what Samuel's plans were, because he was nearing his billionth year with a shift in his internal two stars. They considered the possibilities, but what they did not know, was that Samuel had engulfed a portion of Galasus' dark star. Samuel was a great God alongside the Creator and together in the heavens they were a celestial wonder. This was the ultimate impression in the universe, it was Varco-XVI and the orbiting planets which were a stellar prize of creation.

Galasus fled the theater and returned to his spacious Chamber. Now he dreaded what might strengthen inside Samuel. "I will find another way to secure him," he said aloud. His hand leaned on the rounded windowpane. As Galasus gazed through the window, his eyes flickered when he paid attention to the buried essentials in the universe rippling. They were not obeying the same physical laws as the other objects that were close. Something was not right, and he had never detected this before. It was a rippling dust upsurge attempting to force an approach through a bulging pathway and showing a dark energy. "My dark star or Samuel's flipped too soon. How could this have happened? I have no control over this now," he said and brushed his face. "This change poses a risk to the universe and a danger to him. I cannot believe that neither the council nor I saw Samuel's noticeable dark star in the universe. Now I need to uncover answers." Galasus bowed his head in sadness.

He left his room in a rush and went without stopping to the library. Galasus did not know where to seek the knowledge he required. As he scanned his eyes around the grand room, a sudden flash caught his attention. It was coming from a window where a refreshing breeze swept through and into his hair. Accepting this encounter, he took a deep breath and ambled toward the window. Suddenly, a spiraling staircase popped up in front of him. Galasus did not hesitate to go up the stairs. When he arrived at the top, he met up with a masked warrior. He stopped dead in his tracks and looked right into its intense crimson eyes. Smoke billowed around the warrior, and the area felt as cold as ice. It appeared the masked warrior guarded a shadowy door. Stardust moved up from the base, and there was an image floating on the middle of the door. A bronze triskelion with a monogrammed dark star glittered and it burrowed into the door. Galasus saw it was a Royal crest which alarmed him. He noted a dark and bright star and the Creator's star; it was their coat of arms. But the bright star was dimming on its silver surface. He raised his hand to rub the coat of arms, but the door faded into darkness.

Galasus searched up and down the stardust walls, then he saw an opening through the billowing clouds. Another door had a bronze triskelion with a monogrammed bright star. It stayed on the surface and showed a continuous movement of Galasus' dark and bright star alongside of the

Creator's star. Their coat of arms had separated and placed each part on two different doors. Galasus became very worried.

He strode straight up to it and rubbed his hand over it; the door opened. When he stepped into a chamber, his gaze went from side to side and took in a view of seemingly countless scrolls. They were inside a wide carved out section on a stone wall. This made him wonder why he couldn't enter the previous room and what was inside it. His stomach turned when he noted a passage on the wall. *Estranged dark stars of the universe.* Feeling troubled, he picked up a scroll and read it aloud. "When a dark star leaves a celestial body and joins with another, the strength of this joining will go astray well before its billionth year. A series of spiritual awakenings must take place. Make a mention to the Creator regarding (II) the High Priestess—she is in the Divine cards. Go to the Coliseum where you must call upon the great tapestries."

Galasus' hands went to his head. "This place and these scrolls weren't here before," he said and scanned the area. "When Samuel and I were growing up, we read every scroll in the library. Where did these two chambers come from? And why can I only enter one?" he exclaimed.

Galasus was thankful the Creator had confined Samuel, and he hoped his confinement might put Samuel at ease until he discovered another way to harness his dark star. But now he had learned that the joining of two dark stars contributed to the switch much sooner. Being young at the time, they did not consider this ethical problem, but now they were grown men. He gripped his chin. "Why didn't we figure out what would happen with the two dark stars?" he stated.

But now it made sense. They had both read about the billionth-year epoch. But at the time they picked up no concern that anything would be different. Then he noticed a gold scroll in one of the openings. It concerned the legends of the Coliseum tapestries and the restricted tapestries in the theater. The seal on it could not be opened. He placed it on a table and realized what the meaning of forthcoming events implied.

As he flipped through the rest of the many scrolls, this had him shaking. He realized there were many ways to suppress a dark star, but the scrolls he had gathered contained nothing helpful. Galasus guessed the other chamber contained scrolls about dark legends in the theater since there was nothing here about them. "I know that room is for Samuel, it's for the restricted

15

tapestries in the theater." He gripped the golden scroll in his hand. "Samuel can try to stop me from doing what is right with those scrolls in the other room. So, I must stay true to the lore," he said and bowed his head. Galasus then accepted a gift of strength from the Creator which gave him pause to deal with this dilemma. He knew it was only a matter of time until Samuel would resurface as the Creator could not confine his dark star for too long.

Suddenly a glint of light beamed through the opened door; it heated the seal on the golden scroll, and the scroll rolled open. With both hands holding it open, Galasus read through it, and what he found were three mentions that might prove valuable. A powerful Protostar was in existence on Varco-XVI who could get his time in power from a ruling force that rested deep in the universe. The messengers on Varco-XVI would be able to gain an immense power from the majestic tapestries in the great Coliseum. He also now knew about the Creator's (II) the High Priestess. His head dropped in disappointment; his bold choice for Samuel and his dark star might lead to anarchy in the paradises. "Samuel said we should be cautious because we knew nothing of this force, and he was right," he said sorrowfully.

A different seal appeared on the scroll. It was a card gifted from (II) the High Priestess. He opened it and recited, "Ace of Pentacles, Noble leader Galasus Pagasusesia, Leader of the Imperial Council. You are an all-important decision-maker in the paradises. Place this pentacle in your palm and point it to Varco-XVI and Earth. It's the all-seeing eye for the N-S-E-W. And it is signed by (II) the High Priestess." Galasus picked up and gripped the Ace of Pentacles. Featherlike beams branded the pentacle into his right palm.

He read further on and found something that changed his emotional state; it was about Samuel. His already glassy eyes coated once more with tears. He raised his head high when he noted Samuel was his blood brother. Blacked out below were their birth parents' names. Galasus wiped his eyes and read further. This new information showed him how he must triumph over Samuel. It was a strategy to end two magnificent dark stars that had united. Unknowingly, Samuel had created a disorder in the universe and now he must be stopped. To do this, Galasus must involve the Godly leaders, and the Creator's (II) the High Priestess and her Divine cards. Galasus gripped the scroll and rolled his shoulders back. He understood the flashing pentacle in his hand. Now he must work harder to recover his brother Samuel's real self. Galasus hurried back to his room so he could prepare himself to meet with the Creator.

He calmly entered the Creator's Imperial chamber and approached him. After greeting him he said, "I need to call upon a series tapestry to awaken the Godly leaders of the universe. I call for the Creator's (II) the High Priestess, to share with us her Divine cards. It is a requirement that she arranges this with you and I, my Grace."

The Creator watched him closely. He noticed Galasus was forming his thoughts through the Ace of Pentacles and nodded to him.

The Creator made one room in the library available that Galasus had not seen before. It had his coat of arms on the door bearing his bright star. The other room was for Samuel. "You must work hard by reading the numerous scrolls and deciphering how to rule the tapestries in the great Coliseum," the Creator said. "This requires (II) the High Priestess and her Divine cards. Now you must learn how to confine Samuel's dark star that has gone astray before its billionth-year epoch."

Galasus acknowledged his part in the unfolding of this event, bowed to him and left the chamber.

***

He was quick to organize a majestic ceremony across the Triangulum Galaxy; it was inside a large oval Coliseum on planet Eugleston. When the Imperial Council entered the Coliseum, the marble floor sparkled with brilliant stars. To the right were many colossal stone pillars showing statues of heroes. Seemingly endless rows of poles rising inside a mystic flame sported noble tapestries fastened by coiled ropes. The images flickered with primary metaphors, cups, pentacles, swords, and wands. Galasus requested the great power that rested inside the noble tapestries to be released. It was a celebrated woman who controlled this powerful upper hand. Now (II) the High Priestess would soon have her time in power with her Divine cards, to transform the Heavens' messengers and the Guardians into Godly leaders on Earth and Varco-XVI.

Nine patterned murals on the granite walls showed the Imperial Council. Galasus' Royal Tapestry was next to his marble statue. The Creator had stripped Samuel of his triskelion coat of arms made of bronze and silver.

17

The great seers bowed their heads in shame. His Majesty's brilliant coat of arms was a mirrored image on his Royal Tapestry above his marble statue. Alongside was his Royal clothing, sword, and armor. By revealing his dark star, it was considered an act for imprisonment and allowed for provisional replacements by the Imperial Council.

***

It was not long after his confinement that Samuel began developing a shadow in the universe. Starry flares cascaded through the cosmos as Samuel Raiphualas II mastered a plan inside the black hole. He managed to escape by using his magisterial powers. He did this as the Creator did not strip him of his superior rank, since his purpose was to isolate Samuel long enough to balance his dark star.

Galasus had an uneasy feeling when Sachiel approached him once again. He clasped his hands and stared at him.

"Royal Ruler Samuel Raiphualas II escaped from the black hole," Sachiel said and drifted aside.

As soon as he found out this news, Galasus went in search of Samuel. But he was nowhere to be found, and a great sadness set in. Now he had to set up a meeting to brief the Imperial Council and so he did.

"His Majesty is lurking in the universe. He slipped away from his confinement." Galasus feared what might happen and so he had the Imperial Council's Emissaries scrambling everywhere. This did not work so they needed to slow down and make sensible decisions.

While arranging the legal proceedings, Galasus hoped he had enough time to finish organizing his strategic plan in his bright room. He went straight to his royal chamber and on entering noticed a balcony door was opened. Using this opportunity to send a message while viewing the universe, his triskelion pushed out a spark from his brilliant star. It rippled across the universe and swirled through the stardust. It reached Samuel's birthmark and revealed his message.

Samuel acknowledged Galasus' request. He returned and when he entered the theater, he flaunted his muscular physique in front of all those present. Black rawhide pants covered his lower half, and a new cosmic attachment flared across his lean waist. A Royal Celestial being carried two stars internally, and they were still shifting in his heated core. His powerful double dark star was nearing a final stage that appeared undeciphered by the council or even the Godly man, Sachiel.

Galasus saw the visible veins in Samuel's solid arms and neck were throbbing. Samuel's birthmark on the left side of his neck was hidden by an ice-covered pentagram, and his eyes showed a hue of crimson. He knew Samuel was in the dark room he was unable to enter and had to work even faster.

He went and stood in the middle of the theater to discuss these matters with him, but Samuel turned from him and faced the Emissaries stirring in the crowded theater.

He bellowed, "You Emissaries dared to quarantine me through the Creator? How did that work out for you? I am a superior being who rules alongside of him. You have no power over me." His dark star thundered inside of him. "My dark star acknowledges my privilege and royal status. Now you Emissaries will have to pay attention to how my darkness will work throughout the universe."

Samuel knew that he was too important for the Creator to just banish him, so he once more fitted himself out in his royal clothing and armor.

The Creator knew Samuel was essential for future creation. He raised his right arm to let him go on with his birthright. The Creator turned and decorated him with his coat of arms again and Samuel placed his grand sword back into his sheathe.

Galasus raised his right arm and stared into his Majesty's dark eyes. "Not guilty," he said and lowered his head. Galasus now feared for the Imperial Council's inability to see that Samuel's dark star had transformed. Nine Emissaries on the council had instructions to watch over him. This shocking change with his dark stars had an effect that was pushing the Royal ruler into a dogmatic time span.

They were the Divine children who had been partnered as superior men alongside the Creator. Now Samuel looked at Galasus with sad eyes and left the theater.

It was Galasus who had guided the Emissaries to bring the new planet known as Varco-XVI to life in a painting. The design and execution were flawless but things changed when Sachiel witnessed a staggering force around Varco-XVI. Samuel had revealed his dark star, and he was drifting away, isolated from those close to him. Galasus was the only one who would be able to harness his dark star. Now it was an internal conflict set before Galasus.

Royal Ruler, Samuel Raiphualas II, overpowered the council's decision and remained on his throne, where he sat and suffered in silence. The time was nearing for him to enter into unfamiliar behavior. Samuel brushed his arms when a piercing pain from his hidden dark stars surged through his body. The final transformation in favor of his dark stars was drawing nearer.

"The system Galasus and I trusted betrayed us. I know Galasus can harness my dark star. He instructed the Imperial Council to warn him if I showed any change." His breathing was getting shallow. "He will search through the ancient archives to help me; he is the Highborn Leader." Samuel's thoughts were stirring and the only thing he could think of was to distrust those in authority. His anger was expanding toward the Emissaries.

"Now the Emissaries will meet the only justice I trust," he said and looked up. "I must take personal vengeance on the ones to blame." Samuel felt helpless and disillusioned about how this change with his dark stars would work in the universe.

His trembling hands grabbed his head. He was trying to battle the force within—Samuel wanted to stop the process. But he could not flip the switch when the upsurge hit him. Sorrow closed his throat when his body felt heavy. Samuel's dark star was blinding him with a wrath that would undoubtedly bring on reckless behavior. He leaned forward and placed his hands over his face, inflamed circles coiled inside his murky eyes. The binding phase was final. His dark star was in control.

When he raised his head and stood, his eyes had a dark flickering flame that masked his bright star. Now he was ready to push the great seers of the universe beyond their limits. His dark power was unknown, and his royal decree remained law in the paradises. His Majesty's veiled dark star fueled his bright star for creation. In the earlier epochs, Galasus could restrict his dark existence when it became too powerful. Now those who were the watchful eyes of the universe must face a release of dark power.

Chapter Two
Gabrielle's and Moon-Star's Final Day in the Sacred Garden

Seven days had passed inside the sacred garden. The northern side of Varco-XVI was teeming with life. Its forests were far reaching and thriving above the lush undergrowth. Sunbeams peeked through the canopies, which were layered with an abundance of foliage, shading the plants below. The vegetation and wildlife were more bountiful than Gabrielle could have imagined.

Gabrielle and Moon-Star sat on a bench on this last day. They were expecting Hamuel to arrive and to set up the last stages of their ceremony. The women remained within the setting of the garden and had spent a week preparing for this moment.

"Look at those fish jumping out of the water, Moon-Star," she said and pointed towards the river. "I have never seen that species of fish before." She thought about how it reminded her of her life on the coast of the Maritimes. "I know my attitude as well as yours has changed. We are both focused on our journey. But on this last day I can do nothing but think about what appeared to Michael and me back at the Texas observatory." She shifted to face Moon-Star.

"Do you remember more details from your past?" Moon-Star perked up at her mother's flash of memory.

"I think so. My memory seems to return in patches. My thoughts have been moving in and out this morning."

"You have told me some things from your past when I was growing up, but you suddenly stopped. I do not care if you repeat the same stories again, please tell me about Michael. Tell me everything about this man you are destined for." Moon-Star slipped into daydreaming mode again.

"You sure have an interest in Michael." Gabrielle noticed her eyes were wide and rounded with excitement. "Michael and I were astrophysicists at an observatory in Texas. It was as though we were the watchful eyes of the universe. Michael always claimed he would find a new world discovery alongside me." She gazed at the blue sky intently. "When I think back to it, the lights from the Orion constellation were actually flowing down."

"Oh, where did the lights lead?" she asked.

"One light pointed to the Bakoni Ruins in South Africa, and Michael followed it there. The other, I trailed to the great pyramid of Giza," Gabrielle answered. "Someone had tucked a great wonder in a sphere behind it. That's where I encountered a pyramid made of bronze and silver."

Moon-Star listened to her mother speak as she viewed the river flowing toward the east.

Gabrielle peeked over at her. "That is when everything started to unfold. Michael and I were the only ones who saw those lights streaming down from Orion. Look to the horizon, Moon-Star. The Orion constellation shimmers in the day and night on this planet. Those lights we met, were the spark to this journey. I now have a sharper picture about how it all began."

"Tell me what you recall." Now Moon-Star saw a gleam in Gabrielle's eyes.

"There was a Golden Door within the pyramid. When I reached the gilded surface, it started to ripple." Gabrielle stood and strolled towards the water.

Moon-Star followed her and listened as she talked.

"There was a glimmer; that's when I realized something was beyond the door. It was like a looking glass, and the universe appeared right in front of me." Gabrielle continued as she met her reflection in the flowing water. "I looked at a new solar system encircling a blood moon. There was an object hiding behind the lunar phenomenon. It was this planet."

"That is incredible. The Gods led you to a place of wonder. Can you explain more?" she asked.

"Michael and I worked closely, as we both wanted to find a planet in the Goldilocks Zone. That's a habitable zone in the universe where the temperature is just right to have liquid on the planet, Moon-Star. Just like this one," she said. "I remember when I reached out and took a golden book off the door, it opened. Stardust billowed out, and a God appeared right in front of me. It was Metatron, Moon-Star. He reached out and took me by the hand and led me into the universe, accompanied by Anaelle. Then he placed me on this planet. I now carry his majestic sword by my side." She touched her sword and felt a vibration. "This historic revelation of a new planet is like music in the universe. Moon-Star, this paradise is the last note of a symphony for humankind. As a scientist, I am thrilled at the possibility of human life continuing beyond the confines of Earth."

"I'm most amazed by the part that brought you to me. I'm so happy to be a part of your greatest discovery, but do you miss your life on Earth?" she asked.

Gabrielle met Moon-Star's sparkling eyes. "Heavenly beings brought Michael and me an alternative way of life. The heavens destined me for this moment, and you are all I need."

"I am grateful the Creator selected you as my Mother and Michael as Sun-Star's Father." Moon-Star reached for her mother's hand. Gabrielle shared the sentiment by holding hers. They both took in the emotion they provided to one another.

"Michael and I have accepted our destiny." Her voice faltered as she reminisced about her colleague. "My heart melts when I think of him. I believe Michael and Sun-Star are in the process of their last ceremony today."

"Mother, look." Moon-Star pointed to the shimmering lights that were pouring across the horizon. "Something is taking place in the universe."

***

In the early stages of the disaster, Galasus told the Imperial Council that he was ready to upgrade a tapestry in the Coliseum. He could use the remnants of a massive explosion that Samuel generated in the universe. It was from a Protostar that formed inside the last stages of a supernova. The nuclear fusion had created a unique star named Hamuel. In doing so, it delivered a vital spark to it and Hamuel then achieved his immortal flame from the Creator. His likeness was now that of a mortal messenger on Varco-XVI. Galasus summoned (II) the High Priestess who gave him a spirited card. A grand ceremony then had Galasus embedding the card to upgrade his tapestry and when Hamuel entered the crowded Coliseum, Galasus crowned him as IV-Emperor in the paradises.

"Hamuel, your status has changed," Galasus said. "You now have a grand title in the paradises: IV-Emperor. You as a great Godly Emperor will now be the key to opening a secret passage into Varco-XVI. Your actions will be noticed by Samuel and lead to an uprising in the universe. You must travel fast to the planet in the confines of a dark place that Samuel occupies."

Galasus turned and watched the Emissaries for a reaction. They were motionless as they remained true to their Highborn Leader. "It is now your duty to close the ceremony for Lady Gabrielle and Queen Moon-Star. The celestial beings will face a different epoch in their journey. Varco-XVI's population will meet up with Royal Ruler Samuel. His Majesty calls for the dark tapestries in the theater." Galasus had trouble meeting Hamuel's eyes. He concentrated and went on. "He is a Godly ruler and has many means of access in the universe; his powers are veiled in secrecy. We need to stop his chaotic movements; he will destroy all who come within his reach. In time I must release Samuel's spirit from The Golden Door in Egypt, and find a way to confine him, but this will not be for some time. He uses a mysterious magic, and his dark star now controls a supernatural being. Samuel collected a selection of life from all four corners of Varco-XVI." He stepped closer to him. "My bond with my brother needs your guidance," he whispered. "It must come from the Godly leaders in a way that they can capture him. Hamuel, you can use the powers of the magnetar to annihilate all who follow him when the time is right. There is one more thing, Hamuel. Be mindful of a fitting together the pagans, Saffron, and Efren have." Galasus handed him two bronze scrolls that enclosed the directions for the ceremony. Hamuel accepted the scrolls to finish the last part.

Hamuel bowed his head and acknowledged Highborn Leader Galasus' words about his Majesty and his mandates.

When he left planet Eugleston, Hamuel navigated inside the constellation of Sagittarius on a starquake. This was where he pursued his path, and it was to the most dangerous type of neutron star: a magnetar. In doing so, he harnessed a new power from the densest material known in the universe.

Hamuel understood the true value of the magnetar's greatest force. Gamma rays flared up in front of him, the charge it created resonated through the air as the magnetic field closed around him. The neutron star energized him with the vitality he would need to achieve his tasks. Now, with the magnetar's force, he could transport himself to the sacred garden.

***

Radiant lights in the universe held their attention, and on the horizon was a dust storm. It drifted within the confines of the garden. The ladies observed a male materializing inside the spiraling dust. As the turbulence subsided, an intense light encircled him. It was Hamuel, IV-Emperor, one of many saviors for Earth and the paradises.

When he stepped toward Gabrielle and Moon-Star, they both noticed a coat of arms on his black cloak: a gold triskelion showed the title IV-Emperor. The ladies bowed their heads to him.

"This is your day of reward, Lady Gabrielle and Queen Moon-Star." He wasted no time with unnecessary greetings. "The sacred garden is where you will be in harmony with the Creator." Hamuel raised his arm and directed the ladies further into the garden.

The pair walked side by side; each in a long white dress made of silk and satins. Sacred Boswellia trees lined a path to the garden's entrance. Gabrielle and Moon-Star went through the archway where the trellis was blossoming with fresh flowers. Bustling winds followed Gabrielle and Moon-Star as they neared the hallowed site. They both noticed the pleasant scent of frankincense in the air.

"Please turn to the east," he said and settled before them. "The transformation you went through awarded you the titles of Godly beings in the paradises. When you began your journey on Varco-XVI, you encountered many demands and in turn gained rewards for your successes." He signaled to a small table-like altar. "Put your armor on and set those items here," he instructed.

The ladies stepped forward and adorned themselves with the gifted clothing and armor. Their minds understood the mechanics of revealing and retracting the armor, now hidden beneath their skin. Gabrielle reached into her satchel and removed, first, the silver box from the Creator. She remembered the location where she identified the small silver box. Stepping forward she placed it on the table.

When she reached into her bag to retrieve the next item, she reminisced about how she snatched this golden book from the very face of The Golden Door. She had exchanged the book in the first phase of her journey with wizards Valda and Vance. The wizards sought the mysteries hidden within its pages. In return, she received a treasured item. She gripped it in her hand; it was a glittering sealed golden box. She placed the small box on the table. Gabrielle glanced at Moon-Star as she presented the final two items. The white clam shell from within the Fountain of Enlightenment and her book of destiny. She arranged them on the polished surface.

As she walked away, the silver box transformed. It took the form of a tailored leather pouch. Eight silver coins appeared alongside. Hamuel put the coins in the pouch and passed it to Gabrielle. She took it and held it in her hand.

The white clam shell opened and displayed two shimmering pearls. The golden box glimmered, and the book of destiny flipped a page to the next part of her journey.

Gabrielle's and Moon-Star's shields of silver materialized on their arms. They gazed at the familiar armor. Adorned on each was a vivid engraving of a sun and moon which crowned the triple-crossed swords inscribed on their shields. The emblems shone against the silver. A lily and purple lotus formed as a crest on their shields, and the flowers flickered with an energy.

Hamuel raised his arms and brought in a bolt of lightning. It struck the impenetrable shields and exposed an impression of spiritual allies: Sariel, and Hamuel.

Two loin belts appeared on the table. Inside each scabbard was a jeweled sword. The ladies wrapped them around their waists. Gabrielle slipped her pouch of coins into a pocket on the side of her belt. Then she returned the golden box to her satchel along with the book of destiny.

"Draw your swords," Hamuel instructed. "The pearls will now join with your swords."

The women lifted their swords out of their scabbards, feeling the weight and the power they contained. A slight flame flared up as the pearls swirled into each of their swords.

Moon-Star, who was now a grown woman, was searching for Gabrielle's guidance. She stood by her and nodded. The ceremony and acceptance of many extraordinary relics should have been overwhelming, but the pair took it all in with a great certainty.

He was in the final stages of the ceremony, so Hamuel revealed the significance of each piece they would wear.

"Lady Gabrielle and Queen Moon-Star, you both wear the Breastplates of Righteousness, the Helmets of Salvation, and the Boots of Peace. On your arms are the Shields of Faith. The Loin Belts of truth show the true value of life—it's a spiritual awareness, and it's beyond what is natural. You both carry the Swords of the Spirit, and a life-force rests inside your Lances for Worship," Hamuel said.

"Lady Gabrielle and Queen Moon-Star, you were both born under a moon emblem. Raise your left arm." Hamuel was watchful.

Together, Gabrielle and Moon-Star raised their left arms to accept their markings. He engrained a waxing and waning crescent moon on the top of Gabrielle's left wrist. He turned to adorn Moon-Star with a solar eclipse at the top of her left wrist.

Moon-Star caressed the new symbol on her wrist and acknowledged his statement. She tried to hide the uncertainty in her eyes, but Hamuel saw this. "You are a supreme being, my Queen. Fear not, as Lady Gabrielle is your Guardian and she will guide you through any uncertainties."

"Where will my mother be guiding me next, Hamuel?" Moon-Star inquired.

"Your next destination is to the Coliseum. Later, Raguelle, Metatron, Sariel, and I will strengthen you both in the art of warfare."

She shifted and smiled at her mother. Gabrielle winked at her. They both nodded and accepted these gifts; it was a royal honor. As soon as their heads lifted, they saw Hamuel had two bronze scrolls in his hands.

Hamuel turned to Gabrielle. "Your spirit sits at the left hand of the Creator." He beheld the sky, and a bolt of silver lightning descended from the universe. It flared across the horizon. "The Creator is my strength," he said. His eyes lowered and met Gabrielle's gaze. "These words will be of great value to you, my Lady."

"I will commit these five words to my memory," she said.

Moon-Star noted the passion in Gabrielle's eyes. "Mother." She placed her hand on her arm. "I will also remember these words and mention this to Saffron."

"Now, an ending to the ceremony completes your agreement. You are both in harmony with the Creator." Hamuel administered the Creator's closing power in the garden.

They both drew a deep breath when the whistling wind surged through the garden. The current of air seemed to whisper the words they had both been waiting to hear. "I consecrate you both. The Creator sets you apart, my

Lady and our Queen, from the others, you are both Gods in the heavens." Hamuel bowed his head. "I have completed the ceremony."

Gabrielle and Moon-Star nodded; their faces flushed with happiness.

"Galasus placed a waxing and waning crescent to safeguard this sacred garden. So, too, it will follow you on your journeys," Hamuel noted.

Gabrielle closed her eyes and rubbed the crescents on her wrist. A warmness entered her hand and she wondered what this had to do with the journey, but she knew it would come to her in time. When she peeked over at Moon-Star, she saw the Queen of Varco-XVI staring at the ground.

"Lady Gabrielle and Queen Moon-Star. You are both entitled to all the rights and privileges in the paradises. The Creator graced you both with a boundless spiritual life. Some of your most important skills will flourish throughout your campaigns. This will strengthen you both as celestial warriors."

Nearby, fast moving beams from the universe showed another arrival. Hamuel noticed a man approaching. He drifted aside to let him pass.

From the edge of a spiraling galaxy within the universe, Metatron had materialized within the garden. He stepped down and addressed the pair, "I am the Guardian of the new Covenants, Lady Gabrielle and Queen Moon-Star." Metatron bowed, then turned to face Hamuel.

They both smiled at his familiar face. Metatron was one of their protectors.

Hamuel placed the two bronze scrolls in Metatron's hand along with a silver quill. Now Metatron needed to fulfill his duties for the ceremony.

Metatron unrolled each scroll and penned his signature. One was for Lady Gabrielle, the other for Lord Michael.

He stepped forward. "This scroll is the Covenant for Redemption; this is your spiritual freedom. Lady Gabrielle, you have made an eternal agreement, and this is your sworn oath," Metatron said. "Do you understand the weight of your bond?"

"I do." Gabrielle nodded her acknowledgement.

"So then let it be." Hamuel spoke and added Gabrielle's name to both scrolls.

Metatron raised his arm and brought in a cosmic flame from the universe. Searing flames inscribed the words on both papyruses.

Moon-Star's eyes flickered, and she stepped back. Her mother, with a soft hand, guided her back to her side and returned to her place in the ceremony.

"This is the Covenant for Works of life. The efforts you will put forth, the labors of your agreement." Silver lightning etched these words.

"This is the Covenant of Grace. The beauty of eternal life." Bronze lightning manifested these words.

"Lady Gabrielle, you will be a symbol for humanity, and the Guardian of Queen Moon-Star," Metatron said and bowed his head.

"My Lady and my Queen," Metatron continued, "these are honored covenants." He gripped the scrolls. "I will place these two bronze scrolls alongside the old one. The Creator will display these scrolls to sanction your importance in the heavens. These covenants are unchangeable. The time-honored agreement between the heavens' sacred seeds and you are now in place."

Torrents of radiant lights shone down from the universe, and in doing so, set apart the newly formed covenants.

Gabrielle and Moon-Star bowed to him.

"Thank you, Metatron, for your enlightenment." Gabrielle then asked, "Will Michael be pledging the same?"

"Yes," he replied.

"Say hello to Michael and Sun-Star. Moon-Star and I look forward to reaching them."

"Yes, my Lady, I will tell them both," he replied.

Her heart pounded as Gabrielle thought about Michael. She rubbed her talisman around her neck and closed her eyes. She understood he was on the south side of the planet and she was unsure why they were still not together. She stood tall and returned her attention back to the ceremony. Gabrielle watched as Metatron picked up the written scriptures. He bowed first to Hamuel, then Gabrielle and Moon-Star, before he vanished, returning to the spiraling galaxy with the scrolls.

In the middle of the garden, an astral surge spun stardust in front of Gabrielle and Moon-Star. A blazing light of silver trailed inside a swirl of sparked air. To the women's surprise and delight, three white mares ascended from the circling light. Vaporous flares flowed through the mares' manes. These mares were for their journey.

"My Lady and my Queen," Hamuel proceeded, "there will be a grand celebration this evening at Valda and Vance's castle, and your journey will start at sunrise."

Gabrielle focused on Hamuel. "We come from a sacred place in the heavens and know that life exists in a range of worlds. The Creator graced the universe with the selected ones," Gabrielle said. "But in this world, we have become the selected. I accepted my agreement, and I am honored to be the Guardian of Queen Moon-Star." She reached out and gathered the mares' reins and clutched them in her hands.

Hamuel sensed an uneasiness in Gabrielle, so he watched her closely.

Her hands trembled. Another memory trickled through: Zadkiel. "Hamuel, I miss my brother," she said. "My pledge with the Creator keeps me here with our Queen. I am joined with an environment that involves three low-mass stars. Zadkiel could never join me here. He would never survive on this planet. I wish I could tell Zadkiel where I am, as well as Dr. Knight." She gazed over at Hamuel, hoping for a reassuring response.

When he observed Gabrielle's eyes, he saw that her frame of mind was transforming. Her spellbound state was fading and she was beginning to remember clear-cut moments from the beginning of her journey.

"There will be certain times when you can enter upon reflections from your past, but you must let them settle for now. Focus on the journey ahead, Lady Gabrielle. We will concentrate on these matters when the time comes," Hamuel assured her.

Moon-Star glanced over at her mother. She respected her loyalty to Zadkiel—and those she had left behind.

"Mother, let us have faith that this planet will transform. Meeting your brother here will bring us both much happiness. I am looking forward to this meeting. I hope to be strong alongside of you. Let us trust that this will happen for humankind."

Gabrielle noted her daughter's serious expression and could not help but think she looked more like a Queen with each passing moment.

Hamuel was ready to lead them out of the garden, and back to Saffron. Gabrielle's jewel-like hazel eyes were beaming, and her dark hair drifted with the steady breeze. Her sun-kissed skin radiated from within. A transcendent glow surrounded Moon-Star. Her blue eyes sparkled when Gabrielle took her hand.

New clothing and their internal armor shielded their sturdy frames, including their jeweled swords held in their scabbards. The pearl surfaced along their double-edged blades and gleamed over the formed steel. Gabrielle and Moon-Star showed the Creator they had received their spiritual enlightenment.

Gabrielle pulled on the reins with one hand and held Moon-Star's hand with her other. She led three white mares out of the sacred garden. Then she focused on Saffron as she approached her with the spirit animals.

In the earlier stages of creation, the Emissaries situated Saffron, as a Deity, in charge of a great supernatural power. Several messengers waited outside of the garden, including Raguelle and the High Priestess, who remained as one of Gabrielle's special aides. These women were both strategic defenders for the realms and of significant benefit to Gabrielle and Moon-Star. Metatron returned and stood by the women. Just outside the boundaries of the garden was a great-spirited man, Sariel. He joined Hamuel and stood at his side.

Gabrielle's followers and army of women were covering the landscape. Everybody applauded and gazed at their new stately appearances.

She smiled and handed Saffron the reins to an exquisite white mare. Gabrielle saw Saffron's eyes were bright. The pentacles in her eyes still captivated Gabrielle whenever she saw them.

Saffron leaned over to kiss them both on the cheek. "Lady Gabrielle and Queen Moon-Star, our obligation is to join as one," she said and inclined her head. "Let the forces meet. My Queen, you bear a special motif on your wrist." Saffron gestured to her right wrist.

Gabrielle peered at Moon-Star's sleeve. Moon-Star raised her right sleeve to see her moon symbol and a white pearl which included a pentagram on her wrist.

No one knew that Moon-Star had gained the pagan bloodline at birth. This bloodline was a sacred bloodline for magic users. It could be traced back to the Pagan Gods and Goddesses who were set apart in the heavens by the Creator. Moon-Star was the Divine seed of Michael. This secret stayed with the Creator.

"Where did this image of a pentagram come from, Saffron? Are you her mother?" Gabrielle paused and stared at her.

"My Lady, I am not her mother," she assured Gabrielle. "I donated my pagan blood to the Emissaries. Now I know who the pagan blood was for." She watched Gabrielle closely for a reaction.

"I am touched, Saffron," Gabrielle said. "Moon-Star, you have a pagan bloodline." She understood the pentagram was well-grounded along with her transcendent symbols on her wrist.

"I will teach Queen Moon-Star how to manage her supernatural powers. I will call out directions for you both, and you will understand how we can connect our strengths as one. Draw your swords, raise them in the air, and let this ritual begin."

They both reacted to Saffron's call and stepped in front of her. Saffron stood motionless.

Gabrielle and Moon-Star pulled out their swords. Moon-Star held a solid stance and pointed her sword skyward. Gabrielle and Saffron placed their swords over Moon-Star's. An echo of clanging steel resounded as they made the pattern of three crossed swords. Soon after, Saffron's pupils glimmered. The universe sent down a gravitational wave full of stardust, and it surrounded them. The spirit in the bond set Saffron up with a metaphysical strength. Now she could work through her magic.

The tip of her radiant sword ascended into a flame. Saffron pointed and thrusted her sword down to the ground and unearthed a pentagram. The pentagram illuminated and radiated a light to surround the curved edge of their swords. A power came down from the realms and pulled them into a circle.

Saffron connected with a mighty essence—it was her spirited lifeblood. Saffron drew in the support she needed from a coming together of her ancestors in the heavens. She was a master in paganism. Her signal to her ancestors whirled down a vortex full of stardust, to set up an esoteric ritual.

On the ground, Saffron was ready to place three groupings of lines in the sand to shape across a pentagram. This ritual would represent the Guardian Gabrielle, the seed, and herself.

Gabrielle and Moon-Star connected their minds with Saffron. They watched her eyes gleam as her pentacles sparked and she began the ritual to link them together.

"Three," Saffron said. She extended her hand and buried three lines in the sand to seal the pentagram. "Three is the spiritual aspects of mind and body—the energy." She waved her hand across the pentagram and placed six lines. "Six is the true order of justice, and the frequency." She again passed her hand across to bring to light the ending lines. "Nine, is the cosmic consciousness for a spiritual doorway, with our unity on both sides—it's the vibration," Saffron noted and watched Gabrielle and Moon-Star.

They all continued to blend with the essentials for the energy, the frequency, and the vibration. "I call for this power, now we will meet with our psychic abilities and join as the power of three." Saffron changed her position.

Her pentacles in her eyes shone as she concentrated her powers on the image she had made in the sand. Drawing on the powers from her ancestors and the spirit animals, she cast a spell. The flames from the tips of their connected swords fell to ignite the lines. Red flames blazed until they became silver.

"I have united us with the power of three. This is a great power from my ancestors in the heavens." Saffron lowered her sword, and the ladies lowered theirs. Her dominant power encircled Gabrielle and Moon-Star before the connection was complete.

Raguelle, a supreme warrior from planet Eugleston, stood in the distance. She encompassed herself within a cloud and moved her spirit-self across a path that led to the blue Neptune and left a gift for Saffron there. Raguelle then returned her focus to Saffron and approached her.

Saffron was one of the rulers of the blue Neptune. When she looked skyward, an ember of light spiraled down and reached her. Raguelle offered Saffron a new ability, drawn in from the powers of the paradises. Saffron, without hesitation, accepted the honor. She acknowledged Raguelle as she presented her with a new bond through the blue Neptune. Galasus had allowed an astronomical entitlement to be given to Saffron.

Gabrielle and Moon-Star watched Saffron as she finished embracing the transformation.

"These are paranormal essentials from the Gods; you can raise your abilities to new heights," Raguelle said. She bowed and went back to Planet Eugleston.

Saffron walked in front of Gabrielle, who reached out and gripped her hands.

"Thank you, Saffron, for joining us together," Gabrielle said. "You have infused Moon-Star and me with a greater strength." Her eyes met Saffron's. She could see the effects of her transformation in her eyes. There was a change in her.

"My Lady, we have made it this far in our journey. The Creator commended us with equal rights, ensuring that the power of three will triumph through a committed force," Saffron replied and placed her sword back into her scabbard.

Gabrielle was full of heartfelt appreciation for Saffron's loyalty. Her oath was invaluable. "Saffron, you are an impressive gift from the paradises. Thank you for remaining with us." Gabrielle had a gaze that glowed.

"You're welcome, Lady Gabrielle." Saffron nodded to her.

Moon-Star smiled at Gabrielle and Saffron. The ladies looked dignified in appearance. Gabrielle's cheerful face turned to her noble army and followers. With a joyful tone she announced, "I serve our Queen, Moon-Star, who will rule alongside of King Sun-Star, on Varco-XVI. This is where we will live in peace and harmony. Let no harm come to our Queen. Should I fail my duty as her Guardian, your task is to ensure my daughter remains safe on her throne."

The grand army and followers showed their support for their Monarchy. Cheers of jubilation echoed all around them. "Hail to Lady Gabrielle, hail to Queen Moon-Star," the people said.

"The Creator chose us to safeguard this planet and to crown our Queen alongside of her King. No matter what happens, we will fear nothing that could cross our paths," she said. "We live in a different world and we will adjust. Our training for warfare will begin soon."

Saffron bowed her head. She had no knowledge of what was to happen for certain, but she sensed something was stirring in the realms.

Chapter Three
The Battle Begins

Between equal opportunity and Samuel's unfamiliar brashness, he set off a conflict in the paradises. He used a technique focusing on mysticism to incorporate The Golden Door.

Osahar appeared to the scientists back on Earth as a life form in the earlier stages of creation of the new planet. The Creator set Osahar as one Guardian for Earth and humankind. When he appeared in Egypt, he took on the appearance of a handsome Egyptian man. He gave his wisdom to the scientists and interpreted only what was permitted. The scientists accepted his wisdom and agreed to go along with his advice. They did, however, still keep up their scientific standards of observation. Galasus had acquainted him with a revelation in the higher realms. Now Osahar would guide them on a spiritual and supernatural voyage and be their armament inside the great pyramid.

Osahar was considering what he could tell the scientists. He knew Galasus and the Imperial Council had sworn him to secrecy and that he could expose the Royal Ruler Samuel Raiphualas II's variances.

Osahar saw Samuel's impermeable energy where he had arranged a darkness inside the pyramid made of bronze and silver. He understood Galasus' words: "This is his dark star on The Golden Door." He and the Imperial Council were worried as Samuel was completing his duties as a notable standing inside a darkness they could not see or control. He was in sync with everything in the universe and in control of an extraordinary vitality in the outer space. One of them being a reign over the two Mars planets and a mystic link with Pluto. He also had control inside the Orion constellation. Galasus instructed the Imperial Council that it was time to awaken an assortment of Royal Tapestries in the great Coliseum. They were the impervious protectors for the paradises whose spirits rested inside. Now the council feared that the sinister tapestries in the theater that lined the granite walls might awaken without notice. These were the imprisoned warriors who did not abide by the heavenly laws.

Osahar reflected *I know I am a leading commander who communicated directly with the Creator. I'm an influence his Majesty set forth in the earlier stages for the scientists inside the pyramid. I know I must organize them. They need to be the front-runners for a revelation. But I also know I must be delicate with humanity.*

***

The pyramid worked in silence to further events

Osahar received a private message via the Creator. *The new planetary solar system along with Earth's solar system belong to Royal Ruler Samuel Raiphualas II, and Highborn Leader, Galasus Pagasusesia. At times, address the planets to reflect upon his Majesty Samuel by displaying a 'two' in front of the planetary creations*, said the Creator. Osahar acknowledged the Creator's request and went on when he observed Mira and Temperance from the shining core of the pyramid.

There was a dark star swirling across the surface of The Golden Door. Osahar understood Samuel's presence in the pyramid had led to a turn of events that he could not foresee.

He remembered Temperance—she was a Goddess of a paranormal force on planet Eugleston. When her tapestry unfolded in the Coliseum, it brought to Earth a fine-looking woman. Her skin was ashen, and she had long rippling dark hair. Her eyes were the color purple, tinged by a flame. This mystical woman came to Earth due to a rule from the Creator. But he soon found out that it was not for a good purpose.

Temperance's time in power was unfortunate, as the Creator released her to Samuel. Temperance's stigmata also unmasked her ritual scars for Samuel. Every time Osahar thought about this, his shoulders dropped, and a sadness laid siege to him.

The Imperial Council valued Temperance, and they had lined her tapestry with violet gems. She rested in silence on The Golden Door and would use her hourglass when called upon by Samuel for paranormal aid. Then it happened—a glint of light flashed across The Golden Door. She awakened and showed her radiant eyes; they shone through a violet flame.

36

The spiraling Triangulum galaxy deepened with a flow of vapors and it went straight to her hourglass. A malevolence from Samuel managed to sneak in. Black lightning ignited The Golden Door and the course of light showed an astral energy. Temperance sent a psychic command to Mira.

Osahar perked up and faced Temperance in disbelief. He saw Samuel had ordered Temperance to fasten an astral beam to Mira. Osahar thought about his dishonesty to involve Mira in a mercurial relationship with him. And how he had to show her a false way.

His thoughts were: *Now I must watch this effect through her variable star and how she will behave with Samuel's darkness in the universe.* His mind drifted into deepness. *She does not recognize how she benefited me; it was in a way I don't think she will ever understand.*

He steered his attention toward Temperance and watched her feed Mira with another astral beam. She went on in silence and made a solid connection. Osahar searched around and noticed her hourglass signaled in privacy. Hidden inside the hourglass of time was Temperance's paranormal pull touching Mira.

Mira received her instructions from Temperance, and it was to send a shockwave to a female warrior on planet Eugleston. Raguelle was her name. Her bronzed skin and long straight dark hair which was tied behind her presented her glistening silver eyes. She stood tall and was of an athletic build. Raguelle would keep looking for any lines of attack in the universe. This was one of her powers, which could be seen as a rank on her tapestry. Raguelle was able to distinguish new weapons in the universe, so she was considered a threat to Samuel. He wanted to use her, then have her glorious rank removed from her tapestry.

Mira was now working through a private paranormal pull. She reached planet Eugleston and walked into the Coliseum to confront Raguelle with a supposed difficulty she was dealing with. She approached her tapestry and called upon her. "Raguelle, it's Mira, I have something I must tell you," she said.

Raguelle appeared in the distance and stepped out of a whirlwind. "Mira," she said, and approached her. "What brings you to Eugleston?" A look of uncertainty crossed her face.

But Mira was quick with her shockwave. It arrived at Raguelle in an instant. She primed Raguelle's mindset to fluctuate without warning. Her shockwave added to her deep-seated essence and suppressed it inside of her. A secretive astral beam flowed inside the Triangulum galaxy and created a paranormal enchantment attached to Raguelle. Mira left the planet and Raguelle had no recollection of their meeting.

Now Osahar needed to make sure he was ready for what was coming. It looked as though Samuel had arranged a breach in the universe which would cross forward and turn up where Gabrielle and Michael were. He explored Mira's mindset and saw her positioned inside Raguelle's subconscious. She had a game plan and would enforce a threatened order upon Gabrielle when the time was right and then set up a distraction for Michael.

This would normally have had Raguelle dismissed from the paradises when the Emissaries or Sachiel noticed. But Temperance had blocked them temporarily from recognizing Raguelle's fate in the paradises. She held a great darkness inside of her from Samuel, which no one could get through. It seemed the messengers would notice Michael's embarrassment, and Gabrielle would undergo a mental trance that she would not remember. Sadly, no one would pick up on her forewarnings for help.

Osahar hoped Gabrielle and Michael would be able to pull through this phase. The heavens had sworn him to secrecy on Earth.

Chapter Four
Michael's and Sun-Star's Final Day in the Sacred Tent

Just as Gabrielle and Moon-Star had their last day on the northern side of the planet in the sacred garden, it was on the southern side of Varco-XVI, where Michael and Sun-Star had their last day in a sacred tent where they learned the name of the new planet.

Sun-Star was nervous as they neared the ending of the ceremony. "I have a tightness in my stomach." He looked at Michael and rubbed his belly. "Father, our faith and purpose is to honor our homeland and to consent to a contract with the Creator. We are loyal with the love we have for Varco-XVI, and we will worship this treasure as our home. This ceremony to show courage will be our testament for a grand future. It will give us the stability and the dignity to ensure an allegiance with the paradises' leaders."

Michael observed Sun-Star and saw he was tense. But he had just filled him with pride and joy with his words. "That tightness in your stomach is nothing to worry about, it's called butterflies. You have it in you to be the greatest King on this planet. We will prevail with our destiny and go on with a joyful life. Put your mind at ease, my son; today is our last day in the sacred tent," he said. They continued with the last stage.

Outside of the tent was a vast landscape edging the rivers flowing alongside tall blossoming trees. There was plenty of oxygen filling their lungs, as Varco-XVI was a kind of Eden. Their traveling companions stood in a flat area scattered with small, bronzed rocks, packing the caravans with supplies. The climate was warm, and the sky was clear and bright.

West of the sacred tent stood the celestial army; they were practicing their military tactics. Using their swords, the sounds echoed throughout the area, and the stability of their shields shone in a brilliant light. They were waiting for Lord Michael and King Sun-Star to appear before them. Beyond the panorama was a flourishing meadow crowded with scented wildflowers and an abundance of wildlife was prevalent.

But now the south and north would soon be in contact due to a spirited and superior Godly ruler. The powerful forces he could use on planet Eugleston and the universe would break through and set in their paths.

Michael and Sun-Stars' relationship for their purpose was in the south and in agreement with Gabrielle and Moon-Star in the north. The Guardians of the Sun-Star and Moon-Star both consecrated their spirits under a full moon on the summer solstice. The battle was about to begin.

***

A beaming light encircled the sacred tent. Michael and Sun-Star's last day there ended. They banded together with the Creator as seven days in the sacred tent had ensured they were ready to receive the Divine Spirit.

Their appearance gave them a flamboyant look when they displayed their tailored breastplates and helmets. They slid on their boots and a lift of their arms displayed their shields. One lance rested by their right side. Two loin belts appeared, and they wrapped them around their waist and placed their bronze jeweled swords inside their scabbards. Michael and Sun-Star became one with their symbolized energies, and this powered their armor and weaponry on their bodies.

Michael touched his shoulder. "We will be able to unfurl our warrior attire when called for, just by using the power of our minds."

"Father, my mind is clear. I will protect myself in my glorious armor. And those butterflies, they're gone!"

Michael cherished his celestial gift, Sun-Star, but something was stirring at the back of his mind; something from his past. A sudden memory of his father Immanuel brought sadness. "I am now having thoughts of my father, Sun-Star."

"You remember your father again! It's been quite some time since you last spoke of him," Sun-Star said. He moved closer to his Guardian and glanced into his eyes.

"Yes, and I hope you can meet him. When that day arrives, he will add to my happiness here with you. And I wish I could tell my boss where I am. But you know what, Sun-Star? He is a clever scientist, and I bet he is at the central point of this," he said and watched Sun-Star for a reaction.

"He probably is, because you are a brilliant scientist, and I am sure you left behind enough clues."

Michael smiled at him and hoped he was right. "Gabrielle and I reached out to him before we left the Texas observatory. I went to the South African Bakoni Ruins, and that is where I discovered a portal and superior beings who brought me here to Varco-XVI. This planet has the same qualities as Earth." He scratched his head and looked skyward. "Sun-Star, our families will search to the end of time for Gabrielle and me. But we've crossed over from our existence as being human," he said. "Gabrielle and I now have an astral bond with each other. My heart stays warm when I think of her. No one will take her from me," he said as he bowed his head.

"I know you have a great connection with her and so will I." Sun-Star moved into Michael's personal space. "But when you talk about her, I notice a change in your mood." He sensed his father's overprotectiveness.

Michael had suddenly recalled Josh who had an interest in her, and this changed his mood.

He raised his head. "I feel a possessiveness toward Gabrielle. I appreciate this world and everything in it," he said sincerely. "It will be me alongside of her. We might never meet our families again, so I must keep her close to my heart. Life on this planet offers a cosmic force, no human can tolerate an absorption from these three low-mass stars' emissions. My contract with the Creator is to be your Guardian. Now I must remain focused and deliver you to your Kingdom. When Gabrielle and I work out our agreement, I will plead to the heavens. And wish for this planet to become suitable for human life. But for now, the Creator's plan calls for us to go on with our journey."

Sun-Star detected Michael's sincerity. "There must be a way we can greet Immanuel. Father, I have confidence he will be in our presence one day." He turned to face Michael and showed him his high spirits.

"We've got this far, my son, so maybe one day my father will turn up." His eyes lit up when he peered skyward. Michael respected his father and his boss.

His right hand lifted and gripped his talisman; Michael rubbed his fingers over it. "Around mine and Gabrielle's neck is a safeguarded talisman. The Creator gave this to us as well as you and Moon-Star. When we both appeared on the purple planet we now know as Varco-XVI, we were each given a star baby. I now remember this through this talisman. There is an inscription inside, Sun-Star, and when we arrive at our destination, Gabrielle and I will get this message. Our journey is to reach our destinies so let's stay focused. I want Gabrielle in my arms and your Queen in yours," he said and glanced over at him.

41

Sun-Star's reaction was quick. "Yes. I will remain focused and be by your side. I'm eager to arrive at where these exquisite women are and I want to understand what that inscription gives rise to." He winked and clasped his hands together.

A bright sunlit morning prompted a sunbeam to move toward the ram skin. It unsealed. Both men left the sacred tent and displayed radiance that seemed to encircle them; their presence was striking. The smell of frankincense drew their attention to the numerous Boswellia sacra trees beyond. They stood in a sheltered region scattered with shrubs and small trees where the Creator gifted Michael a sanctified tent full of weaponry. In the distance, Efren stepped closer to them. He revealed a broad grin. Three notable black stallions stood beside the sacred tent. Their dark, piercing eyes met with Michael's. He approached one horse and placed both palms on its neck and stroked a dark mane. He raised a set of leather reins and passed them to Sun-Star.

"Wow, Father. What a magnificent contribution from the paradises. I'm confident these honorable horses will serve us well."

Michael and Sun-Star had picked up the finest crafted garments in the sacred tent. They were both wearing long, black, hooded cloaks, leather boots, gloves, and jeweled armor. Luminous swords hung by their port sides with a brilliant amethyst that coiled through their blades with a glint. Impenetrable bronze shields were bound on one arm. Embedded on their shields flashed a symbol of justice. An image of a sun and moon was alongside a symbol of Sariel and Hamuel. Their shields held a motif which resembled swords.

Paul, one of eleven men who tracked the sacred tent in secret, came back to address Michael.

"Lift your left sleeve, my Lord. It's time for you to accept King Sun-Star's symbol."

Paul formed a whirlwind in his palm and engrained a sun symbol on top of Michael's left wrist. Their eyes flashed as they looked at each other.

"When you are ready to settle this evening, please accompany me. This evening will be your last stay at the house, but I will return in time," Paul said.

"Thank you, Paul, for your part in our journey and for placing my son's symbol on my wrist. We look forward to your return," Michael said.

Paul nodded to Lord Michael and King Sun-Star. "You're welcome," he replied and left.

Sun-Star did not hesitate. He took Michael's wrist. "This image is impressive; you are my father, and I am privileged to be by your side."

Michael paid close attention to Sun-Star. His gentle voice resonated, "I am your Guardian, Sun-Star, who raised you, and yes, I picked up the right to be your father. You will always be my son."

When he witnessed Michael's reaction, Sun-Star's smile could not get any fuller. He treasured Michael's remark.

Efren arrived, Michael offered him a huge grin, and raised a set of leather reins in front of him. "A mighty steed is yours, Efren."

He brushed the horse's mane. "A priceless gift from the Creator, thank you, Lord Michael."

"Look at this, I have my son's symbol." He flaunted his left wrist in Efren's face.

"What a distinguished mark, my Lord." His pentacles brightened as he studied Michael's unique impression.

"The sacred tent holds many weapons, Efren. We will need to sharpen our skills on how to deal with these superior items."

"Yes, Lord Michael, I will be helpful in how to implement training for these weapons."

"I'm missing something." Michael crossed his arms and examined him. "Is there any wine left?" he asked.

Efren laughed. He stepped in and grabbed them both into a powerful man hug.

"Welcome back." Efren's curious eyes scanned over them. He settled back. "You both look dashing," he said.

"Thanks, Efren, I guess my father hasn't changed," Sun-Star said. Using his mental powers, he removed his armor and dashed ahead.

Michael glanced over to discover Sun-Star was rooting for a chalice of wine.

"Bad news, my Lord, the wine barrels are empty. But the wine carafes are full. Priorities meant our assistants should harvest and store wheat, fruit, and vegetables for the journey. This part of the planet does not have any grape vines. We might locate some grape vines further ahead. The dark forest is plentiful in the way of meat and poultry, and the rushing rivers yield plenty of fish. Our bodies absorb a force from the universe, as we still require a mortal strength, my Lord. There is enough food stored in clay tubs," he said.

Michael followed Sun-Star, as he was nearing a table where the wine carafes were. "Sun-Star wants to guzzle the wine," Michael said. "But he's not excited when it comes time to stomping those grapes." They both laughed.

"Thank you for continuing the hunt and regulating the food for the next part of our journey. I am glad we have you here, Efren." Michael paused with a grin. He stepped in front of Efren and gave him a good handshake. He then removed his armor through the power of thought.

The wine carafes and chalices rested on the wooden table. Sun-Star almost flattened the ground with his new boots when he ran over to get a chalice and his black cloak lifted in a warm breeze.

Michael looked surprised and feared they might have remained in the sacred tent for too long. He wondered if Sun-Star had become stir crazy.

"Efren, does Sun-Star seem different? He's filling way too many chalices with wine!" he asked.

They glanced over at each other. "No, King Sun-Star just enjoys his wine," Efren replied.

"Let's go over there before he sets up his own party." Michael realized Sun-Star was in a festive mood.

Michael and Efren strode toward the timber tables. The army waiting for them glanced over at Lord Michael and all bowed. The celebration started with everyone welcoming Lord Michael and King Sun-Star with firm handshakes. There was a grand feast of lamb, wine, fresh hot bread, pheasant, beef, vegetables and fruit, and an assortment of desserts. Sun-Star grabbed a plate and heaped a variety of food on it and gave it to Michael.

"Thank you, how thoughtful. You gave me plenty of my favorite meal: pheasant." Michael turned to Efren. "The hunt for pheasant is plentiful in the vast forest." His mouth watered at the sight of this delicious food.

Admiring the view of the tower of food on his plate, Sun-Star loaded another one up and gave it to Efren.

"Well, my King, look at this bounty." Efren looked up and smiled at him. His head went back down to stare at his plate. "My Lord, our King has quite the appetite."

"Let's eat, I will never finish this," Michael said.

"Come on, Dad, get that delicious pheasant in you. This is, after all, your favorite meal. There is warm bread in front of you and I loaded another plate with a variety of desserts," he said and placed both hands on his hips.

Michael looked at an enormous plate towering with an assortment of desserts. Beside it was another plate loaded with sliced bread plastered with whipped butter. He watched Sun-Star stuffing his face and taking advantage of every minute.

They enjoyed their meal and talked about their next destination.

"Well, what a magnificent feast. Thank you, everybody for such an impressive spread of food," Michael said.

Several attendants glanced over and smiled at Michael; they took away their plates. Sun-Star leaned back in his large chair. He was stuffed to the brim.

A sense of duty redirected Michael's thoughts, and he leant towards Efren to talk. "I have absolute confidence in you, Efren. I understand the weapons inside the sacred tent show the journey ahead is no minor task," he said. "Efren, your imperious rank must be for these approaching campaigns."

Efren countered. "You know I am honored to be at your service, my Lord. The skills both of you possess on this planet are about to become greater. Lord Michael, King Sun-Star, we will join with our spirits and be as one." Efren got up and bowed to Michael and Sun-Star.

Michael and Sun-Star glanced up at Efren. They both got up and contemplated how this could happen.

"Efren, what do you have in mind?" Sun-Star inquired.

"Oh, my King," he said and pointed at Sun-Star's wrist. "The pentagram image is on your left wrist."

Sun-Star raised his left sleeve, to reveal a superb mass spiraling on his wrist. A fueled flame arced to encompass a perfect pentagram, and a brightness shielded his adorned sun and black pearl.

"Pagan blood at birth gave you the freedom to continue with the supernatural, my King. Your superior spirit will permit us three to serve as one," Efren said.

"King Sun-Star, a greater power awakens in you." Efren's enigmatic eyes blazed over his pentacles. "Your spirit is mighty, my King."

Sun-Star had gained the consecrated pagan bloodline at birth, and he was *the Divine seed of Gabrielle. This secret stayed with the Creator.*

Michael stared over at Efren and needed to know. "Efren, by any chance is Sun-Star your son?" he asked.

"No, my Lord, I am but a contributor to King Sun-Star's pagan blood. Lord Michael, you accepted your covenant from Paul, you are King Sun-Star's Guardian and Father."

"Look at my left wrist, Father, I must learn how to take care of this additional force," Sun-Star said and raised his arm in front of him.

"Let me look at that," he said and glanced down at his wrist. "I'm sure Efren will ground us alongside of his magic." They both looked straight into Efren's eyes and wondered what he was about to do.

"My Lord and my King, I will signal directives. A metaphysical relationship will join our spirits." Efren paced around them.

"Are you ready to receive orders, King Sun-Star?" Michael suggested.

A jolt into Sun-Star's side from Michael's elbow signaled him to follow his lead. He accepted, and a tilt at their waist showed they accepted Efren's call.

Words were raised in an enthusiastic tone. "Yes, I will support Efren's decrees."

Michael faced Efren. "We are at your service."

Efren beamed and bowed slightly to Michael and Sun-Star. "You both have an outstanding blend of the Creator's magic inside you," he revealed. "I recognize what enhancements we can control, our spirits as three can infuse. We will become privileged as a superior pressure on this planet. Lord Michael, before we set up, the Creator established a valuable script within your mind. Let him receive your voice."

Luminous vapors hovered above Michael. He faced skyward. Clustered clouds drifted in and concealed his muscular frame. He drew a hefty breath.

"I, Lord Michael, call up the covenant. When I received your Divine spirit from the heavens, I pledged to be the Guardian of Sun-Star and to protect the sacred seeds." He bowed.

A light cropped up in the spacious horizon, and mystical flares showed Michael that the Creator received his message.

Michael and Sun-Star unfurled their armor and removed their swords from their scabbards. They crossed them over each other. Efren's sword joined in and contributed to a scorching flame. Three crossed swords created an impression in the grand universe. Michael's army gazed up as each man reached for their scabbard and unsheathed their sword. Raw steel clanged as the army presented their sword and crossed them over each other's. Efren's dark, enigmatic eyes lit up and an image of astral flares mixed inside his hot opaque eyes and reflected both pentacles. The ground shuddered, and solar flares rooted Michael, Sun-Star, and Efren inside a bronze pentagram. In the distance, a golden sky rumbled, and a spiraling galaxy released an ethereal cloud. The mixture enclosed strong vapors and carried them inside a radiant veil. It swept around their unwavering frames and then slipped away in a torrent. Efren bowed and lowered his sword; Michael and Sun-Star followed. Efren had created the power of three for a great strength they would need on Varco-XVI.

"Thank you, Efren," Michael said. "Sun-Star and I have merged with a phenomenon. The power of three will prevail. This is a superior ability you have brought into our bodies and minds. My life on Varco-XVI will be to reign alongside of my son. I thank you for your loyalty to us and the paradises."

Efren saw how Michael had transformed into a worthy man. "I will be at your service without end, Lord Michael and King Sun-Star."

Michael reached out his hand and Efren came back with a firm handshake.

They stood in silent contemplation for a moment.

Sun-Star perked up. "Well, look who is moving our way," he said and directed their attention to a person walking towards them.

Dante showed up and offered a welcome. "I'm sure glad to see you, Lord Michael and King Sun-Star." He clasped his hands and bowed. "Oh, and you as well, Efren." Dante had a quirky grin on his face.

Michael looked at Dante's face which now had a puzzled expression on it. "Thanks, it sure is good to see you too, Dante. How are you?" Michael asked.

He patted his head and was figuring out how to respond to Lord Michael. "Well, I can't get any rest. You know, Lord Michael, that I suffer from nightmares." He started fidgeting with his hands.

Michael crossed his arms. His face held a troubled expression, with a touch of concern. "How long has it been since you slept? And tell me what's going on with these nightmares?"

Dante shivered. His bewildered eyes went cross-eyed, then he snapped out of it and straightened his posture. He shook his head which cleared his view. "Well, since I met you, my Lord, I haven't experienced a normal night's sleep." His dark eyes stared up at Michael. "For the last seven evenings, there have been several hazy creatures drifting in the night sky. Numerous masked men in black armor set out from a freezing forest on creepy horses. I hid here and there and watched them roaming all over the place. Lord Michael, I nearly froze to death," he said with his teeth chattering.

Michael examined Dante. "Are you okay?" he asked. "You seem cold, it's best to put on a jacket." He looked at Dante closely. "Dante, please keep us informed if these dark dreams appear again, I want to know."

"I will keep you posted, my Lord." Dante took a deep breath and wandered elsewhere.

***

Beyond the landscape, a whirlwind of fire appeared. It was Sariel. He walked through a spiraling mist and greeted Michael and Sun-Star. Sariel saluted them on their last day.

"Lord Michael, King Sun-Star, you are now one in harmony with the Creator. To have blended privileges with Efren is a glorious achievement," Sariel said.

In the distance, a light stretched across the ground. Raguelle drifted in on the tails of the spiraling Triangulum galaxy. Her arrival was imposing and they witnessed a magnificent soldier stepping forward. She nodded and approached Sun-Star. "I will give you, King Sun-Star, an additional inner force," Raguelle said and paced around him.

Two suns moved inward and solar flares rushed across the blue sky. The ground vibrated when the sunbeams attached to Sun-Star's body. Raguelle swung both arms to lift him into a magical inferno. This was the ultimate blending for Sun-Star's internal flame. She called up his amethyst and sank a violet flame into his sword. Sun-Star's pentagram encircled a radiant blaze.

Raguelle turned to Michael and nodded. "I will put a zenith over your spirited sword. Your magnificent sword will drift without restriction during each battle and serve you, my Lord."

Roiling through Michael's sword was cosmic dust, and Raguelle activated his amethyst with a violet flame. She stared into his watchful eyes but then stepped back as she had a thought of uncertainty. She cleared her mind and proceeded. "Your amethyst is from the Creator; a perfect jewel powers King Sun-Star and your magnificent sword, my Lord."

Raguelle turned away from Michael and extended her psyche to join in with the paradises. When she raised both arms, she pulled in a galactic wind. The roiling wind sparked a flame, it then spilled across the enlivened sky and spearheaded straight down to her. Raguelle gripped a slice of the universe in her hands, and Galasus handed her a card. She pointed a shaft of light at Michael, then Sun-Star and Efren. The Three of crossed Swords was embedded across their left upper arm.

She shifted and faced Efren. He met Raguelle's gleaming eyes as she said, "The great Nile is a source of your water and needs to be protected. I will give you a special gift, Efren; brace yourself."

He nodded in agreement and a flare exited her fingertips. She pierced his torso with a special power.

"You can now get yourself nearer to the blue Neptune."

Raguelle then informed Efren of the great power she had attached to him, which would add to his skills.

With a burst of energy, she exclaimed, "This is a personal bond I gave to you, and it is a privilege. You can now meet with Saffron inside an uncharted domain. The Tree of Life will lead to a greater elevation of consciousness for you, Saffron, Lady Gabrielle, and Lord Michael."

Raguelle nodded, and then set out in a stormy mist.

Sariel walked forward. "Lord Michael and King Sun-Star, you have both been filled with a radiant spirit from the universe. Efren and I will guide you to address these cosmic strengths and I will equip us for simulated warfare. Please join me before nightfall." Sariel bowed and drifted away.

An immense force of space dust arrived on the planet from the Milky Way Galaxy. The ground rumbled. An imperial sight arose beyond the southern horizon. The empyrean hurled two raging neutron stars into view, and stardust showed a spirit-like hand cloaked around Hamuel. A deafening blast ricocheted through a host of astral flares to shadow the ground. He stepped through a cluster of circulating particles and a primary path took him to Michael.

He faced him and said, "In spirit, you sit at the right hand of the Creator, Lord Michael. The following words are of the utmost importance."

Hamuel lifted both arms and sent a riveting flare skyward. He gazed at Michael. "Who is like the Creator," he said. "One day you will have to make a decision about allowing your life to continue or death to come; you will find out when death is near, my Lord. Place these words in your subconscious mind, and keep them there. Use these words when the time arises." A sudden breeze swept across the landscape; heavenly flares circulated and tinted them with a glow.

Michael bowed and acknowledged Hamuel's guidance. "Thank you, Hamuel, for these righteous words, I will never forget them."

"I have returned with more gifts, Lord Michael. They're organized in your sacred tent; your spiritual army now controls many weapons."

Hamuel continued. "Lord Michael and King Sun-Star, you wear the Breastplates of Righteousness, and the Boots of Peace. On your arms you have a sense of balance through the Shields of Faith and you wear the Helmets of Salvation. You show the Loin Belts of Truth sheathed with a Sword of the Spirit, and by your sides are the Lances of Worship," he said and raised both arms. "Lord Michael and King Sun-Star, you are the Divine seeds of the Creator." He nodded and a galactic flame pulled him away.

Sun-Star turned and stepped in front of Michael. "Father, I will never fail you with those words. I will remind you when the day comes, you can count on me." Sun-Star stood immersed in Hamuel's words and he was certain it was his responsibility to prompt his father.

Efren bowed to Lord Michael in agreement.

Michael considered his noble men and walked to them. "My brothers-in-arms, our second destination is not too far ahead," he said. "We are armed and the Creator chose us to protect this planet and to crown our King alongside of his Queen. Let us not fear what could cross our paths. We are alive in a different world, so we must adjust. Our training for warfare will begin with the messengers soon. Let us enjoy this amazing day together."

On the timber table, an assembly of chalices overflowed with red wine. Michael, Sun-Star, and Efren raised their chalice. A thump together signaled them to say, "Cheers."

Efren bowed his head for a moment as a coiled brightness entered his vision. He could not interpret it but he suspected something was shifting in the realms.

Sun-Star interrupted Efren's thoughts by saying, "So, Dad, no more wine?"

"No, we must keep a sharp mind, so it's best to put the chalice on the table, Sun-Star," Michael said and waved his hand at him.

Efren laughed. "My King, we have no more wine." He pointed to the empty wine barrels.

Sun-Star had an idea. "I will stop drinking this delicious wine," he said and watched the sweet wine run along the edge as he swirled the glass, "If you do, Dad." He glanced over at his father and hoped that his heartfelt words would inspire him.

Michael did not hesitate to throw out his wine which splattered on the ground. His army followed his lead.

"Does a big chalice of goat's milk sound good, Sun-Star?" Michael wrapped up his comment with a grin across his face.

He reconsidered. "No, just a thought, let's fill these wine flasks with fresh water."

Sun-Star smiled at him. "Terrific, I knew you had it in you."

"You bet, my son. We're set up for battle. Sun-Star, your safety comes first, we need flawless judgment for what threatens us. When you were old enough, we amused ourselves with the stomping of grapes. Then you started throwing grapes. Efren and I were eventually wearing grapes. Then we finished with grape mustaches as we drank our glorious wine," Michael slurred and laughed. "Those were great times. But I did sense you had some issues with the stomping of grapes." He leaned over and gave him a nudge.

Sun-Star eyeballed Michael. "Oh yes, memorable days." He nodded and showed Michael a grin. "We put together a load of fun, and I look forward to future wine making, Father."

Efren gazed over at everybody and realized they had disposed of their wine. He placed his hand to rest on his chin. "I have the only chalice of wine left. What should I do?"

Michael and Sun-Star watched him. He flung his chalice up in the air and the wine flew out to land on Dante's head.

"Nice shot, Efren," Dante said as he detected a taste of the dripping wine.

"Dante, you remind me of Dad, Efren, and me, when we soaked ourselves with that glorious wine."

"Yes, my King, I can picture you all having an amusing time producing it. And I know you enjoy the festivities that go along with preparing the wine, my King."

Sun-Star stared at Dante and shook his head in amusement.

Dante walked away dripping in wine; he licked his lips and headed over to a stream to take a bath.

Michael and Sun-Star regrouped and spoke to their men.

Efren then became serious and shared, "I have come to learn that Lady Gabrielle commands an all-female army."

Sun-Star regarded Efren. He then turned to behold his men-in-arms. "My brothers-in-arms, later today simulated warfare will allow us to train to be exceptional warriors. This will be conducted by the mightiest warriors on this planet," he said.

"Father expressed to me inside of the sacred tent, that life, wherever it be present, is the fruit of the Creator's seeds. But we here on Varco-XVI, are the selected ones. That makes us a proud diversity of the Creator's plan to protect this planet. With a Celestial army, we are the spiritual beings who will strive for a lifetime in a peaceful world. Etched upon our impenetrable shields is a whirlwind filled with numerous swords. We have Sariel, Hamuel, and my sun and moon, and a justice symbol on our shields. Dante placed four pentacles on our shields—the powers of earth, air, fire, and water will serve us well. A fifth detail also came from the Creator, and it enlightened my father and I in the sacred tent. This spiritual gift is an element that will charge all shields to be impenetrable. My army, we will dedicate ourselves to this journey. Let us move forward with open hearts and reign over this beautiful planet."

The crowd cheered. Sun-Star had a deep feeling stirring inside of him and he found his inner voice. "Thank you for your faithfulness in journeying with me to meet my Queen. Efren has also informed me Lady Gabrielle rides with a spiritual army, and they're all female." Sun-Star raised an eyebrow and waited for his army's reaction.

Michael, Efren, and the army rose to address their King and applauded him.

Sun-Star raised his chalice. "Cheers to my family, and my brothers-in-arms, let us stay focused and reach these magnificent women."

They raised their chalices filled to the brim with water. "Cheers," the people called out.

Chapter Five
The Godly Ruler Sachiel

Nestled inside the Triangulum galaxy, is where planet Eugleston housed Galasus and his Imperial Council. Galasus called upon Metatron who then left The Golden Door and went to the Coliseum where he met him and the Emissaries in the council chamber.

The heavens had adorned Metatron with a jeweled breastplate interlaced with gold chains. He wore hand-crafted leather sandals and rawhide clothing. His bronze shield decorated with silver etching rested on his left arm and his left side bore a new jeweled sword.

Highborn Leader Galasus Pagasusesia walked ahead to greet him. "Metatron, I have set up a meeting where you will meet with a Godly man. Your decree will come to you when you leave the chamber and go to Varco-XVI. Get ready for a new phase in the universe," he advised.

Metatron bowed to Galasus, then to the Imperial Council, and drifted away.

Metatron arrived on Varco-XVI, and he looked upon Sachiel. "I know you are a courageous sentry in the universe who will not abide by change. When you searched the universe, you discovered what could be our doom." He bowed his head to him.

Sachiel faced Metatron, ready to tell him about a big change in the paradises. "A prominent God stirred up a darkness in the universe and on the western side of this planet. He is gaining followers at an alarming rate. I have expanded my control through the pink Jupiter and Earth's Jupiter. Alongside to help me is a Deity who accepted a metaphysical directive. She is part of the pink Jupiter plan."

The Deity sheltered behind a rainbow cloak and she was hiding their meeting from prying eyes. Metatron looked away and fixated on Sachiel.

Sachiel's dark eyes focused on Metatron. He had important information to share that would have serious repercussions.

"I deliver news about a privileged star named Royal Ruler Samuel Raiphualas II, and your brother Sandalphon. As you know, a guarded star rules alongside the Creator. Together inside a planned dimension, they created this paradise. The Creator and his Majesty noted and marked another world as useful for human life," he said and paced around Metatron.

"When the Creator placed Samuel's spiritual being on The Golden Door in Egypt's pyramid, it was his bright star in control. But his dark star was stirring up a plan. Galasus, the Emissaries, and I did not notice any changes to him or the universe. I am in contact with the Creator, as well as Samuel, who is opposite to him. Samuel's dark star took a spot on The Golden Door without anyone noticing and his placements on this new planet await his command," he said. Sachiel understood the Creator always withheld evidence to some extent when a celestial dark star went off course.

"The Imperial Council's Emissaries failed to see his Majesty's dark star had gone astray. They did not report this to Galasus. He could have reined in his dark star. I watched his dark star hovering over Varco-XVI as it was trying to connect but went offline. The council needed to find a way to repress his dark star. His Majesty went to trial and became livid with their judgment, so the Creator removed him from the realms and put him inside a black hole to calm his dark star. He stays a supreme being in title and abilities, but he succeeded in overshadowing his bright star," he said and sent Metatron a pained look.

Then he broke eye contact and continued. "When I looked back in time, I saw a gravitational tug in the universe. It rippled inside of a super-heated shockwave. Samuel's movement across the universe was undetected. But I knew something was not right, then I saw Samuel's dark star. Samuel escaped from the black hole and slid inside a raging pulsar. Now he plans to destroy Earth and reign over the planet he and the Creator made," he said and shook his head.

"Metatron, his dark existence now controls a nearby supernova. Gamma-rays and neutrinos from a collapsing star stay buried someplace in the universe. The solar neutrinos from the core of the Earth's sun, stream him an infinite source of energy. He hid a mixture of the universe's real meaning; this hidden secret worries us because he alone can create a nuclear-powered force. It will be greater than anything we have ever known. Now we must look at our Majesty, Samuel, as the enemy who will give rise to an unknown force," Sachiel said. He pondered about the dark tapestries in the theater. His last meeting with the Creator allowed him to understand that the truth of this matter would never become known.

"The Emissary's decision to dismiss Samuel was the best course of action. His confinement by the Creator gave Galasus enough time to find what he needs in a bright room. The Creator let him know about the tapestries in the Coliseum and the theater. Galasus is awakening many Godly leaders of the universe," Sachiel said. "Samuel's clever escape made him eager to get revenge on the Emissaries. I forewarned Galasus and he made it known to the Imperial Council. Samuel's bright star still lingers in his celestial body, but his dark star soon took over." He looked at Metatron and saw he was in deep thought; he was tapping his sword by his side.

"Samuel gained a dark room and will unleash the dark warriors from the theater tapestries. He also gained an authority within the Orion constellation," Sachiel said. His eyes widened and with his brows furrowed, he continued. "He will wield many dark tapestries above a tomb on the west side. Two dark tapestries belong to a great power, and these are two evil spirits. Metatron, a great God named Ramiel will work alongside of Samuel," he said. Sachiel saw Metatron closing his eyes and lowering his head.

Metatron then reminisced about the celestial being, Ramiel, who wielded a grand power in the realms for both the dark and bright side of creation. Metatron was fearful of this man, but knew many would come to aid him, in his time of need. He blocked out this thought and continued to listen to Sachiel.

"Ramiel will raise these two dark spirits to execute Samuel's hidden plan in the universe. Their function will be to destroy Earth and go into battle for Varco-XVI. Far away, Samuel positioned three red dwarfs to orbit his dark star. They wait in balance for a meeting; this will be catastrophic. I expect in time his dark spirits will drift these red dwarfs into the Oort clouds. In addition, they will boost up the gamma ray levels. This mixture will generate an imminent-Earth explosion, to wipe out humanity."

Sachiel crossed his arms and took a deep breath. "I have searched through Samuel's history and I have a sense that time had stopped somewhere. Samuel is an ancient God and watched over by the Imperial Council. It is Galasus who holds the reins for his dark star. Something created a ripple in space, and when this created confusion for everyone, they all missed his transformation. I caught his actions when it was too late. The universe will now face the opposite side of his brightness."

Metatron put his hands on his head. He could not believe the force they would face from Royal Ruler Samuel Raiphualas II, whose bright star had been reversed, and his dark star had taken over and gone astray.

Sachiel continued as he began to explain about the others that Samuel had involved.

"Samuel crept his way through the universe where he took himself back in time. There was a place where he found an extraordinary being of power who bears a tapestry in the Coliseum and the theater. He apprehended this woman's tapestry in the dark room and then secured her in the underworld and expects her rebirth," Sachiel said.

"A promise by the Creator allowed Samuel an option of cards from (II) the High Priestess. She handed over her Divine deck to the Creator for Samuel, to embrace a collection of dark cards in secret. Galasus must now counter these cards, so he arranged for Osahar to introduce a range of cards to the scientists on Earth inside the pyramid. This phase in the plan draws nearer. Samuel now commands (II) the High Priestess' most valuable card: XIV-Temperance. She is on The Golden Door and operates an hourglass. We can follow her sands in time, and we can also watch Samuel's phases, and they are changing quickly. His dark seeds roam in every corner on Varco-XVI."

Sachiel gazed into Metatron's troubled eyes.

"His spiritual and supernatural essences remain deep seated in Egypt on The Golden Door. Samuel also secured a variable brilliant star, Mira, in the earlier stages of creation. His dark star dragged her in from the Cetus constellation and sent her straight to the Triangulum Galaxy in secret. Osahar has an attachment to her, so we must stay alert. Mira is now present there in the form of a high-spirited woman; she works her shockwaves in the universe for Samuel to use," he said and continued.

"Samuel holds sway over two Mars, and he instructs Pluto. A step up of power flows across the universe, and a breath of malice fuels countless neutrinos across The Golden Door."

Sachiel looked at Metatron with glazed eyes. "You know what this means, Metatron; it's the billionth year. Galasus continues to read the scrolls of the 'estranged dark stars' in private. He now knows that those in authority have a position that leads to a great power. Our heroes of the universe might amend Samuel's dark star as they have done this with estranged dark stars before. But Samuel holds a greatness inside of him we do not understand. Let us hope this Highborn Leader will survive and put a stop to the chaos we have experienced for billions of years."

Metatron bowed his head and recalled the great apocalypses that had almost ended all in existence. He gazed at Sachiel and bowed for him to continue.

"Galasus has summoned the tapestries in the great Coliseum. He is also aware of the dark powers buried for billions of years. Samuel controls the dark stars entrapped on the tapestries inside the theater," Sachiel said and knew his most important goal was for their survival. Any small threat could lead to a bigger one.

"Samuel now leads an offensive in the realms. This led to a delay in humankind to be able to live on the planet. Varco-XVI's environment shows three low-mass stars; this disengagement has not taken place. Gravitational waves stream one hundred years away from Earth and show a dark and bright view. New sanctions ruled by Galasus will bring us a diversity of Godly leaders and Guardians–they will safeguard the Creator's seeds. You are one of these leaders, Metatron, and soon you will receive your reward in the realms from (II) the High Priestess. Her Divine deck has been awakened."

Metatron bowed his head and thought about how Samuel's plan had devastating consequences for a celestial planet. The outcome would cause a revolution in the universe. This judgment involved humans and the Creator's mature beings to follow a prophecy.

"Sandalphon served Samuel due to a force not seen by anyone. A personified form of your brother sits in silence on The Golden Door, his sword a direct match to yours."

This update disappointed Metatron. "A guarded star met his billionth epoch to refurbish his stars, and this came to him too early, and the Emissaries missed this? His Majesty developed a hostile intent for Varco-XVI and Earth; this will be an uprising in the universe. Now it involves humankind and drew my brother away. How could this have happened?" Metatron asked and shook his head. He looked at Sachiel and wondered if he was strong enough to stand up against the opposition.

His brother's misfortune overwhelmed him and Metatron dropped to his knees. Dark pressure from a Royal ruler had overwhelmed Sandalphon and his Majesty would create havoc on Varco-XVI, throughout the universe, and make his way to Earth.

"The paradises make ready for battle," Sachiel said.

"I understand my brother's soul is forced to stay on the ominous side of the planet. We share the same privileges from the heaven's hierarchy, and Sandalphon carries one of the mightiest swords," Metatron said and stood.

"Hemmed in by a dark dominance is a bronze serpent, and it controlled Sandalphon with its venomous bite. This removed his inner enlightenment with a poison from beyond the realms. Now he defends a monumental tomb where an overpowering influence awaits resurrection. Galasus put strict orders to the Imperial Council. The Emissaries will not interfere. But I detect two menacing spirits; this pressure matches no other," Sachiel said.

"Samuel possesses an esoteric castle and a cryptic pyramid on the northern side of Varco-XVI. This is where he operates a galactic energy. There is a warning which hovers over The Golden Door. A power arranges for seven gates to open. This is for the woman he apprehended and it's a troubling confinement in the underworld. Samuel has grown to worship her. The last gate will deliver his first rule from the underworld. She is sister to a genuine Queen. He will be ready, and this new woman will be his Queen. A quick victory is what Samuel searches for, and Earth will fall into a darkness filled with ominous spirits," Sachiel revealed and understood this was a dangerous set-up in the making.

"Galasus has been working tirelessly reading the archived ancient scrolls, and we hope what Galasus is uncovering is enough to stop him. But now we must prepare for the worst outcome in the universe, for Earth and Varco-XVI. Samuel's dark entities will be his lead to a tiresome battle. They will weaken the Guardians and possibly bring death to them all," Sachiel said. "Galasus informed me that a human spirit can put an end to Samuel's dark star when it's his time to appear on the planet. To destroy the paradises' nefarious power, you must show the Breastplates of Righteousness, the Helmets of Salvation, the Boots of Peace, the Shields of Faith, and the Loin Belts of Truth sheathed with the Sword of the Spirit. Two Lances of Worship must pierce his heart; only this force can contain Samuel's dark star. Galasus will summon a righteous leader who will arrive on this planet. This is where he will assemble a power to contain his Majesty's dark star," he said.

Metatron understood Sachiel's message and this made his journey even harder because not only did Gabrielle and Michael bear these items, but so did the King and Queen.

"Look upon the heavens, Metatron, and lift your energies so you will obey the sacred laws. If Lady Gabrielle and Lord Michael reach a specific point on the planet, Samuel will summon the great God, Ramiel, who will raise the two dark seeds. They will both then change over to a dark living entity. Alongside the tomb, Sandalphon controls a menacing bronze serpent. Lord Michael and King Sun-Star's protection are Efren and Sariel, while Lady Gabrielle and Queen Moon-Star have Saffron and the High Priestess and Raguelle. Gabrielle and Michael also have Hamuel and Sariel, as they work on both sides of the planet. Hamuel, is a new Protostar who holds the lead with a remarkable force from inside the depths of the Orion Nebula. He is also an IV-Emperor in the paradises and these are the highest powers over the universe. Galasus managed to put forth many to mingle in time. He is the Highborn Leader who will work out a solution," he said.

"Osahar is an outstanding Guardian; he is a watcher over The Golden Door's actions and a protector of humans. Powers from beyond connect to him and deliver him precise guidance. Call on direction from him but make certain your words are in good faith as his mindset belongs to the Creator. Mira will spiral out her shockwave for Samuel. How matters stand has led to a disturbance for Osahar. Keep watch of these conflicts on Earth, to see if you can help him in any way possible. Stay connected to Lady Gabrielle and Lord Michael, as they will listen to what you have to say. The west side's terror will bring you a deep sadness. Restrict your concerns during this stage for Sandalphon. Your position in the heavens is to watch over creation and to guard a heavenly entrance. Metatron, your oath is to defend the paradises when called upon. The battle begins."

Metatron stood tall as he thought through Sachiel's urgent report. His fealty guided him to establish an immediate plan. He could not intercept Sandalphon, but he could react to approaching issues.

"I plead to you, Sachiel, for my brother's forgiveness. Sandalphon holds no conscious understanding of what possesses him."

"If you fulfill your duties as a Guardian and do not go to the west side where your brother is, the heavens will receive you," Sachiel said. "Great responsibilities are ahead, so be a skilled watcher over creation."

Metatron's heart softened for his brother. He hoped that this would not weaken him. "Please let me travel alongside Lady Gabrielle?" he asked. "She owns my sword, and she will never command Sandalphon. We both offer the same powers."

"Be at ease with Lady Gabrielle, her human strength possesses an infinite vitality. She opened a direct line of contact with the Creator, and an attachment between Lady Gabrielle, Queen Moon-Star, and Saffron, forced them to become the power of three. Lord Michael's human strength has a similar basis with Sun-Star and Efren."

Metatron stood straighter and pulled his shoulders back. "The Guardians will face these testing times, and they will triumph; I have faith in them," he said. "Lady Gabrielle and Lord Michael will remain motivated by those around them."

"Do not mention what will cross their paths. Just work alongside them and when the time comes you will be able to aid them in the battle with a mighty force. Sariel perceives everything, as he is one with the Creator. So just inform Efren and Saffron. The High Priestess already knows about Samuel, but she is sworn to secrecy. Make them conscious of our Majesty's dark star," he said.

Sachiel informed Metatron of the nearing of an overpowering dark star which riddled the realms with his ruling. Metatron needed to figure out how he could help Gabrielle and Michael when they reached this unknown force from the west side. This secret tomb there was awaiting resurrection. His brother Sandalphon would use the bronze serpent to move around the planet.

Metatron, vowed to secrecy, swore he would be cautious as no one knew when the dark entities inside the monumental tomb would awaken.

"Metatron, you are one of the greatest in the heavenly hierarchy, a master of the highest power, and a chancellor in the celestial realm. The Guardian of The Golden Door's gateway to heaven," Sachiel said. "I can tell you this, an aid for you carries a miraculous force. It will show up inside a hidden place within Orion. Keep this in the back of your mind."

A spark of light allowed Sachiel to conclude, "You offer a never-ending power; Sandalphon controls the same power."

Metatron bowed to him and responded, "My brother does not realize that a darkness settled upon him; I pledge to stay away from him."

Sachiel saw Metatron was ready. He drifted away in a flame.

Flailing around in Sachiel's flame was a Deity. She peered over at him to show off her rainbow cloak. A woman out there was camouflaging Sandalphon on the west side and Metatron could not see him. A Deity has a requirement in that she must connect to a reign greater than herself. Sachiel pledged a promise to her and she could do nothing else but rule alongside of him so she could reach her destiny.

Metatron looked around and then left in a flash.

He turned up at The Golden Door in order to find a route of access to the sacred garden and then followed it. Hamuel surfaced in front of him.

Metatron dropped to his knees and pleaded for his brother's forgiveness. "I am the protector of the new covenants in the heavens, my mind is still focused on my brother, so please forgive me, Hamuel," he said.

His trembling hands reached up and he offered the scrolls to Hamuel who took them from his unsteady hands.

"Metatron, Sachiel will soon secure your mind from the thoughts of your brother. What you have placed in my hands, stays honorable. I will protect these sacred scriptures until you are ready to receive them for Lord Michael."

Metatron nodded and pushed forward to The Golden Door. He then bowed his head and sent a psychic message to Efren, Saffron, and the High Priestess:

Royal Ruler Samuel Raiphualas II is the nefarious dark star. He is now plotting to rule the universe. His bright star converted, and he controls an energy within Orion. A dark army and his dark seeds roam everywhere on Varco-XVI. They are ready for battle, so stay silent and use your magic.

Meanwhile, Hamuel gazed out at the universe and noticed a shooting star. Streaks of black lightning ripped through the cosmos, which signified a forewarning. The paradises' prophecy was about to materialize.

Chapter Six
A Pyramid Made of Bronze and Silver

Across the desert sand, an Egyptian police troop bustled about. They placed barricades around the perimeter, securing a twelve-foot fence around the Great Pyramid of Giza. The explanation for the closure was: *The pyramids are undergoing emergency restoration. Please use other available sites.* The barricades made it so that no tourist or curious observer could see what was going on around the pyramids.

It was June 20th, 2015. Within the pyramid made of bronze and silver it was June 20th, 2115, a hundred years ahead. Teams of scientists managed to join the action online from eleven countries around the world. They were supporting Project Solar Escape, and a secret mission inside a previously undiscovered pyramid. While some scientists traveled to inspect a portal in the Bakoni Ruins in South Africa, Dr. Knight took his own crew with him from his Texas observatory. The others that had stayed behind hooked up with him online in the pyramid made of bronze and silver.

Ben deliberated with his teams of scientists. "We're still struggling to figure out this phenomenon taking place deep within the colossal pyramid and in the Bakoni Ruins. This door still has the same images we originally saw of glittering chalices, jeweled swords, and glowing lanterns. Vines still climb on the edges and intertwine with scepters and sequined spears," he said and gazed over at The Golden Door.

A colossal door with embedded moving images spread out along the back wall and stood tall. The ramifications of this discovery were so huge that they had to work fast to keep it all a huge secret. This global project was now veiled under a cloak of the highest security clearance.

"At first no one could understand what was before us." Ben stopped and looked over at his working party. "But you clever scientists have kept yourselves together and continue to study the phenomenon's developing on this Golden Door," Ben said and knew he had a strong organization who had the ability to concentrate on anything. They all had curious minds, which kept them active to the events transpiring.

Strange pillars of light flew across The Golden Door. Ben looked around. "I am sure glad I uncovered and then deciphered the link that scientists Gabrielle and Michael left me," he said. "At the Department of Astronomy and Astrophysics, Gabrielle and Michael observed the Orion constellation connecting a light to areas on Earth. This dynamic signal in the universe then lured my leading scientists to Egypt and to South Africa."

Rising lights from Orion created a partnership between eleven countries' observatories involved in Project Solar Escape. These countries were now reporting their data to Dr. Knight in the pyramid in Egypt.

Ben resumed. "We discovered Michael found a portal in South Africa's Bakoni Ruins and he is on a distant planet. And Gabrielle was inside this pyramid made of bronze and silver but is now on the same planet. Egypt's observatory linked up with the Orion constellation. Messia attached a beam of light to the pyramid and expanded an element of power across The Golden Door. This was inexplicable and perhaps the grandest experience to take place in human history," he said as he was pacing in the sand. "Our task is to figure out this new pyramid and the attachment it has with South Africa's Bakoni Ruins. Let us move on with our day."

***

Inside the pyramid was a control room where several scientists worked day and night to study the paradox of The Golden Door. It was a door and a portal but appeared more like a looking glass where reflections of a myth came in from far away. The screens in the control room hooked up with the other eleven countries and showed the scientists the door inside the bronze and silver pyramid.

Ben's stance was firm in the sand. "The challenge is to identify how we can get onto this planet. This is where two of my leading scientists went missing. My sons Blake and Josh studied the Bakoni Ruins and ended up in a whirlwind of trouble. Now they are traveling on the planet's eastern side to set up a Kingdom for the King and Queen." Ben shook his head from side to side as he thought about this.

Sandra Collins, who had identified the Temperance on the door, walked over to him and presented him with a data sheet. "Well, Ben, we're setting up a fresh schedule this morning. The pyramid continues to assemble a significant source of energy from the universe, and sometimes it makes me feel peaceful and other times overwhelming."

Ben turned to check The Golden Door. She stepped to his side and went on. "Good news. Today is the summer solstice. This pleasant morning just opened with two magnificent full moons on The Golden Door. Look."

The two brilliant new moons caught Ben's attention. "Well, this is something, Sandra. Our data revealed several moons have cropped up on this Golden Door, and they have a range of phases. I'm hoping this might be a positive arrangement, but these two moons are peculiar." Ben crossed his arms. "They're uniting with a reddish halo. Okay, let us arrange a close study on these new moons; keep me posted on the universe and how it connects with this pyramid. Thank you for the updates."

Osahar approached to tell them the good news. "Ben, I can now reveal to you the planet's name. Varco-XVI is the name his Majesty presented, I will return soon," he said.

"Great, now we have a genuine name," Ben replied. "Thank you, Osahar, we will see you shortly, I hope."

"I got it, Ben," Sandra said from across the room. She added it to her large index, and joined it to the other mysterious phenomena they had come across.

Chapter Seven
Two Blood Moons

Overall, her deep-seated duty and her love for astronomy motivated her. Sandra headed the team that studied the images on The Golden Door. As she stared at it, something caught her attention. She spun around and an alarm rang through her mind.

"It's happening again," she yelled to Ben.

He paced right over to her and gazed at The Golden Door. Vague images took shape and played across the surface, as though it were a pool of mist that took shape to tell a story. The scene that stretched out before them showed two fiery blood moons.

"This view is spectacular, and it's developing on this Golden Door," Ben observed. This enigma was certainly fascinating.

"These mystifying moons are evolving. Now I can look at the two suns behind them; their celestial bodies are eclipsing." He considered these two moons and two suns. Ben was on familiar terms with the meaning of these celestial moons and suns. He knew that something was nearing.

"Keep watch," Ben said. "We know this Golden Door will transform to indicate future predictions. I hope Osahar and his colleague Mira come back into the pyramid soon. He is our life force and guidance to these inconsistencies in the universe. If we didn't have his guidance, I am sure we would be dead by now," he said and showed the scientists a distant stare.

A strange wind coursed a path through the pyramid and as the team watched, Sandra's paperwork on her desk fluttered everywhere. She shrugged as she cast a brief gaze over at Ben.

Ben shook his head and mumbled, "Where did that wind come from?"

A secure satellite linked the countries of Project Solar Escape to the pyramid which allowed for rapid communication.

Italy chimed in and could be seen on the main viewer on a wall of monitors.

"Hello, Marco here, good morning," a voice said.

Ben looked up eagerly. "We're just getting started, Marco, thanks for joining in. What do you have for us, my friend?"

"Ben, the universe is presenting us with a series of flashing lights. They stream down somewhere here in Italy, then to an exit. Our systems show us a link inside Orion picked something up here right under our noses," he said. "Gaseous clouds sped upward with some sort of image inside."

When the scientists in Egypt heard this, they changed their focus to Italy and checked out what was taking place.

Frank in Texas chimed in on screen. "Hello, Ben."

Ben turned his interest to Texas on his home-based monitor. "Hi, Frank, what do you have for us today?"

"Ben, Lota Orionis exhibits a singular brightness and stores something huge. A ray of light just released an orb, and it is revolving around Orion. There's a weight of dust clouds and it's now headed straight to the pyramid."

Frank directed their attention to a live view. The sight of Lota Orionis on screen showed the scientists a multiple star system in the equatorial constellation of Orion. It is the eighth-brightest partner of Orion, and was fast becoming an impressive sight in the universe.

Ben put his coffee on a stand and stepped over to The Golden Door. His keen eyes followed a rapid advancement in the universe, moving in at a startling rate.

"I need more predictions on The Golden Door. We have a rush of outer space energy coming down to the pyramid again." Ben motioned with his hands. "I can see it now; it connects to the door." Ben measured the remnants from a supernova, and they watched the celestial vapors balance on the door. "This cluster of dust shows the Crab Nebula, and the remains encircle a large object." His sharp mind whirled through possibilities since he could decipher most metaphors as they cropped up.

"There's an extraterrestrial dust molding something inside the Crab Nebula." He examined the door. "I can see these combustible gases; they show giant claws are on the rise," Ben pointed out.

Bright and distinguished in form, the Crab Nebula whirled into sight. Soon after, a galactic flare stemmed from a vaporous claw. Immense astral winds veered downward and cut a line right across Egypt's Tropic of Cancer. Gassy clouds flipped the claw across The Golden Door, it slipped back inside the Crab Nebula.

Ben followed the Nebula's progress. "Widespread movement in the universe sparked an upturn in the Pleiades. This order of hot B-type stars is in the constellation of Taurus. It is among the closest star assemblies to Earth," Ben said as he fiddled with his pen and studied the vaporous outlines on the door. "There's a bulge of cosmic dust inside the constellation of Taurus. Incoming vapors just offset a release of seven blue stars. These stars cover a silhouette and rotate above the pyramid."

A shockwave moving through the interstellar medium came down and vibrated through the pyramid. A heaviness jolted the scientists from side to side. Colorful vapors circulated in a transcendent presence, which then linked up with The Golden Door.

This sudden change inside the pyramid took control of Ben and he became aware of the nearness of a celestial being. He walked onward and wandered into a peacefulness. The Golden Door was radiating from side to side with solar flares; two dynamic blood moons brought to life an essence inside the pyramid.

His eyes lit up. In view was the constellation of Taurus outlining a man in a white cloak.

Ben clinched his hands close to his chest. "The Crab Nebula and seven blue stars hold siege to this man in the constellation of Taurus," he said, and signaled upon the scientists to be on the alert to the events that were unfolding.

***

An entrance outside the pyramid appeared as a spinning staircase when opened, and an eddy of a glittering darkness when closed. It was next to Osahar and Mira's tent. They then left their tent and entered the pyramid.

Ben gestured to Osahar. "I'm sure glad you are here. Movement in the universe swells with ghostly images; look what image stilled and become peaceful on The Golden Door. Spectral vapors in the constellation of Taurus confine a man inside the Crab Nebula. Do you know him?" he asked.

Osahar crossed his hands over his chest. He advised, "I see a powerful man secured his time in power on The Golden Door. He intends to open the wrought-iron gates. This man will open a passage for the selected who are the otherworldly leaders. For now, study his spiritual existence."

***

The arrival of the righteous man had begun when Galasus went to his bright room and discovered another ancient scroll. It had a gold crest stamped in wax and when he popped the seal. Galasus could release a virtuous God from the heavens to go to Earth. But at this point in time, he was not aware of who this great God was.

***

The great man's aura-like radiance showed the scientists the latitude was 23.5 degrees on the northern side of the terrestrial Equator. The summer solstice was in the northern hemisphere and the Sun had reached an all-out declination. Flares went north and cut a straight line over the Tropic of Cancer. Intergalactic dust mixed with a protective vapor for the seven spinning blue stars, whereupon a star cluster hid an important God. He had accepted a mission in secret from Galasus—to be on Earth to map a passage on The Golden Door. The pyramid shuddered when his medallion and eight-pointed star came into view and became fixed. This man in his white cloak revealed his crossed keys on an ancient medallion. He clenched the keys and raised his hand to lock in with a power from the heavens. Scientists listened to the universe rumble. Galasus had now involved a symbolic man to unlock the mysteries that were allied with creation.

***

Galasus now knew who this man was. He informed Osahar who understood a protector would shroud himself inside a haze on The Golden Door. This was where he would wait and expect his chapter, then he would reveal himself in the great pyramid.

Chapter Eight
A Metaphysical Change Leads to Simulated Warfare

On planet Eugleston, inside the great Coliseum, was where Raguelle's magic rested deep inside her tapestry. She arrived on Varco-XVI a spiritual warrior who specialized in combat. But she was also famous for impressing Galasus and the Imperial Council. Her rank came from her great strength of mind and it served her well. Galasus ordered the Imperial Council to have a strict chain of command with ranks based on acts of heroism. But an unforeseen force was now a part of her fame, hiding as a shadow in the universe. She would work to rule in secrecy on the dark side when summoned by Samuel.

Eight stars in Orion took the shape of a glistening pearl. The gathering of lustrous stars shaped above Varco-XVI.

Raguelle was currently with Gabrielle and Moon-Star. She triggered her gemstone in her sword and her powerful arms wielded the sword back and forth thus projecting an astral flare. "I am your spirit protector," she said and placed her sword to her side. "I am one of the strongest female commanders in the paradises, and a watcher for the planet. Congratulations on your last day," she said and paced over to them. She stood fixed to encourage Gabrielle and Moon-Star in a pure attitude for combat.

Raguelle reached out and shook Moon-Star's hand. "I bring you a moonlit effect, which will gleam upon your request." Her firm grip passed a spirited element to Moon-Star, as well as her final mindset. "This spiritual attachment will give a heavenly attachment with the orbiting moon," she said and bowed to her Queen.

She turned to face Gabrielle. With a powerful grip, she took her hand and pulled her close. Raguelle also gifted her with a precious item. A glossy pearl now lay in her palm. Raguelle sealed her hand around the precious stone.

"Thank you, Raguelle," Gabrielle said. She freed her hand, and with a glint in her eyes, she met Raguelle's gaze.

She leaned toward Gabrielle and whispered, "Carry this pearl with you, my Lady. An essence rests inside and you will need to call upon this pearl in time." Raguelle stepped aside.

Gabrielle clasped the pearl then tucked it away in a side pouch. She knew how powerful this connection with Raguelle would be.

Raguelle left to go to the Coliseum, but when she got there, Metatron made her aware that he would prepare Gabrielle and company for simulated warfare that day.

***

The sky thundered and a tremor brought Hamuel forward, surrounded by radiating stardust. He stepped out of the inferno and joined Gabrielle and Moon-Star.

"I have your last preparations before you go to the Coliseum," Hamuel said and nodded.

His body sparked with luminous flames; clouds formed around him. He shocked the ground and streams of cosmic dust spread over Gabrielle, Moon-Star, and Saffron. The universe grew in an interstellar movement and revealed a supernova. At the heart of the cosmos, the stars changed color and sparkled beyond. There was a great supersonic passage expanding in space, and it was now hovering around them. Hamuel passed a power to Gabrielle, Moon-Star, and Saffron. Galasus had given him a card to brand the Three of crossed Wands on their upper right arm. He stepped away to leave them inside a supernova. Hamuel drifted away in the stardust.

The cosmic dust lifted, and they were now ready to head out to the Coliseum.

"Are we ready, my Lady and my Queen?" Saffron urged. She escorted the spiritual horses over to Gabrielle and Moon-Star.

"Lead the way, Saffron," Gabrielle responded.

Saffron tugged on the reins and they proceeded to the new planet's Coliseum where they would learn the art of warfare. White horses galloped along a dusty road. The scenery consisted of a tailored landscape and included the aroma of fresh flowers. Gigantic clouds hovered over the ground and through them an impressive Coliseum on Varco-XVI could be seen. As they trotted through a set of gates, silver lightning flashed up and down the marble pillars. This energy passed a heated vigor through their bodies. Gabrielle identified an immense force inside. She moved closer to Metatron who was standing to receive them at the pillars; he reached out and took Gabrielle's hand as she dismounted. Metatron stepped over to Moon-Star and greeted her. He gripped her hand as she dismounted. He turned to Saffron, and she too dismounted.

"Grand army, please move into position. The time has arrived for simulated warfare," Metatron said. "These pressures we will meet are a sample of what can be lurking on the planet. Let us prepare for an actual battle."

He neared Gabrielle. "Lady Gabrielle, please step forward," Metatron said.

"I will teach you how to unleash the magic in your mighty sword. But first, let us focus on your inner strength."

Metatron prepared Gabrielle to be mindful of the enemy. An image of a female warrior appeared in the distance. As Gabrielle watched the figure move closer, Metatron circled his left hand above his head, indicating to Gabrielle to pay attention to her surroundings. Gabrielle picked a diamond-tipped spear off the ground, and whirling the spear through the air, she faced the warrior.

"Corner the enemy, drive them up toward a barrier and strike with a potent charge; waste no time. Many weapons are at your side so use them in sequence." He added, "Hit your mark."

Gabrielle moved back and forth on the alert. The moment arrived to create a diversion. A flash whirled out from her sword. With force, she pierced the heart of the simulated warrior with a diamond-tipped spear. It dissolved.

Metatron explained further. "Get geared up for the next, change direction, and consider the sky. There you will discover if more of the enemy move closer."

She looked skyward to find numerous shooting stars crossing the spirited universe. An animated glow inside the Orion Nebula revealed a source of energy which would aid her. It passed a magical gift through Gabrielle's body. She felt the energy and was ready to learn how to use this incredible power.

"Now use your sword, let's continue the battle."

She positioned herself in a balanced stance. Her impenetrable shield rested on her arm. Both hands held a firm grip on her sword. A shuffle of her feet allowed her to move across a pile of dirt. She sliced her sword in the air, creating a swooshing noise. Gabrielle sensed a dynamic new strength in her upper body. As she whirled from side to side, raw steel filled the air. Her persistence withstood Metatron's attacking force. A purified pearl could be seen glistening on her sword's surface and together with her shield, they formed an illumination like no other. No darkness would fall upon Gabrielle during battle. The illumination even blinded Metatron to the point where he could no longer lay siege to Gabrielle.

Metatron shifted to the left side and raised his arm. He stepped toward Gabrielle.

"Congratulations, Lady Gabrielle. There's a determination inside you and it's impressive. You're ready for battle."

She placed Metatron's gifted sword by her side and turned to watch Moon-Star who was approaching.

"I'm amazed, Mother. I hope I can fare as well in combat as you."

"Thank you. I have full confidence in you," Gabrielle replied and tapped her on the shoulder to give her the go ahead.

Metatron walked over to Moon-Star and Gabrielle watched to see how she would hold up in the simulated battle.

She arranged her shield on her arm, then hauled out her sword. A twist of her feet in the sand angled her in front of Metatron. Her weapons took on a life of their own and a moon phase illuminated the entire zone.

Metatron couldn't follow Moon-Star as the brilliance surrounding her blinded him. He gestured to Gabrielle. "I understand our Queen stands ready."

As they walked to her, Gabrielle and Saffron clapped their hands. "You're incredible, Moon-Star," Gabrielle boasted. "I'm proud of you. What a tremendous demonstration in showing Metatron your moonlight effect. It was very clever to use this dynamic weapon."

She brought her in closer and hugged Moon-Star.

Metatron then continued with the simulated warfare. He focused on the female army to exercise their specialty weapons.

Gabrielle, Moon-Star, and Saffron stood ready to participate in the battle. Gabrielle commanded the spirit animals to join the war zone. "Spirit birds circle the perimeter, spirit animals secure the territory and set up a barrier."

Ahead, thirteen bright orbs took the shape of wild boars, and were now charging towards the army. Anxious horses fired up the dirt with their hoofs. The army pulled back on their crossbows and six orbs took the shape of large nets and plummeted over the wild boars. Several soldiers dismounted and drew their swords. With a robust push they sliced the ghostlike images of the wild boars to pieces. A cloud lifted from the ground and formed the shape of spectral horses. Apparitions coiled in the clouds and dark soldiers materialized on the backs of the horses. The female army launched a military course of action and guarded themselves with their impenetrable shields while attacking the figures. Spirit animals watched the sword fights and moved in a diversion to finish the dark spirits. Soldiers removed several ethereal images out of action even quicker. The tone of war filled the Coliseum and more dark warriors on horseback closed in on Gabrielle, Moon-Star, and Saffron, so they formed a circle.

Moon-Star's pentagram burned with a flame on a curved edge and displayed a bright moon—it shone over her white pearl. Saffron's pentacles in her eyes lit up, and Gabrielle's body glowed via an esoteric merger. Gabrielle and Moon-Star stared at the moon and drew in a moon segment. A surge of energy bolted toward Saffron. She absorbed a dynamic moonbeam. The entire section lit up with the power of three, and cosmic dust whirled. Saffron's pentacles brightened and she sent a rush of silver lightning to Gabrielle and Moon-Star.

"Engage in battle, let's wipe out these dark spirits," Gabrielle commanded. "We will be triumphant."

Simulated warfare was no match for Gabrielle, Moon-Star, Saffron, the army, and spirit animals. They conquered the reproduction foes and moved forward.

Metatron looked to the crowd and applauded. Gabrielle reached out to Moon-Star, Saffron, and her army. She nodded to the spirited animals and praised everybody. The grand army fell back into a military formation.

When Gabrielle looked up, there was a moon that appeared to be blood red. Silence fell upon them.

The army stayed tightly packed, awaiting Gabrielle's command.

"My army, now you must become infamous with the use of your powerful weapons. Your swords are lightweight and have a very sharp edge.

We must learn how to use the terrain and the weather," Gabrielle said as she raised her shield and held her glittering sword at her side.

The female army gripped their silver swords by their sides. Complex engravings inlaid in bronze were in their grips. They had an extremely strict chain of command, with ranks based on the use of their weapons.

A portal appeared in the distance which drew their attention as it spun out an orb dripping blood. Slowly appearing inside of the orb was an iron statue of a warrior. It held two large swords in its hands, and the sparkling etched symbols on the iron grips showed the swords' previous victories. Then a host of sparrows flew by, creating a distraction along with a blazing hue of green shooting across the sky.

Saffron used a system of her magic to shapeshift the spirit raven, hawk, fox, wolf, and bear into iron. Their spirit animal's teeth blazed with streaks of white lightning. Then a catapult appeared with raging balls of fire set in iron. The army used their stealth to maneuver into a highly precise formation. Archers pulled back their bows, now set with iron arrows, and the quick moving infantry were ready to use their iron lances and swords. The army moved up in a tightly packed formation to use a tower of shields.

Then wooden walls cropped up around the iron warrior, where mythical tapestries, weapons, as well as statues of Gods and corpses and skeletons were set on the walls for a distraction. Trip wires, snares, and spiked pits surrounded the iron warrior.

Saffron and Moon-Star looked at Gabrielle.

"My Lady, it is you who must defeat the iron warrior," Saffron said and nodded her head.

The iron statue came to life, and the warrior swiped the two swords in the air.

Gabrielle removed her jeweled sword and wielded it above her head.

"My army, set up the catapult to release the iron ball of fire."

The catapult swung and an iron ball of fire flew in the warrior's direction. This burned down the wooden walls and everything disappeared but the warrior. Suddenly it stepped down off the pedestal and crossed the swords over its chest.

Gabrielle focused on the target. With the thought of victory in her mind, she and the army needed to fight with a newfound strength.

But, as a powerful gust of wind blew across the battlefield, it produced a stinging spray of sand and limited their visibility. Then a major tremor forced the combatants to the ground as the flow of combat shifted the entire battle in an alternative direction.

Gabrielle looked to the heavens for her guidance. A radiant light shone down on her and everybody saw this. She raised her sword and fearlessly charged toward the iron warrior. The sound of clanging steel filled the battlefield. Spirit animals moved in and took hold of the blades of steel with white lightning that sparked from their sizzling teeth. This lightning held the blades back for Gabrielle and heated the statue. Now she could pierce the statue's heart with her magnificent sword. A thrust of the sword went through the melting steel. The iron warrior disappeared, and simulated warfare was over.

She walked over to the army and saw they were back in formation and bowed to them. They bowed back to her. Spirited animals stood by her side and hovered above and transformed back into their natural shapes. She looked skyward and smiled and then down at them. "My spirit animals, you are a splendid gift from the heavens, thank you for your protection."

Moon-Star and Saffron hurried over to Gabrielle. "You completed the challenge! What an accomplishment," Moon-Star said and shook her hand.

"My lady, you are quite the force to be reckoned with and the spirit animals surely gave you the distractions you needed in the battle."

Gabrielle nodded her head to them; she was speechless.

A sudden change in the sky and a flash of silver lightning caught Gabrielle's attention. Cosmic dust surrounded them. Hamuel's hand reached out from the dust and a motif of the Seven of crossed Wands was etched on the top of their right upper arm, branding them superior warriors. Her army had turned the simulated warfare in their favor and gained a heavenly warrior rank.

Moon-Star faced Gabrielle. "We are the fighting force, aren't we?" she expressed.

"Yes, we are. When we join as the power of three, our strengths are powerful and constant," she replied.

In the distance, a spiraling galaxy touched down and Sariel exited the blistering gases.

Sariel approached Gabrielle and Moon-Star and remarked on the magic within their shields.

"Everybody used their shields successfully. I am impressed," Sariel said. "These shields hold important energies. The symbols are key and set in motion a self-protective barrier to make them impenetrable. Call upon your shields when the time is right, and supporting forces from the paradises will be ready to aid you. Gabrielle, Moon-Star, Saffron, you will realize when the moment is right to use the power of three." Sariel bowed.

Saffron looked at Gabrielle and Moon-Star and focused her gaze. "The great Nile is ahead. Lady Gabrielle and Queen Moon-Star, you both own a positive vitality and have embraced a para-psychological skill. This force, along with mine, will unleash a wave to reinforce the Nile. Protection of these waters is necessary. Our companions loaded the caravans with supplies and are waiting to depart."

"Thank you, Saffron," Gabrielle replied. "We will secure the waters on Varco-XVI," she said. With her arm raised, she waved to the companions to start their journey back to the castle.

Gabrielle, Moon-Star, and Saffron's fight for survival had led to a victory in the simulated warfare. Hamuel returned and stood by Metatron, and Sariel, and they acknowledged their leadership. The paradises' leaders bowed and disappeared in a cascade of light.

Spirited white horses trotted out of the Coliseum with their riders; they were ready to travel back to the castle for a grand celebration. Suddenly, Gabrielle's mind became muddled, and she was uncertain as to what this was. She decided to keep this to herself.

The High Priestess, who stood by and monitored Gabrielle's performance, noticed Gabrielle was uneasy. So, she used her psychic power and identified a weakness inside Gabrielle. She wondered what this drawback was and if she was ready.

Chapter Nine
A Distraction Within the Simulated Warfare

Companions cleaned up the campsite and organized the caravans for the next leg of their journey. Michael, Sun-Star, Efren, and the army had eaten a splendid meal. The time had arrived to practice simulated warfare.

Michael thought about a special man who aided them since the beginning of their journey. "Paul is a noble man, Sun-Star. He will be of great help when the time comes."

As they walked toward their stallions, Sun-Star reacted to Michael's words. "Yes, Paul is an honorable man. I feel safe and sleep well in the concealed house he provides for us. How about you?" he said and peeked over at him.

"I do too. But, let me tell you something, that house will disappear tomorrow. Paul will return one day. So, for now we will live on the land. Tonight will be our last good night's sleep. So, you might see black rings and bags begin to form under your eyes as we continue. The battle is about to begin," he cautioned.

Sun-Star gave his father a quirky look. "Well, let's hope we don't deteriorate too much before we reach our destined women, I want them to recognize us," he said and frowned.

Efren pushed his cloak to his side and mounted his stallion. "I know a girl who makes potions with herbs. You can rub a special blend on those dark rings and bags under your eyes," Efren said and howled with laughter.

"Thanks, Efren, I can't wait to meet her," Sun-Star added and rolled his eyes.

Stirrups clanged as heavy boots filled them. Everybody mounted their black stallions and galloped along a scenic trail. This was their home; it had a wide range of different plants and many species of animals. Fruit trees and a vast, varied collection of edible plants, and safe drinking water to a certain extent hid the terrain among the trees. Michael was in an upbeat mood. The seemingly endless landscape showed a territory embracing tall oak trees, that towered out of the Earth and brushed the sapphire sky. The curling branches spread out with giant sun-spotted leaves and created a lambent shade. A river flowed alongside of their path and curved beyond the trees. Spirit birds soared in the clear sky; spirit animals continued to stride by their side.

Michael's adrenaline triggered an alert as he saw what was ahead. A stone path led to a set of pillars. Fire radiated along the carved edges. Metatron surfaced between two burning pillars. A tug on the reins brought Michael to turn his stallion. He faced the army. "Dismount your horses," he instructed.

Michael, Sun-Star, and Efren dismounted and took a step toward Metatron.

Metatron, in turn, faced Michael and Sun-Star and bowed. He looked to the heavens and was ready to receive the scrolls from Hamuel. They dropped into his hands.

"I am the protector of new written covenants. Lady Gabrielle and Queen Moon-Star have completed the last day, my Lord."

Luminous rays shone down and opened the scrolls. Metatron read the contents out loud for everybody to be familiar with the covenant. The grand army stood in attentiveness.

"This is the Covenant of Redemption. Lord Michael, you have made an eternal agreement with the Creator. This is the Covenant for Works of life and the Covenant of Grace, for eternal life." He bowed and continued. "The Creator set you apart in the sacred tent, my Lord and our King from others, you are Gods in the heavens," he said and bowed once more to them. "This covenant is unchangeable and established a legal agreement between the heavens and the Creator's sacred seeds. It stipulates your relationship as the Guardian of Sun-Star. This is your sworn oath you agreed to in the sacred tent. Do you accept the last stages of this bond, my Lord?"

"Yes, I am honored to be the Guardian of Sun-Star," Michael said as he touched Sun-Star's shoulder.

"I am honored to have you as my Father," Sun-Star said and gripped his shoulder.

Metatron penned Michael's name on both scrolls and nodded to him.

And so, it was. Michael and Sun-Star's mental focus unfurled the Breastplates of Righteousness, and the Helmets of Salvation enclosed on their heads. The Boots of Peace encircled their shins, and bronze blades slipped into the side of their boot pouch. They both carried the Shields of Faith and showed the Loin Belts of Truth sheathed with the Sword of the

Spirit. Lances of Worship rested by their side. Leather gloves covered their hands and their adorned cloaks draped over their shoulders.

Metatron watched as the armor became visible and said, "The scrolls are now in place." Michael thanked him and they shook hands.

Metatron continued. "Lady Gabrielle and Queen Moon-Star understand the covenant, and they both understand you are a Guardian of Sun-Star. They're ready to continue on their journey, my Lord," he said.

"How are Gabrielle and Moon-Star?" Michael asked, his eyes blazing in intensity.

"They're good, Lord Michael, they say hello."

This brightened Michael. He glanced over at Sun-Star. "What glorious news Metatron brings to us."

"My Lord, I must arrange the Coliseum for simulated warfare," Metatron said and inclined his head. He then left in a blaze.

"Well, that wasn't so bad now, was it?" Michael said to get him started.

"Father, here we go, let's get on with it." Sun-Star had a big grin across his face and added, "I need to see what kind of cleverness you plan on using for combat." He raised an eyebrow.

"Well," he glanced over at Efren, "let's go, I'm sure I can entertain you," and he winked.

Remounting their stallions, they pressed on through the two blazing bronze pillars. Scenic paths helped to inspire them as they set their minds to the upcoming warfare. They arrived at a massive Coliseum on Varco-XVI. Rising high were leading columns made of limestone. Stucco adorned pillars displayed a sun and moon along the trim. Circular walls exposed marble, the surface had a glossy finish and upheld a black and white banner. Efren turned his stallion and signaled the army.

"We are now ready to learn the art of warfare, let's push forward," he said.

As they entered the Coliseum, the army went into a sequence and awaited their training.

Efren stopped his horse and faced the grand army. "Hamuel delivered many weapons, and they currently rest by your side," he said. "Training starts with an organized pattern. These weapons can shapeshift to set up a grand force for battle. The heavens gifted us with the knowledge of the terrains and these extraordinary weapons. You are a part of a formal chain of command," Efren said and raised his shield. "Grand army, your psyches are reinforced through the Creator. Impenetrable shields and magnificent weaponry give Lord Michael a high-ranking army. We will stand on guard to King Sun-Star; we will protect and fight alongside Lord Michael," he said.

Efren's right hand moved to his left side and he clasped the hilt of an imposing bronze sword and pulled the forged blade out of its scabbard. He pointed it skyward. Sparks flew everywhere when he swung his black stallion to face Michael and Sun-Star.

"We will fight until death," Efren said. He was a patriotic man who was fiercely loyal to Michael and Sun-Star, but also to the paradises.

The grand army raised their polished bronze swords and called out, "Hail to Lord Michael, hail to our King Sun-Star."

Efren continued. "You will use crossbows, spears, shackles, chains, swords, daggers, axes, nets, halberds, and whips. Prepare to dedicate yourself to learning how to master these weapons. Lord Michael's army will become unequaled in military intelligence," he said.

Greeted again by Metatron, Sariel and Raguelle approached the Coliseum and walked toward Efren.

"Army, please dismount," Efren said.

As they dismounted, Sariel approached Efren. "Brace yourself, as you will contend against me," he said.

Efren looked over at Michael. "You got off easy, my Lord, I have to battle my father," he said and shrugged his shoulders.

Michael and Sun-Star faced Efren; they were both affected by his words.

"I never imagined you as Sariel's son, Efren!" Sun-Star said.

Michael put his hands at his hips. "Well, Efren, your father is the leader of the celestial army, and we have his son by our side," he said and faced Sun-Star. "What do you think of this?"

"To have an accomplished father and son in our presence is inspiring," he said.

"Efren, I hope Sariel goes easy on you," Michael said and rubbed his hands together.

"I hope so too, my Lord." Efren grinned in return.

Raguelle approached Sun-Star and bowed to him. "Come this way, my King, you will battle with me," she said and directed the way.

He peered over at his dad. "I can't fight a woman," he said. "Let me team up with someone else."

Efren turned to Sun-Star. "Raguelle is a superior warrior. Beware, my King, strengthen yourself." Efren reminded him, "Let no women drift you aside from your purpose, other than your Queen," and winked.

"*Aw*, my Queen; she's worth fighting for, Efren."

"Good, show her your strength," Efren said.

Michael turned and faced Metatron. "Well, I assume I have to partner with you?" he asked.

"Yes, my Lord, we will engage in combat, but first I must address your army."

Metatron approached the army. "Celestial army, pair up on the ground and on horseback; be ready." He walked toward Michael.

Michael stepped into the middle of the Coliseum to challenge Metatron. He hauled out his sword and waved it without delay. The amethyst glowed within his sword; it generated a flare to fire in each direction. Metatron tried to corner him against the Coliseum wall. But he broke free. Michael twirled around and met Metatron's sharp edge; they crossed their swords. You could hear the aggressiveness in the clamor that rang around. Metatron was teaching Michael his footwork, and how to use his peripheral vision.

Sun-Star was cautious of his surroundings, as Raguelle would be a mighty foe. Raguelle peeked over at Michael, then turned back to face Sun-Star.

Sariel and Efren stepped aside and monitored their actions. Efren shuffled around in the distance which broke Michael's concentration and he turned to look at Efren taking weapons out from under his cloak. He then glanced over at Sun-Star to see what was happening in his battle. Metatron drew his sword and placed it at Michael's throat. His eyes widened as Metatron moved in for the kill.

Efren knew he needed to work on Michael's focus as this incident could have caused his death.

Michael glared at Metatron and shook his head. "I should have remained focused," he said. "I brought my attention over to Efren when he hauled out those weapons, then to Sun-Star." Michael slipped his sword to his side.

"Yes, my Lord, watch me, pay no interest to them over there. Let's take a break so you can refocus."

Michael glanced over at Sun-Star and saw an extraordinary display of courage. He showed several dynamic strikes during his battle.

Raguelle saw King Sun-Star's technique had authority. She took a brief glimpse over at Michael as she was curious about his distraction.

The grand army clanged their steel blades against each other while practicing and mastered their weaponry on many degrees.

Michael realized he could have lost his life and this awareness made him cautious.

Efren tossed whips, chains, axes, shackles, and spears, into the middle of the Coliseum. Spirit animals moved forward on the sandy ground and awaited their command.

He raised his arm. "We will take forward our spirit animals, they stand awaiting their commitments to advance into battle," Efren said.

Spirit birds' large wingspans could be seen soaring over the horizon. They spiraled across the vibrant blue sky, camouflaging themselves in the dense clouds. Spirit animals prowled nearby, searching for their guidance. Metatron set up several mirrored images in the distance. An animated dragon angled inside a galactic mix of dust; two giant bats swooped overhead. On the ground, they saw great lions breaking through a tower of vapors. Beyond the Coliseum, dark masked soldiers ascended from the ground and mounted phantom stallions. Waves of dust raised countless soldiers.

Efren passed a command. "Choose a weapon on the ground and use it to destroy these dark spirits."

Sun-Star finished his training with Raguelle and moved close to his father. He was the first to take two glittering diamond-tipped spears. Michael picked up two whips. Efren took the chains. Sariel seized the axes. Metatron gained the shackles. The grand army split into two groups. The first group removed their swords and raised their shields to their chest; they followed a guided formation. A section of the remaining army moved aside. Crossbows were raised and loaded with jewel-tipped arrows. Michael's high-powered army was ready to learn how to hit their target.

Before they went into battle, Michael directed a stare at Efren. "Please help me focus," he said. "I don't want to surrender in the battle."

"My Lord, you need to ask the universe. Call to the heavens, ask the Creator to shield your mind before you go into battle."

"Thank you, Efren." Michael, at first, struggled to find this path in his mind.

"Now, my Lord, let's go kill these dark spirits."

Earlier Raguelle had glanced over at Michael and her concentration became cloudy. She had thoughts that she might have caused Michael's distractions somehow with her psyche. She departed from the Coliseum.

Spirit animals worked together to force the dark spirits to go in a precise direction, right toward the grand army. In an intense spiritual achievement, the army adhered to their formations and used their weapons with a violent charge to wipe out numerous simulated dark spirits. Sun-Star moved in and hit his first mark. A dragon with blinding jeweled eyes hovered overhead. Not one strike, but two glittering spears pierced the dragon's body. The army followed King Sun-Star's mighty blows. His successful hits brought a gigantic dragon to the ground. Rising dust filled the Coliseum, while a mirrored image of the dragon stayed noticeable.

Leather grips coiled around Michael's hands; he was instinctive with his whips and cracked them in the air. They wrapped around two enormous bats and he watched them disappear. Sariel threw his axes into the lions and erased them. The army controlled their weapons and shields of protection and extinguished the ghostlike warriors.

Sariel glanced over and noticed Michael was a bit dazed. He drew him away. "Lord Michael, make Efren aware if you are uneasy. Efren's my son, a Guardian to you, he will battle until death. Remember his words, they will serve you in your times of need. Your heart is still soft for your son, it's imperative you look after yourself, be on guard. You have the skills and the mindset. You're ready, Lord Michael."

"Thank you, Sariel, for your loyalty and Efren's. I turned my head during a battle. How foolish of me," he said. Michael had a confused expression on his face because he had completed his actions without thought.

Sariel contemplated his distraction. A thought flitted through his mind but he couldn't hold onto its meaning. He wondered where the thought came from.

Metatron approached Michael and placed one hand on his shoulder. "My Lord, let's continue, it's time to defeat the dragon." He handed him a set of shackles.

Michael accepted the shackles and wrapped them around his arm. Then he said, "I'm ready, please help me understand my strengths."

A pillar of light flickered over Michael.

"Lord Michael pleaded to the heavens," Efren said. "He is looking for his inner strength."

"Good, what you said must have triggered him. Now, as he calls for guidance, he secures the ability to meet the Creator's light," Sariel said and glanced at Efren.

The simulated dragon remained motionless on the ground, a triumphant strike by Sun-Star lodged two spears in its right side. He had weakened the dragon. Now Michael must finish the test.

Michael placed the shackles on the ground and walked near the agitated dragon. A twist of both wrists snapped the two lengthy whips he still carried.

"Spirit animals, come forward," Michael said.

The dragon's eyes opened and watched his every move.

Michael lifted his shield for protection. The dragon's large mouth widened and directed a firestorm; one blistering flame after another bounced off his shield.

Sun-Star feared for his father and moved towards him to help him.

Efren seized him and stared into his eyes to explain. "My King, your father's battle requires focus. Lord Michael needs to manage on his own, or he will fail. Have faith in him."

When Efren's pentacles lit up, Sun-Star absorbed his words and nodded.

Michael's tone became loud and forceful. "Spirit animals, surround the dragon," Michael commanded.

The spirit birds, in turn, were setting up a disturbance by beating their wings as they circled the dragon's head. Spirit animals charged toward the dragon, they hid inside a transcendent sphere and rearranged a mound of dirt beneath it. A coil of dust flew up into the dragon's bright eyes. Michael tightened the leather grips around his hands and lifted both arms. A quick snap of both wrists extended the whips fully until they coiled around the dragon's mouth. His firm stance and strong pulling force shut the dragon's mouth and put out its fire.

"Efren, throw those chains over here," Michael said as he was backing up.

Efren moved forward and tossed the chains at his feet.

"Spirit bear, hold these whips in place," Michael said and quickly brought the whips down to the bear. The bear opened his mouth and gripped the whip handles and pulled on them hard. He observed the ample target and picked up the chains and the shackles. A glow developed around him, and he pulled on his inner strength. Two large chains rolled in his hands; he tossed them toward the dragon's flapping wings where they interlocked. Drawing himself closer, he clamped on the shackles. The dragon, whips, chains, and shackles disappeared. His mission was complete.

He rubbed his head as an uneasy feeling ran through him. A quick turn brought him to face the west, from where he could hear a propelling force. It was a swooshing noise from far away. Michael glanced up. Using his mind's eye, he saw a black dragon in the distance and followed a flash of emerald triangle eyes. Now visible, it spearheaded a passage for the Coliseum.

Heat coursed in his veins; Metatron's body came to attention. "Sariel, a sinister spirit ascended from the dark side. This dragon is not simulated, it moves towards Lord Michael. Should I intervene?" Metatron asked as he was reaching for his sword.

"The arena shimmers with his light, Metatron. Lord Michael has secured a celestial bond, and he upholds a superior strength. Let him go ahead, I have absolute faith in him," Sariel replied.

Michael was ready for this unforeseen encounter. Strapped on his left arm was an impenetrable shield. The shadowy entity was gliding in from the far west end of the Coliseum. Huge wings flapped and brought in a violent breeze. Blazing fireballs struck Michael's shield. The dragon moved closer. Michael set his stance and braced for the battle. Large daggers rested on both sides of his high leather boots. The moment was perfect; he removed both daggers and raced toward the dragon. Long blades hurled through the open air and pierced the dragon's throat. Spirit birds soared over the dragon's head to build up a turmoil, and soon Michael was close enough to jump in the air. He heaved his sword out of his scabbard, while his impenetrable shield withstood the fire-breathing dragon. His amethyst flashed in his sword, and he swung his sword with an imposing charge, and cut off the dragon's head.

When the head struck the ground, a booming noise filled the Coliseum and the head rolled in the crowd's direction. Michael's feet were back on the ground, his watchful eyes examined his surroundings to find he was secure. Michael's breathing was heavy as he contemplated what he had just achieved.

Metatron turned to Sariel. "Lord Michael adjusted his inner strengths, he wiped out an actual dragon. Sariel, Efren should inform Lord Michael of his magnificent kill."

Efren overheard Metatron mention it was a real dragon, so he approached Sariel. "I should tell Lord Michael he killed an actual dragon; he is triumphant." He looked skyward and saw a mist of dark clouds hovering above them.

"Yes, tell him," Sariel said.

Efren moved aside and knew his Father connected to this incident somehow.

Sariel used his psyche and brightened a dark cloud. In secrecy, he released an actual dragon to force Michael into a frame of mind to be with one with the Creator. And it benefited him. Michael managed to clear out a mysterious attachment that led his concentration in the battle astray.

The crowd applauded. Sun-Star showed his ecstasy for his father's performance. "Father, you finished it," he said and rushed over to congratulate him.

When Michael found a connection to the Creator in the heavens, he pulled himself into a willingness to engulf his cosmic flame. That was when he could focus on the darkness and go for the kill.

"Sun-Star, we have to stay focused. I believe our practice with simulated warfare ended with the final dragon," he said and examined the Coliseum.

"I understand how important our techniques are. The true battle awaits us."

Michael stood tall and glanced into Sun-Star's eyes. "What do you think of my cleverness now?" he said and tilted his head to the side.

"You're a distinguished warrior." Sun-Star gripped Michael's hand and showed his respect.

Efren wandered over. "Well, look at you." He walked around Michael. "You remained outstanding, Lord Michael. Congratulations, two dragons in one day is impressive," he said. "My Lord, look over there, your army is receiving a superior rank from Galasus."

Michael watched his noble army raise their left arm to receive an honorable rank. Cosmic dust drifted in from a distant galaxy. It reached the celestial warriors and etched a motif on the top of their left upper arms. The Seven of crossed Swords branded them as superior warriors. Michael saluted his warriors; they saluted back.

"My Lord, the black dragon you killed was real. It moved in from the dark side, unforeseen. Metatron picked up the forewarning. Sariel said you're ready for battle, as your stable strength secured you a victory."

Michael's eyes lit up as he turned to face his kill and noted it didn't die out like the simulated one. Efren raised his arm to signal the spirit animals. Those that consumed flesh encircled the dragon and devoured it.

"Father, what a remarkable achievement! I was worried for you," Sun-Star said. His eyes could not get any wider.

"This test showed me how to release my force for combat. My inner spirit craved a bond with the Creator, and my heart became warm. When we battle the darkness, Sun-Star, our minds must stay sharp. Whatever is ahead we can battle, so, we must be fit. Our inner selves will grow with discipline and bring us the ability to succeed," he said. He stared into Sun-Star's eyes and sensed he was now preoccupied with the dangers he would face.

"The power of three will be a pressure resembling no other. I grew stronger through my fears of you dying. And I gained a sense of purpose watching you battle. It's so strong now I can do nothing but think of winning," Sun-Star said. "I will face the darkness and hold fast to your beliefs. Together we will uphold our connection with Efren." He stood tall and showed his father he was ready.

They both looked over at Sariel and Efren and walked towards them.

"Now there's a great fit together. They're a powerful force to have with us. I'm glad you got your turn to face your fears too. Are you okay?"

"Yes," Sun-Star replied.

Just before Michael and Sun-Star joined them, Efren expressed to Sariel, "Lord Michael became one with the Creator, but I will still watch him closely."

"Yes, he is ready, but keep a close eye on him. His confusion came from an unknown source; it was not from him."

"I know you will uncover who diverted him, Father, and be the one to put an end to this magic."

Sariel's thoughts about this drew him away, as his inner essence detected who had distracted Michael.

Michael and Sun-Star, seeing that the conversation between Efren and Sariel was over, mounted their stallions.

"See you in the morning, Efren," Michael said.

"Yes, my Lord and my King. Get a decent sleep." Efren laughed. "Oh, and the wine is off limits," he said.

"Efren, it's not fair to mention what I can't drink: a nice chalice of wine," Michael said, then sat high on his horse. "I killed two dragons today!" His grin could not get any wider. "When we reach our destined woman, we will have many stories to tell. I say that will be a good reason to drink plenty of wine." He leaned forward in his stead and gave Efren a big grin.

Efren grinned back and agreed.

Michael and Sun-Star headed to the acacia house and met up with two men who stood ready to pick up the reins as they dismounted. They stepped inside the house where a sudden aroma of fresh bread wafted to them. Sun-Star licked his lips when he noticed a large spread of food on a long wooden table. The men and their wives prepared Lord Michael and King Sun-Star for their last supper at the house. A basin was offered where they could wash their face and hands. Incense was burning, and it lingered with a sweet smell; a tranquil mood relaxed the warriors. Michael sat in a special chair and Sun-Star by his side. A bright light shone down on both. Paul and his family saw this. They moved to their knees and pleaded to the heavens for a protected journey for Lord Michael and King Sun-Star.

As they enjoyed their last feast, Paul approached Michael and presented him with a vial.

"This is a spiritual oil, Lord Michael. The time to use this oil will be made known to you."

"Thank you, Paul." Michael slipped the vial into his loin belt, securing it in a compartment.

Paul faced Sun-Star. "King Sun-Star, there's a greater power you will need in time," he said. "Be perceptive, as this attachment involves your

Queen." Spiraling stardust reached the top of his right wrist and he was branded again with a small lunar eclipse.

"I will be diligent when this power from the heavens emerges, thank you, Paul."

He bowed and left.

"Sun-Star, let me have a look at that," Michael said.

Sun-Star showed him his right wrist.

"You have a lunar eclipse on your wrist. That's not something you see every day," Michael said. "Tomorrow is a big day, you know." Michael stretched his arms and yawned.

"It sure is, let's have a decent sleep tonight."

"I will hit the hay like a ton of bricks, and sleep like a baby tonight."

Sun-Star looked around. "Hay? Bricks? A baby? I'm confused." His puzzled look made Michael laugh.

"Son, back on Earth, we have a wide range of words and phrases. Now you're getting a flavor of my easy-going speech. I am sure we will nestle in some hay somewhere on our journey," Michael said. "But in that case, we won't be sleeping like babies, we will be roughing it," he said. He turned and watched Sun-Star for a reaction.

Sun-Star took a breath. "I sure hope not," he said. "My bed is what I need because I need to sleep like a baby." He glanced at Michael and realized he was grateful for what he had. "I will try to be comfortable and adjust to this change as it comes."

Michael opened the door to find two bathtubs full of water. There was an assortment of clean garments and towels arranged on their enormous bed. They both had a warm bath before they retired.

Elsewhere, while Michael and Sun-Star become peaceful and slept, Sariel explored a predicament. He met with Raguelle.

Gabrielle and Michael would want victory. Spiritual and supernatural warfare was imminent, and this could bring them both unimaginable consequences. Stormy weather was ahead for Gabrielle and Michael. Winning the battles for the rule of Varco-XVI and Earth was now at stake.

Chapter Ten
Mira and Osahar

The universe sparkled with billions and billions of electrifying stars. Inside the Orion constellation was a bond of seven in the middle of the Crab Nebula. A spirited man's existence was revealed through a cluster of stardust. He was an out of the ordinary man who was deep-seated on The Golden Door. Galasus knew his calling coursed through the galaxies. It amounted to a joint decree that offered a superior force. The interior and exterior part of this pyramid connected with a metaphysical order. An ancient civilization was nearing the pyramid.

When a female Deity's intensity gathered speed inside the Orion constellation, this woman associated herself with two Jupiter. She triggered two suns and two moons to eclipse. Animated stars rippled inside a gravitational wave; two crowns and two thrones glittered inside of the Orion Nebula. Osahar acknowledged the Creator provided guidance through several moon phases. He looked back into the realms, and he watched Gabrielle and Michael's children flourish in the vaults of the blood moons. The Cartwheel galaxy increased with a stable path, it entered the Lenticular and Ring galaxy and wrapped around a storm. Dust blankets twisted and boosted an uprising. Massive stars collapsed and inclined toward the constellation of Sculptor. In the distance were shiny stars rotating with a roundup of treasures. Blue stars lined the frame of a black-and-white raven. He was aware that two supernatural beings would be impressive on Varco-XVI.

Osahar led a brilliant star to believe she could be human and witness the development of a new planet. He knew Baten Kaitos was a contributing cause for Mira's shockwave, along with Deneb Kaitos and the neighboring stars. Astral shockwaves flowed with an immense potency to Mira. When he saw her famed shockwave roping in a coiled spine, and her cosmic dust led to a great astral tail, he had to act fast. He tricked her and took something from her brilliant star; he hid it in the realms.

Later, the Creator made Mira's essence build up into a prototypical woman. But her balanced shockwave in the universe shifted from an

Sylvie Gionet

unknown source, it ended in a fallout that weakened her. The paradises' law called for a long-term agreement, but Mira parted from the decree.

Osahar, gazed at the northern sky; it showed him the constellation of Cetus. A stable form of power was an everlasting connection for Mira.

The Creator arranged for Osahar to remove Mira from the universe and place her on planet Eugleston so she could be a part of the prophecy on Earth. When he dragged Mira in from outer space, it was at a shocking pace. Galasus countered with a gravitational tug. It passed in a neighboring star called Menkar. Galasus instructed Menkar to go after Mira's continuing star trail when the time was right. Mira's fame stayed accessible in the celestial realms. Now Menkar will hunt for a misplaced shockwave in secret loaded with cosmic relics. When the quest for a loss of mass showed up in the universe, it would give Menkar an opportunity for the prophecy which he had held in reserve.

When Samuel went through his scrolls in his dark room, he found out about Mira and her protected area on planet Eugleston. Now his dark star occupied her in life form. He had managed to gain a portion of Mira's shockwave and forced her to attach three low-mass stars to hover above Varco-XVI. No humans could withstand this force of three low-mass stars over the planet. Her pledge with the universe would now aid Samuel's purpose—to put an end to the heavenly creations on Varco-XVI and Earth. But before his planned destruction. Samuel had kept a selection of spirited captives on the bronze and silver gate on Varco-XVI to fight and live by his rule. Mira's variable star added a superior strength to The Golden Door. She continued to send her shockwaves to Samuel. Mira's stardust extended an isolated malevolence to join with his dark star. When her shockwave finally ends, Mira will drift into an abyss inside the universe.

Once Osahar learned of Mira's plight, he knew he had to meddle with the situation.

Ben and the scientists appreciated his and Mira's faithfulness; they understood something was troubling them.

Strong arms wrapped around Mira. "I can't support the council's decision to let you leave."

Mira marveled in the depth of commitment in his dark eyes. Later she expressed in a quiet voice. "Our devotion to the heavens is undeniable," she said and took a deep breath.

He felt his heart warming. "I will call upon this judgment and plead for your forgiveness. I will call upon the heavens to search for the heart-shaped rose gem," Osahar said. He knew of this gem as it was used to save many stars that were headed for extinction in the paradises, millenniums ago.

***

This heart-shaped rose gem was in the mold of a heart-cut stemmed rose; Galasus had read a new scroll in the bright room and instructed the Emissaries to connect to a spiritual force in the heavens. He noted that this prized gem would turn over a metaphysical healing for stars that were once not destined. The Emissaries acknowledged his request and informed their Highborn Leader the gemstone would drop down from the heavens into a mountain range on Varco-XVI's east side. But they were not sure when this would happen.

***

As one who longed to reverse her collapse, Osahar's mission was to call for Mira's forgiveness. This revered gem could save her and hand over a permanent continuum of being mortal. Osahar committed himself as a Guardian on Earth and for Varco-XVI. He would need Ben and his team to help him search for a way to recover the treasured gem.

Osahar waved his hand over the animated door. Six swords showed a robust flame throughout the universe. The Creator placed the yin and yang of six crossed swords above Metatron. Supreme specialists were there to reinforce Gabrielle and Michael on Varco-XVI. But was their celestial firepower enough to defeat an impenetrable God?

This man was a God, and Galasus placed him on The Golden Door. His white cloak stirred up a synthesis of hazed stardust to darken his silhouette. In the galaxies' deepness, a series of perfect stars stretched out a different dominance. He set them aside in a secretive sphere. A rapid eruption of solar flares reached Orion; a gravitational pull towed in the sphere. An explosion in Orion hurled out seemingly countless diverse warriors. They pressed forward to the pyramid.

Chapter Eleven
Professor Isaki Lourens

The universe showed the value of a creation, one of them being Pluto. When the scientists studied the icy dwarf planet on The Golden Door, a whirling dust cloud accompanied by methane, curved downward and placed a tomb on Varco-XVI's western side. The scientists suspected it was not safe because it was a dark tomb. Ben hypothesized a setting with Pluto beyond compare. So, he phoned a valuable associate for advice.

"Isaki, how are you my friend?" Ben said as he paced through the sand, phone to his ear.

"Wonderful, Ben, it is so nice to hear from you. What have you been up to?" Isaki asked.

"I need your help. The Space Agency gave me clearance to talk to you. I am in Egypt and in control of a top-secret project."

"You're in Egypt! Tell me where and I will come. I am in Cairo with some family, and they want to go shopping. I know my scientist friend is here for a good reason."

"I hope I am not interrupting your family shopping."

"Oh, heck no, this will get me out of it. Besides my wife has all the credit cards—she can shop all she wants. Olivia understands my life and its sudden emergencies, so take no mind to it. Please tell me more."

"You bet, Isaki, say hello to Oliva for me. Anyhow, the universe is spreading out a phenomenon. Pluto holds an unbroken movement; a gravitational pull permits it to travel in and out of the Earth's solar system. I believe you're the person who can make any sense of Pluto's actions. There is dark matter around its glacial surface," he said and signaled to Sandra. "One of my scientists is sending you our location. I will explain more when you arrive."

"I'm on my way, I will be there in about twenty minutes or sooner once I hail a cab." They hung up.

***

Sandra glanced at a tall, dark, dapper man coming into the pyramid. She teetered toward Ben and her stilettos sunk in the sand and she turned her ankles. She took both shoes off and poured out the grit, while her bare feet nestled in the sand. Ben watched her and shook his head from side to side.

She ignored him. "Professor Isaki Lourens is here, he's on his way through the pyramid."

"Thank you, Sandra." Ben hurried across the pyramid to meet him.

Professor Isaki Lourens was an independent scientist in South Africa. He too had a network of experts from around the world. His aptitude was extensive in Astronomy, Cosmology, and Astrophysics. Ben thought Isaki might explain Pluto's unusual passing.

Ben reached out to shake his hand and then introduced him to the team. He showed him The Golden Door. Isaki's eyes brightened when he saw the great wonder and knew what he had to do.

"Welcome to the great inexplicable pyramid," he said and crossed his arms. "Can I get you a drink?"

"No, thank you, maybe later."

"I see you brought something with you," Ben said.

"Yes, the Space Agency contacted me, and sent a package to my hotel room and this was in it."

Isaki opened a hefty sack and lifted out a unique apparatus. He set it up and touched a button. A ray of immense energy reached The Golden Door. This allowed him to halt any progress on the door and deposit a marker in outer space. A new opening enlarged on The Golden Door; a laser pulled in Pluto. Stardust burst out with a vivid streak.

Ben watched Isaki in wonderment. When he turned, he caught a sight on the door. Isaki's equipment had an optical beam that reached a cryptic passage. An orb swallowed dust and pulled in an object. Isaki stopped his apparatus.

Isaki turned and faced Ben. "I'm ready to report," he said.

Ben followed Isaki's setup and saw he produced an apparatus he had never seen before and used it with an unusual technique. He stepped closer to him to listen. This was when he knew Isaki surely knew what was going on and his time was now to intervene.

"Pluto's orbit follows the Earth's sun as a dwarf planet. This classification of theory rims the edge of our solar system and promotes two shielded missions. It turns out, that Pluto develops an aggressive approach to Earth with a metaphysical form. This cosmological creation stays solo; Pluto will serve alongside the bright and dark side of creation."

The scientists remained perplexed and deliberated on how this could have developed.

Ben acknowledged his words. "Pluto's moons move inward; along the way they dodge planets. This outer space alignment does not hamper the solar system. But what's interesting, is Pluto creeps in to set up an uprising on this Golden Door. It attracts dark matter on its surface and slips out. These actions continue to be a concern. Who's working this?" he asked.

Isaki's closing statement ended with a proposal. "I will go with this apparatus and investigate everything. This analysis could take some time, so please be patient. Ben, let me suggest something."

"I'm listening," Ben replied.

"Scientists explore the universe for intelligence, but they also want to connect with the spiritual unknown. This exploration broadens to one hundred years into the future. When you enter a deeper awareness, an entrance will show a paradise. We need to bring to light a hidden clue in the cosmos." Isaki focused on Ben. "The Creator selected us to carry out this journey. Pluto is important. I had been waiting for your call and the delivery of this apparatus. As scientists, we must search beneath the spectrum. The heavens encourage us to take notice."

As his gaze bounced from place to place, Ben revisited Isaki's theory. "One hundred years ahead," he said. "The Space Agency actually brought us together for this campaign. They must have known I was going to call you for this. Isaki, take care and study Pluto's dust to the best of your abilities, I know you will find some answers to its orbital pattern and darkness."

Ben gripped Isaki's hand and gave him a firm handshake. Isaki gathered up his apparatus and left the pyramid.

Chapter Twelve
Two Celebrated Creatures

Gabrielle and company traveled back to the grand castle after their simulated warfare. She was a bit off balance, but the aroma of fresh plant life drifted in on a summer breeze and put her at ease. There was a striking brightness up ahead. Myriad flickering beams blended through the leaning branches and touched their faces with a warmth. Streaming pastel colors, orange inside a tint of yellow and a hue of blue stemmed in from the northern horizon. Natural surroundings feathered the clouds with a silky luster. Riding upward on a grassy path, they continued to an outlook where they saw the massive castle decorated by gleaming sun beams. An enchanting view and the aroma of frankincense caused Moon-Star to take a deep breath. Boswellia sacra trees were plentiful in a valley beyond. Stone pillars entwined with flowering ivies surrounded the large oak trees. Grassy paths with stone slabs guided them to the castle, as they trotted through a peaceful scenic route. A grand army and attendants traveled alongside, and in tow were carriages filled with fresh supplies.

When they reached the castle, Moon-Star leaned over and handed Saffron something. She accepted the piece and slid it into her pocket. Valda, Vance, and the High Priestess had prepared a celebration. The trumpets sounded to announce their arrival, large wooden doors opened, and they went through two silver gates. Saffron dismounted, stepped over to Gabrielle and Moon-Star, and picked up their reins as they dismounted.

"My Lady, we must arrange for our next journey. But, first, we will enjoy a grand celebration this evening, here at the castle. We will join you later at the gala," Saffron said. She shifted her cloak to one side and waited for her reaction.

"Thank you, Saffron. I can't imagine surviving here on this planet without you," Gabrielle said.

"Oh, Saffron," Moon-Star added. "There is something within you." A glow surrounded her, and the radiance captured everybody's attention.

"Mother, are you noticing this about Saffron?" she said and turned to Saffron and went on. "Am I right?" Moon-Star asked.

"Yes, my Queen, this awareness you see in me will show up in time, so definitely keep that in mind." Saffron nodded. She flailed her long ivory cloak and proceeded onto the castle grounds. Spirit animals, attendants, and the grand army traveled across a stone road. Spirit wolf and Moon-Star's owl stayed alongside of them.

Moon-Star turned and faced Gabrielle. "See, I told you, a long time ago, I knew it. I knew there was something more than just special about Saffron," she said and tilted her head.

Gabrielle glanced over at Saffron and together they walked through the castle grounds.

"Yes, she certainly is unusual, and holds a deeper secret," Gabrielle said and pondered. "I expect we will understand this mystery in time, my dear. Let us go inside, we have much to look forward to today."

They both walked toward a set of monumental pillars. Flowers twisted over climbing ivies which wound around the pillars from end to end. Large ivory limestone steps led them directly into the castle. Gabrielle became fascinated with the torches on the stone walls. They burned with an incredible fire. One burning flame flickered with a mysterious glint and she noticed an odd murkiness on the spacious marble floor.

Moon-Star bumped into her arm and startled her. "How far is the promised Kingdom?" she asked.

Gabrielle snapped out of her daze and said, "I suspect the Kingdom you and your dreamy King will rule, is a lengthy journey ahead."

"Did you have to point out my dreamy King?" Moon-Star sighed and rolled her eyes.

"Okay, you're becoming dreamy again, straighten up," Gabrielle responded.

As Gabrielle and Moon-Star advanced, they met up with Valda and Vance.

"Lady Gabrielle, we keep something impressive for you. Come this way please, let me show you both," Vance said.

He pointed the way and escorted them through a chamber not too far ahead. When they reached an elaborate acacia wooden door, a whirlwind swept through the chamber and poured a curve of cosmic dust to glisten in their eyes. Silver lightning streamed along and exposed a sparkle through the mixture. Gabrielle and Moon-Star noticed a large white fossilized dragon blending in with the woodwork. Two silver jewels flickered in its peering eyes.

"Look, embedded in the bronze and silver framework. It looks like a design inside the glow," Moon-Star said and gazed at it.

Valda pointed to the door. "Those are the watchers on the acacia door, you can see their reflective eyes in a mist on the edges of the door," she said as she pushed open the giant doors.

They stepped forward and walked into a large dungeon with a line of torches blazing on the stone walls. In the distance, a turbulence swirled in the uneven sand. Something huge was coiling in the back in silence. An abrupt movement revealed a misty silhouette. A black cobra slithered into plain sight beside a big white dragon.

Gabrielle felt discomfort and wrung her hands as she waited to find out what the apparitions were all about. Spirit wolf and owl rested on a stone slab beside them; something was keeping them calm and silent. Gabrielle locked eyes with the white dragon and a sixth sense joined them mentally. Whispers resounded in the hollowed room and the cobra slithered through the sand. She lost her sense of calm and became fearful—which was confusing. She stared over to Valda and Vance and noticed they seemed to be under some sort of influence. She stayed silent.

Moon-Star was in a daze. She peeked over at Valda and Vance. "Who are these fascinating creatures?" she asked and stepped closer to Gabrielle.

"These celestial creatures belong to you, Lady Gabrielle; you are their ruler. The time will come when a noble soldier will bring them into a spiritual existence, then later, they will transform. But for now, they will stay in this dungeon," Valda said.

Vance bowed to the dragon and the cobra. He turned to Gabrielle. "They are both ideal for you and our Queen's protection. The day will arrive when you will contain these creatures inside your realm."

Gabrielle saw a blinding light in front of her. None of the others could see it and it became difficult for her to withstand this energy. A beam of light hidden in the universe stayed in her sights and interfered with her state of consciousness. She placed her trembling hand on Moon-Star's shoulder. "Take me to Saffron," she said and tilted to one side, trying to keep her balance.

The spiritual dragon and black cobra lowered their heads onto the whirling sand and closed their mirrored eyes.

Moon-Star saw Gabrielle panicking and gripped her hand. She moved quickly and withdrew her from the dungeon. Now she needed to know what was wrong with her mother.

Valda and Vance closed the wooden doors and hurried to see what was wrong with Lady Gabrielle.

A distress signal through Moon-Star's mental consciousness reached Saffron. *Come into the castle, please hurry. Something is not right with my mother.*

The spirit owl flew out of the castle, but the spirit wolf stood by her side, entranced.

Saffron detected Moon-Star's cry for aid and ran to the castle with the High Priestess, spirit animals, and several soldiers. The grand army stood on guard. As Gabrielle collapsed, Moon-Star grabbed her around the waist. She went down to the floor, and Moon-Star fell with her. Confused and upset, she cradled her mother in her arms.

"What is going on with my mother?" she said to Valda and Vance.

They both appeared muddled and were not able to answer their Queen.

Moon-Star feared for her mother's wellbeing and her trembling hands held her mother's weakened body. Her blue eyes were watery and glossy. A quick glance confirmed that Saffron had joined them. She kneeled beside Gabrielle and placed her hand under her head to support her. "My Lady, what's ailing you?" Saffron asked.

Gabrielle was immobile. Saffron looked over at an emotional Moon-Star. "There are no warning signs as to a spiritual attack, my Queen. Spirit wolf is by her side and detects no danger."

Saffron joined mindsets with the High Priestess, and later shifted back to Gabrielle. She picked up a disturbance inside her mindset, but it faded too quickly for her to recognize what it was.

Saffron's eyes flared and set alight the two blazing pentagrams therein. She searched Gabrielle's mindset to look for any hidden clues. Faced with what had taken place, she discovered nothing ongoing in Gabrielle's mind.

The High Priestess kneeled. "Lady Gabrielle, can you understand me?"

She turned her focus to Saffron. "I believe combat fatigued Lady Gabrielle; she requires rest and nourishment," she said, and stood.

Gabrielle opened her eyes and fixated on Moon-Star. Saffron and Moon-Star helped her up and shuffled her along the sculpted marble floor. Her eyes wavered as she examined a darkness swirling on the curved floor. Her firm grip on Moon-Star and Saffron enabled her to close her eyes.

Valda and Vance were both unclear as to what was taking place. Saffron and the High Priestess realized they did not understand Gabrielle's circumstances.

Female warriors surrounded Gabrielle and placed her on a wide bed. The High Priestess passed Moon-Star a chalice of wine.

"See if your mother will drink this wine, my Queen, this will soothe her," the High Priestess said.

Moon-Star worried for her mother. "Mother, please have a sip of wine." As the chalice reached her lips, Gabrielle took a sip.

"Lady Gabrielle, can you describe how you felt inside the dungeon?" Saffron asked.

Gabrielle gazed up at her. "I'm not sure what happened," she replied. Her pupils were large and murky. Saffron leaned in and touched Gabrielle's hand to try to enter her psyche once more, but something blocked her.

The High Priestess reached in to rub Gabrielle's palm and focused on her mental stability. Confusion set into the High Priestess. There was a change in Gabrielle's mindset, and it showed a dark alteration was in her presence. This unexpected change forced the High Priestess and Saffron to be alert of their surroundings in the castle. The High Priestess showed concern with these recent developments. She needed answers. Something was blocking her ability to reach what Gabrielle had seen. Then a sudden opening in her psyche streamed a clue; the High Priestess detected two blocks. Now she could consider how to devise a plan to recapture Gabrielle's troubled frame of mind.

They both understood Gabrielle would progress through many transformations in her way of thinking. This conversion came from beyond the Creator and was unfamiliar to them both. Their occult rituals would help them hunt for hidden symbols. The High Priestess left the room.

"Now let us get rested, Lady Gabrielle. We'll keep a close eye on you," Saffron said and looked over at Moon-Star.

"Saffron, did you know my mother has two celestial creatures waiting inside a dungeon?" she revealed.

"Yes, my Queen, I knew of their existence," she replied. "Lady Gabrielle will get these creatures in time, now you both need to rest, and we will eat soon."

Saffron sat in a high-backed wooden chair beside the bed. They relaxed, knowing there would be a splendid celebration this evening.

Moon-Star rested by her side and managed to fall asleep for a few hours. Gabrielle tossed to one side and tried to relax, but she could not. She closed her eyes so Moon-Star could get the rest she needed.

Chapter Thirteen
A Second Sight in the Paradises

It was a clear sky and nighttime in Egypt. But there was a misty dust cloud rolling along the desert, and it headed for the pyramid.

There was currently a dream-like feel to these places and the scientists inside the pyramid and those in South Africa examined the Orion constellation on the celestial equator. They continued to reveal paranormal developments on planet Earth and in the universe.

During the shift change they all saw something was happening.

Osahar entered the room. While striding toward The Golden Door, he raised his hands and pushed out a burst of stardust from the middle of his palms. He connected with the universe and opened a passageway. A flood of dust swept in and fastened itself to the pyramid. It funneled through the bronze and silver arteries and entered The Golden Door.

Osahar had created a blockade inside the pyramid; now it was time to justify the prophecy that would bring a paranormal force throughout the universe.

"I will describe the celestial partnership within Orion and the well-known constellations," he announced, his tone serious.

Ben and the teams gathered around to listen to him.

"It's imperative everybody understands Gabrielle and Michael's purpose, along with Josh and Blake's. Cosmic secrecies blend inside the Orion constellation, and an apparition aligns at the center in a launch position," he said.

Osahar needed to share several metaphysical symbols with the scientists so he turned to face them. He then set up a protective sphere around them so that the meeting was in private. He radiated calm and his eyes focused as he scanned through The Golden Door and sealed off the universe. He was now in command of The Golden Door.

"I'm ready to explain some of what is happening," he said. "Entrusted to the heart of Orion is a call for transmissions of a continuous light to envelop eleven countries. A blissful transition enclosed a unique solar system, along with Varco-XVI. More dimensions inside the universe will come forward. Orion's Belt is the most prominent and identifiable constellation across the night sky. Ben, you did a presentation in Italy and this meeting was for a team of selected scientists from around the world," he said. "You named it Project Solar Escape. These scientists can examine the Orion constellation during the day and night. Orion's influence limits various functions. The Golden Door symbolizes the universe around the clock," he said and walked across the room.

White lightning crossed along the door, and he uncovered a significant point directed at the prophecy. "The Creator uncovered (II) the High Priestess who holds a superior rank in the heavens and the Divine cards. She has turned over a diversity of heroic leaders from her deck of cards. You are now ready to meet a spiritual and supernatural existence this evening," Osahar said.

He paced through the sand and returned to his discussion. "The universe formed a support inside the Milky Way Galaxy. Your world will meet many unexpected settings in the universe. It is now time to point out this spiritual creation," he said and set forth with his views. "Mira, in part, collapsed as a brilliant star and we both arrived on Earth with Metatron. Our decrees come from the Creator. The power I control stays hidden; in time you will know where I come from. My leadership is for everybody's safety. Gaze upon the majestic Golden Door, ponder what the heavens have proven. It's a transition you can now follow. Several righteous leaders interact to reinforce Gabrielle, Michael, Josh, and Blake. They're primed for a predestined divination."

Osahar was ready to introduce an exceptional man. "His absolute power leaves physical changes throughout the universe; this man is an honored essence who controls most of the Orion constellation. I will familiarize you with him tomorrow evening," he said and nodded.

He met Ben's gaze and went on with his report. "The resulting celestial alignments are important; we will have plenty to interest us. I present to you, the purple planet, Varco-XVI." He raised both arms and faced The Golden Door.

"The Creator set a path for Michael and Gabrielle on Varco-XVI. Spiritual and a supernatural guidance takes them to their destiny. They're both humans who, in spirit, stay by the right and left hand of the Creator. Before Gabrielle and Michael left Earth, celestial messengers removed a seed from both. Solar movement in the universe coupled a new sun and moon, and the planets overshadowed a Deity associated with two Jupiter. Branding flames from the two suns and two moons served as two blood moons, and stimulating solar flares led to creation. Cassiel and The Tree of Life connected with Gabrielle and Michael. The Creator delivered to Gabrielle and Michael their seeds into being: a King and Queen to rule Varco-XVI. Their children grew up, according to Raziel, through The Fountain of Enlightenment. They're now twenty years old. I cannot tell what child came from which seed, Ben. But I do know a female Deity fertilized their seeds in a blood moon. Gabrielle raised Moon-Star on the northern side of the planet. Michael raised Sun-Star on the southern side. Gabrielle and Michael understand these two Royals are not theirs."

Ben took in this latest information. News of Gabrielle and Michael raising their own children on Varco-XVI had him speechless. But eventually he managed to utter, "Gabrielle and Michael each have their own offspring on a purple planet. And to top it off, they do not even know these seeds were their own children. I can't even imagine what this outcome will return. Osahar, where do my boys fit alongside of Gabrielle and Michael?" Ben stared at him with an inquisitive look.

"Josh and Blake were the selected seeds," he replied. "You and your wife are the selected too. Their mission is to set up a grand Kingdom for a King and Queen. Their instructions will come to them from the heavens. And they are more than capable of their purpose. Josh and Blake must follow through irrespective of Gabrielle and Michael's outcome. Josh and Blake's mentality are one with the Creator. I trust no one can pick up on their plans or impede their capability of working on the new planet. But meddling from unfamiliar sources might alter their journey," Osahar said and went on with more.

"Josh and Blake have many advocates, craftsmen, craftswomen, and assistants, messengers, and Guardians. A grand army is available for their safety. Your sons each carry an exquisite amulet around their necks from Cassiel. These amulets have a hidden portal for the Bakoni Ruins, which will be reachable for space travel soon."

Ben had trouble absorbing the information. "How am I going to explain this to my wife?" He ran a palm over his mouth and uttered, "Please continue."

"At the center of the universe there is a steady gravitational wave that fine-tunes the Orion constellation, and it connects with your world. In the Milky Way Galaxy, Earth's solar system and a new solar system both orbit around their own sun. Varco-XVI is the new planet. There is a vast range of Godly leaders in the Triangulum Galaxy, they will show up in time," Osahar said and saw Ben glance around who appeared tense.

"Eleven countries joined in with your Project Solar Escape. Unknown to them they contributed their seeds to a race in the earlier stages of this divination. Australia's connection brought the Big Dipper and Little Dipper to spread their spherical seeds which multiplied over Varco-XVI. The Fountain of Enlightenment contributed to the speedy growth of women and men, they became a new mortal race. Many seeds moved beyond the planet, to produce a paradise elsewhere. Female and male companions care for Gabrielle and Michael and their Monarchs; a supportive, diverse society bonded in a pledge."

The representatives of the eleven countries applauded. The scientists all knew there was a meaning for their connected seeds. They were real and part of a destined divination. Now their purpose became known. The planet needed a population, and they were the contributors.

"Project Solar Escape merged with eleven countries; we have a link with a prophecy. Someone placed this joining in all our mindsets in Italy. How incredible," Ben said.

"Orion is the celestial heart associated with these changes. Aides from the heavens will contribute to a grand bond inside the universe," Osahar said and continued. "A Pharaoh and Queen rest on The Golden Door. I will advance to an understanding soon and learn more based on their purpose."

"What you have mentioned so far has provided us with a good explanation. Superior entities balance the cosmos," he said and now realized that Osahar was a diplomat from the paradises. "Osahar, you have helped us to understand what is before us, and we thank you for being here," Ben said.

Osahar raised both arms. Blended planetary dust swept across The Golden Door. The Orion constellation brightened the universe.

"Tomorrow at 7 p.m. you will meet the Godly leaders and Guardians, and alongside of them will be an unparalleled woman," he said and withdrew from the pyramid.

Chapter Fourteen
The Creator's (II) the High Priestess Reveals the Primary & Channeling Cards

During the day, Ben and the scientists prepared by setting up new cameras and prearranging the teams. There was a fresh development in the universe, and Osahar was to communicate this to the scientists this evening.

The moon was above Osahar; it was bright and secured a moon beam to embody his spirit. He formed four lines in the desert sand which took the shape of a sacred scripture. He had sent forth a plea to Highborn Leader Galasus Pagasusesia for urgent action on Earth. He was now being informed of (II) the High Priestess and Galasus' choice of cards. His hands covered the scripture. Osahar entered the pyramid, and his opaque eyes flashed. Roiling inside Orion was a glimmer bound for his intense view. White lightning struck the pyramid and hemmed in an unbroken attachment to him. A high-ranking meeting was set into place.

Ben and the scientists were attentive when they noticed Osahar entering the pyramid.

He paced toward them and lifted both of his arms in a gesture to signify he was about to deliver important news. "Greetings. The Creator awarded the High Priestess with a reign in the Monarchy," Osahar announced. "She is (II) the High Priestess, and she embraces a great power over the tapestries of prominence. In the Triangulum Galaxy on planet Eugleston inside the great Coliseum and the theater, sit the spectral tapestries. The Coliseum houses the Godly leaders, while the theater holds their evil adversaries. At the beginning of creation, she attached images from her Divine deck of cards to the shadows of all the tapestries. I informed Highborn Leader, Galasus, that we are now ready for her support. In secret, (II) the High Priestess chose many commanding cards from her Divine deck to awaken the tapestries in the Coliseum."

Flamed white lightning whirled inside a haze, and astral dust opened The Golden Door. Osahar brought in several diverse beings and his essence summoned a shockwave to close the door.

Ben and the scientists gazed at these mystical characters; their likenesses stood mirrored inside their tapestries, awaiting a calling.

"(II) the High Priestess and her Divine cards will power a life force to transform the messengers and Guardians into Godly leaders."

Osahar stopped and absorbed a brightness on the door; he was in mental communication with (II) the High Priestess. He found out that Galasus had acquired a selection of spirited cards. They were primary cards, alongside of channeling cards for the great messengers and Guardians on Earth and Varco-XVI.

He acknowledged them and went on. "These channeling cards start with Cups and have awakened. They will mark the journey to symbolize Galasus' master plan. Sharp Swords on Varco-XVI take hold of a flash of lightning from a hidden force in the universe. Pentacles carry a paranormal degree, an absolute power arcs in from beyond the domains. Perfect Wands uphold a weight from the galaxies, and a magical dust weaves inside a passage on the planet. Primary cards are the Godly leaders in the paradises. They're encircled by a weight in the universe," he said and bowed his head.

"Eleven observatories use refracting telescopes and a special lens. Their superior view allows them to examine the visible light, and this region rests inside the electromagnetic spectrum. Scientists, you are the eyes in the universe," he said. "Ben, please introduce your countries and I will tell you how it works. Please start with Egypt," he said.

"Right away, Osahar. Sandra, can you please bring the Egyptian observatory on screen?"

"Done," she said.

The monitors were flashing as all the linked countries were in line to announce their connections to a historical event transpiring in the universe.

"Hello, Ben, teams, and Osahar. I am Ammon Daher, the leading scientist at the Egyptian observatory. The observatory's telescope has a magnificent lens. It joins with Meissa, which holds a double star companion. This marks Meissa as the shining one. An excellent star among a sequence remains inside Orion. Meissa carries a superb energy, and it secures a permanent link to the pyramid and The Golden Door," Ammon said.

"Thank you, Ammon," Osahar said. "Two celestial warriors stand at top of the heaven's hierarchy. Both warriors are equally in command of a higher power. They're the Guardians of The Golden Door and the gateway to heaven. Metatron gained a channeling card from Galasus in a private chamber on planet Eugleston, a noble title from (II) the High Priestess, King of Swords. But Sandalphon changed his agreement to a purpose that remains unknown, and did not receive his title from Galasus. When his time in power surfaces, Galasus will inform me. Sandalphon received his channeling card King of Swords from Samuel in an undisclosed place."

A mirrored image moved up onto The Golden Door—it was Sandalphon. He was now inside an eerie fire and wore a crest on his black armor bearing the King of Swords.

"Metatron stands alone protecting The Golden Door; he keeps a different Covenant and defends the gateway. His new rule as the King of Swords makes him a powerful Godly leader for Gabrielle and Michael. He once carried one of the mightiest swords in the universe," Osahar explained.

It now concerned Ben. "Osahar, when we first started examining this pyramid, Sandalphon linked up with Pluto and alongside of him was a viperous bronze serpent. Did they go to Varco-XVI?" he asked.

"Yes," Osahar replied.

Ben's forehead furrowed as he frowned and his angry eyes glared over at Osahar. "I'm not thrilled," Ben stated. "Metatron's brother is on this planet, lurking around with a viperous bronze serpent." Ben twisted and looked intently at the two noble soldiers. "Why did Metatron's sword disappear?" he asked.

"Metatron donated one of the mightiest swords in the universe to Gabrielle," Osahar replied.

Ben waved his arms in the air, then slapped them to his side. "Gabrielle carries one of the universe's mightiest swords. Is that if she has to confront Sandalphon?" he asked.

"I cannot control or guess what Gabrielle will face; her spiritual symbol is one with the Creator. But what I can explain, is that Metatron and Sandalphon have become part of an Egyptian spiritual afterlife. For millenniums, they have secured this gateway in the universe. Their existence comes from South Africa, home for the Solar Egyptian Calendar," he replied.

Ben nodded as he thought about this new information.

Osahar pushed out a mist on The Golden Door; he waved and presented Temperance. Her mystical embroidered gown and dark hair flared through an outpouring of astral dust. A transformation took place in front of him, and above Temperance's head, an image could be seen where the dark parted. Serpents joined and formed a black and white sea serpent; this unusual creature folded around itself inside a purple mist. Her right hand overturned her hourglass and the sands of time passed over to the next chapter. The switch on The Golden Door provided a fresh view.

He acknowledged this and continued with her title. "She's a primary card, XIV-Temperance, her mystical violet eyes hook up with (II) the High Priestess's view. Her essence bonds with the Divine cards, but Temperance is reversed in her deck. This removed her power to join with (II) the High Priestess. The Creator cloaked her involvement with Varco-XVI and Earth. This reverse led to an isolation to (II) the High Priestess. His Majesty Samuel controls Temperance. She maintains a bond with his dark star on this door, and it's impenetrable. I cannot uncover his Majesty's judgement and how this will affect us, Ben. But I receive messages through my state of mind from the Creator. Temperance is off-limits, and so is the dark star. We will take a short break," Osahar said as he waved his hands over The Golden Door. "I will return soon to further my exploration; new information has come my way." He left the pyramid.

His power over The Golden Door had Ben reaching out to the scientists. They talked about the Godly ruler Samuel, who moved in a force on The Golden Door. They had no control over his supernatural attachment, as it reigns through his dark star. Ben and the teams waited patiently for their Guardian to return with more knowledge to share.

Chapter Fifteen
An Esoteric Importance—Divine Cards

Perfect mixtures of colorful dust encircled the pyramid. Osahar returned and waved a hand over the gilded door. The arrival of (II) the High Priestess mystified the scientists, and continuing onto The Golden Door was a representation of her.

"The Creator set the High Priestess in Gabrielle's path," Osahar said. "She oversees protecting Gabrielle, Moon-Star, and all who follow their journey. An influential power arises from beyond; it is in a dimension not known to any. The Creator roots her state of mind through a secretive occult power in the universe, where she uses an esoteric magic. (II) the High Priestess has a steady balanced power; this seats her on the heaven's throne. Study her image before you on The Golden Door. She holds a crystal ball in one hand, while her sacred book and Divine cards remain in the other."

Upon The Golden Door, the seam of a vortex opened. A burst of smoke unfurled the High Priestess as a misty spirit.

She looked Godly in her spirited mist as he continued to address the scientists.

"(II) the High Priestess commands an order with her Divine cards and tapestries," he said. "Her surrender of many tapestries from the Coliseum to Galasus will now aid us in this divination. Now I must also tell you about a Royal ruler who picked up several useful cards from her deck. This came upon her by the Creator, and he returned a likeness of these missing cards to her deck. She keeps balance with seventy-eight cards. These dark cards belong to the tapestries in the theater and will unfold to me soon."

Seventy-eight Divine cards fanned from one side of The Golden Door to the other, and vapor trails left an ember of light. Metatron awakened and collected the cards. Scientists looked in awe when he showed his luminous sapphire eyes. He pushed the cards into a sphere and back into the realms, then he returned to his position in stillness.

"Supremacies allow the High Priestess to help Gabrielle with forthcoming developments," he said as he walked up and down through the sand. "Michael picked up a legacy from the High Priestess. It is a primary card. 0-Fool: Dante. He's a male who wears a peculiar outfit," he said. "He builds up a unique sixth sense for Michael. Dante can go inside Michael's dreams to discover any uncertainties. For example, he can forecast approaching crusades. When they met him on the bronze gate, he placed the Four of Pentacles on their shields. Sun-Star gained a fire, Michael gained a whirlwind, Efren a drop of water, and the fourth pentacle allows Dante to watch over the land they walk on. A fifth element is a magic from the Creator, it shrouds their impenetrable shields," he concluded. "The High Priestess exists in the realms as the celestial Mother, a noble woman who enjoys high rights in the celestial realms. She remains a prominent aid to Gabrielle and 0-Fool: Dante stays with Michael."

Osahar turned and accepted a spiritual card. "The High Priestess encouraged the Creator to appoint a front-line card for Gabrielle and Michael. VI-Lovers. Their love for each other would allow a spiritual and supernatural connection to the Creator. This selected couple will build up a romance on their spiritual journey. But temptation ascends between two opportunities, they will need to open their hearts to a painful discovery," he revealed.

Ben paid close attention to a mist unveiling on The Golden Door; a darkened form of Gabrielle and Michael showed their commitment to the Creator's actions. They both wore exquisite armor and look like Gods. He clasped his hand to his chest and took a hard breath. "I accept their missions and I believe that all they have been through will help them overcome any obstacles and that they will have a prosperous reign. Osahar, I believe they will both make true decisions. Please proceed," he said.

Curved black lightning swept across The Golden Door, and unbalanced clouds positioned the likeness of two wizards.

At this, Osahar continued his brief. "Valda wears a long colorful cloak. Embroidered on her cloak are supreme images; she uses the bright side of wizardry. Vance wears a long black cloak and it marks his cloak with otherworldly images; he uses the dark side of wizardry. They are wizards on Varco-XVI, and their mission conceals a mystery. They both relate to a primary card, XII-Hanged Man. The Creator positioned a glorious castle on the new planet when it was at its final formation, along with wizards: Valda, and Vance. But they exhibit a setback with the Yin and Yang in the world of wizardry because they are both off balance. This is one card the Royal ruler gained; he has a minimized attachment to them," he said.

Ben shifted to look at these spiritual beings from a different angle; they all contributed to so many different changes in the universe.

"These Godlike leaders are alive in the universe," Ben said. "They're made of stardust and take the likeness of humans. How incredible," he said and crossed his arms. Then he reflected upon a dark, Godly ruler on The Golden Door. "There's a difference in the paradises that makes a judgment. Fellow scientists, we understand what is beyond this door. But to reason with a dark star is something we humans can never dream of negotiating." A spark of black lightning moved across the spacious door. He was planning and encouraging the teams of scientists to be prepared for what was about to unfold in the universe.

"Creation in the universe comes in many forms, and the study and sharing of knowledge that this prophecy exists is something scientists have a desire for," he said. "Life is plentiful on planet Earth and that the Creator can continue creation elsewhere is remarkable," he said, and paused to reflect a starry gaze at this fascinating woman. "We stand indebted to (II) the High Priestess for the surrender of her Divine cards. She places these cards amongst the great tapestries in a place we never knew to be real. Now these Godly beings stir with a new cosmic strength. This force for Earth and Varco-XVI is our front line of protection," Ben said and turned to face the scientists. Cheering echoed through the room. Scientists from eleven countries were now aware of a dark star and the heavenly leaders of the universe. A willingness to work together and help to defeat the dark star settled in.

"Let me explain even more," Osahar suggested. He waved his arm across The Golden Door.

The outline of the country South Africa illuminated on The Golden Door; a sand swirl stirred a passage to Orion.

"Hello, Ben, teams, and Osahar. I'm Andricia Pillay who leads the scientists at the South African observatory. The observatory's telescope points one lens, and is the leading eye aimed at the Orion constellation. The broadcast connects South Africa to the Orion Nebula. Inside the nebula there is a rise and fall shockwave," she said.

"Yes," Osahar replied. "The heavens mixed the youngest star inside the nebula. This enforced a supernova to expel a mixture of gaseous clouds across the universe. The Anunnaki is an eternal ancient civilization who appeared on Earth, but who remain concealed from humankind. The Bakoni Ruins remains as treasured ground, and a secret portal reaches Varco-XVI. The Orion Nebula connects with this pyramid. There is a great image of a paralleled sword hidden inside the Orion Nebula. This sword is for Metatron, since he gave his grand sword to Gabrielle," Osahar revealed. "Metatron, will need a grand sword in the paradises as his brother holds one as well."

Osahar trusted Metatron's sword was not perceived in the realms when he gave it to Gabrielle. He faced The Golden Door, and paused for a moment, so he could prepare himself for what was about to unfold.

Chapter Sixteen
IV-Emperor Hamuel

Twelve electrifying stars brightened the universe, and the star pattern took the shape of a spectacular black hole. Streaming lights in the universe set down a likeness onto The Golden Door. The scientists watched in awe at the appearance of the black hole on the door; even the copy looked lustrous and powerful.

This gathering of superior elements signified an enlightenment was about to take place; it was for a man who escaped from a great darkness. He now had a hunger for the Emissaries.

Osahar stood in front of The Golden Door in silence as he thought about a great man who had observed the Royal ruler since the beginning of his reign.

"Sachiel's power moves him beyond creation in secrecy. He is a watcher in the universe. When he looked back in time, he watched Samuel escape from a black hole and move through the universe. Then he grasped a hideous line of attack waiting to happen and reported this to Galasus," he said and continued.

"Sachiel also reported Samuel to the great warrior Metatron, along with additional information about his brother Sandalphon."

The desert sands whirled inside a warm breeze; a quick wind progressed through the pyramid. Osahar gazed solemnly around him. Rising dust caused the Orion Nebula to change shape on The Golden Door. South Africa's observatory showed a vision inside the heart of Orion, where vigorous vapors shifted to form a man's image mirrored from where he was. He wore a black cloak and cosmic flames surrounded him. He balanced himself inside of the Orion's vapors and came into view. A path in Orion uncovered a Protostar: Hamuel.

"Galasus crowned Hamuel as IV-Emperor on planet Eugleston, a Divine card from (II) the High Priestess. He reported the startling news about his Majesty to Hamuel, whose dynamic force enable him to connect to everything in the universe. Hamuel possesses a psychic ability to see and communicate with Galasus and the Creator. His spiritual creation as a

Protostar, will now allow him to a revelation. Hamuel plans to transform Earth and Varco-XVI. Two Mercury in the Milky Way Galaxy aid him to take part in a disguised relationship. Far-off in the universe, Hamuel embodies a spirit empowering an unbound gravitational wave. Inside a multi-verse, his pledge entitles him to set up a divination within Orion. Resplendent lights marked a special full moon, and Hamuel's silhouette connects with Gabrielle and Michael. They both have a spiritual connection to him. This man of many mysteries exists alongside a prophecy and he uses nearby supremacies to defend our sacred laws. Hamuel is a celebrated man in the paradises, and we are placing our faith in him that he is our salvation." At this, Osahar bowed his head.

Ben accepted who Hamuel was, and understood he was a superior Protostar who would even up the prophecy.

Then an arched flame streamed across The Golden Door. Raziel brandished his white cloak and showed his likeness on the door, surrounded by a spiraling galaxy.

"He's a Guardian from the celestial realms," Osahar said. "A great man who upholds his status quo in the paradises. His pledge embodies an allegiance to follow and protect creation. His primary card is presented as: X-Wheel of Fortune. He represents an everlasting movement throughout the universe; the rise and fall of an unexpected judgment in the universe will forge ahead. This man who is an expert ruler and a Guardian of the Divine Guidance, safeguards the mysteries of the Creator. He's the bearer of the Fountain of Enlightenment; this spiritual fountain carries faith and wisdom. He protects a positioned portal in the Bakoni Ruins, and connects with the South African observatory. Raziel upholds the universe and his position to the Creator is close to the throne. A sanctioned decree combines him with Cassiel and two Saturn," Osahar concluded.

Osahar swung his hand and made the image clearer on The Golden Door. Ben's Texas observatory zoomed in on The Golden Door. Varco-XVI illuminated alongside it and the scientists eagerly watched the elegance of creation.

"Betty Grant here! Hello, Ben, teams, and Osahar. Project Solar Escape originated here at the Texas observatory and with me. I have scientists Frank Connors and Linda Stevens who have connected three scopes to monitor the universe. A permanent link has the telescope aimed at the Orion constellation, Varco-XVI, and one special lens can look deep into the billows of Lota Orionis."

"Yes, the brightness of the strong x-ray shows the making of a grand sword," Osahar revealed. "A potent link from Lota Orionis and Earth contributed a connection to Varco-XVI. The planet covers a geographical arrangement equal to Earth."

He continued. "Ariel will now appear as a mirrored image on The Golden Door. This male encases himself in a blue robe. He's a lion in the universe who protects Earth and Varco-XVI. He is a watcher of everything that is and is to be in the universe. Ariel is the Guardian of the native spirit animals. He's a superior warrior who is the keeper of their sacred wisdom. His primary card: XXI-World. Uriel is a female who rules alongside of him."

A white robe draped over her shoulders when she appeared on the door. "Uriel has been situated as a persuasive ruler for Earth and everything that is and is to be in the universe. She generates a rare magnetism to secure her unseen forces; a flame from the sun shows her guarded fire as it swells across the universe. Ariel and Uriel's fellowship are to support the supernatural delegates in the universe. Uriel's flaming sword has a loyal link with the throne and she can grant pardons. These two leaders from the paradises offer a gracious love for a majestic sovereignty. The Creator and his Majesty reached a perfect finished cycle for Varco-XVI. If we look at the result, Varco-XVI and Earth are both in harmony. These planets are magnificent and orbit in their solar systems in perfection," Osahar said.

He watched a new flow of light move across The Golden Door. Within the Orion constellation, Lota Orionis was infusing a defensive wall with two stars. It lit up to show Ariel and Uriel were using the stardust to outline a grand sword.

Osahar went on. "Ariel and Uriel now have the Ten of crossed Swords and are forging an honored sword inside Lota Orionis. They will store this magnificent sword inside the Orion Nebula. A sacred placement in the equilateral triangle will power and conceal an ionized sword. When the great sword of Orion surfaces on The Golden Door, an arc of hydrogen will prime the celebrated sword. Then it will drop into the palm of a Righteous Leader. During a dynamic part of Michael's campaign, he will call upon Uriel for her aid."

Ben stared at several monitors, taking in the representatives of the countries and how they were handling the revelations. Eleven countries recorded what was happening in the universe day and night, and they were now able to link how Godlike leaders connected with Orion and the planetary alignments inside the Milky Way Galaxy. Ben was thankful he had a team of scientists who had stayed back at his Texas observatory as they were also part of the key to the unwinding of a prophecy.

"Now it all makes sense how we are in the heart of a paramount meeting that calls for the heavenly leaders," Ben said. "Noble scientists, we must keep up with an unprecedented broadcast from inside the cosmos. Osahar is showing us how an eternal connection transmits a spiritual and supernatural fitting together." He turned and nodded his head for Osahar to continue.

Osahar lifted his arm and cast a shadow over The Golden Door; dark clouds encircled Italy.

"Hello, from Italy. I am Marco Abelli and the leading scientist for this observatory. All the countries' telescope lenses have a wide field of view. These generous gifts originated from Ben here in Italy. But my good friend also gave me a special lens which is superior in strength. It shows a dwarf planet mixing an energy in the Kuiper belt. This lens stays aimed at Mintaka and Pluto. The ice dwarf retains a band, and it encloses a dark essence further than Earth's Neptune," Marco concluded.

"Pluto remains the barrier for dark spirits," Osahar said. "Mintaka harmonizes as a multiple star system in the constellation of Orion. Alnilam, Alnitak, and Mintaka make a magical connection through the power of three stars. Mintaka synchronizes your attachment. Pluto carried two dark entities to the western side of Varco-XVI. There is one dark card inside the tomb, and it's masked. These individuals stay dormant. Pluto will go on bearing dark matter on The Golden Door; we cannot interfere," he said and watched Ben for a reaction.

"Ramiel is a male." He slipped on a white cloak. White lightning progressed across The Golden Door and unveiled him in a mirrored image. "His time in power drew a primary card: XI-Justice. His ruling delivered the XI-justice card to the Emissaries for a privileged star, Samuel is back in the realms as a Royal ruler. In spirit he waits on the ethereal part of this Golden Door. Ramiel serves Samuel and Galasus in the paradises. Balance and virtue act with the best intentions for two sides of a prophecy. A pledge card awakened him to raise whatever his Majesty places in a monumental tomb and to work alongside of Galasus. Ramiel is the thunder and terror who awaits his orders inside an enigmatic galaxy. He draws nearer. Ramiel's movement in the universe builds on an unforeseen power, this sequence operates alongside the rising of Pluto."

Osahar faced Ben and added, "I know where Sandalphon stays. His Majesty obtained his essence in the earlier stages of creation. Ramiel now oversees the western side and a monumental tomb. Sandalphon guards this tomb along with a bronze serpent."

Ben now understood where Sandalphon had gone with the intimidating serpent. He bowed his head in disappointment.

Team Italy understood they would predict when two dark spirits would awaken inside a monumental tomb. This knowledge primed the scientists to push forward.

"Let's believe, my friend, that this observatory can forecast these ties," Marco said to Ben. "We will pursue these dark spirits when they show up in a starry pattern and are ready to unleash. Our networks will remain constantly on high alert."

"Thank you, Marco," Ben replied.

Osahar waved his hand over The Golden Door once more. Mystic clouds glided across to show Canada.

"Hello, from Canada. I am Liam Adams and the leading scientist for this observatory. A powerful telescope tips a lens to connect with the new silver Mercury, and Earth's Mercury. We have a partnership with the Orion constellation, and it's Rigel. Betelgeuse can outshine Rigel, but the magnificent star is dimming. Both stars work together to bring a bond to generate a mighty brightness," Liam said.

"Raphael," Osahar said. "A male who wears a white cloak stands before you. He secured a primary card: VIII-Strength. He rules the silver Mercury and Earth's Mercury. Raphael protects the north, his bond in the heavens is as the healing one."

The universe presented an outbreak of astral flares; it struck the pyramid and extended along The Golden Door. Chamuelle arrived inside a nebulous haze.

"Chamuelle, a female, adorns herself in a white robe. She pledged to a primary card: XX-Judgment. She sees the Creator and is a member of the order of spiritual forces for Galasus. Chamuelle carries an eternal flame of love; she can build up your heart with a thirst for a good life. She is an angelic mediator who can shape-shift into many forms."

The Golden Door shimmered as a celestial windstorm passed over it and brought Turkey into view.

"Hello, from the Turkey observatory. I am Adlet Sezer. A large telescope joins with one primary lens; this enhances our views on the pink Jupiter and Earth's Jupiter. Our partnership remains with the Orion constellation Alnitak. A triple star system in the constellation of Orion, Alnitak is a primary star in Orion's Belt along with Alnilam and Mintaka. The magic of three spreads a liveliness throughout the universe," he said.

"Sachiel is a Godly man who rules the pink Jupiter and Earth's Jupiter," Osahar revealed. Sachiel's black cloak covered his broad shoulders as he appeared as a mirrored image.

"His primary card: V-Hierophant. Sachiel transmits a brilliant light along the universe and Earth, he is the spirit of mercy. His presence promotes an angelic man who can silence emotions, and this gives him the power to forgive. His ability to see celestial views take him beyond the dimensions to recognize who has gone astray."

Images of Egyptian relics swirled on the edge of The Golden Door, and dust clouds burst out to illustrate the two Egyptian figures that remained on the door from the earlier stages for the scientists' observations.

"Turkey, your connection to Alnitak will breathe new life into the Pharaoh and Queen and send them to Varco-XVI soon," Osahar said. "These Royals entrenched on The Golden Door display no risk at present," he concluded and mentioned. "Prepare yourselves to meet an astonishing woman from the paradises." Osahar paced through the sand and stood in front of The Golden Door.

Chapter Seventeen
A Shooting Star Showed a Cloak of Many Colors

The teams sat back and watched as Osahar raised both arms. He was reaching for an attachment in the universe and pulled in an electrifying piece of energy in both hands. He pushed it through outer space to mark a path for a shooting star. Absorbed in his orders, Osahar brought in an energetic roiling stardust to spread throughout the pyramid. The scientists were watchful as this captivating scene spread without a sound and presented a multitude of vibrant hues. Inside was the image of a woman.

"Her name is Jophielle, and a specific oath placed her to govern alongside Sachiel."

Streaming colors exhibited a rainbow cloak draped over her shoulders.

"Jophielle claimed a primary card alongside of the Creator: XVII-Star. A potential opportunity is located ahead for her. Past and present meet to prepare Jophielle for a specific approach. She has a balance between heaven and Earth, and her vow permits her to be the Guardian of the Book of Wisdom, along with a rank next to the throne. She can shape-shift into a trickster, to consider the bright and dark side of the prophecy. Jophielle can be seen when a flash through the universe brings to light a shooting star. She owns a coiled shockwave which leaves a splendid trail of colors across the universe. The Creator protects her. She requested a role to play on Varco-XVI, and is ready to gain a deep secret from Sachiel."

Osahar saw Sandra approaching. "We will take a break and I will be back to continue," Osahar said and moved aside into the darkness.

She sauntered over to report some new information. "We have everything on record, Ben, and I expect this will make generating the processes easier. Over there is some fresh coffee and food. Ben, please have a break," she suggested.

Sandra pointed to a table set up with an assortment of food and drinks. Then she showed him a desktop computer. Ben angled his head to look at an expanded computer screen. Astral alignments with the paradises' leaders showed how eleven countries were associated with them. An index graph showed the channeling cards and primary cards. They were attached to tapestries bearing the Godly leaders and tapestries bearing the dark entities. Another graph showed the Orion constellation, two solar systems, Earth, and Varco-XVI. The Triangulum Galaxy and planet Eugleston were on the map. They placed a big cork board on the pyramid wall and a white board near a group of scientists helping her. Sandra had drawn Cups, Pentacles, Swords, and Wands on a white board.

Ben wondered what she was doing with the white board. But he remembered she had a connection with Temperance on The Golden Door in the earlier stages of their discovery. She had explained the Temperance's existence in terms of a fortune teller. So, he let her go on with her business. "Thank you, Sandra. Your methodology looks promising so please keep me updated on any progress. I'm going to have something to eat. I must relax for a moment and call my wife to let her know everything is fine here and with our boys," he said.

A little while later, Ben finished his coffee and was ready to continue. He watched Osahar walk out from the darkness. Ben got up and walked toward The Golden Door and gestured for Osahar to continue.

Inside a swirling dust cloud, China surfaced.

"Hello, from China. I am Bing Cheng and the leading scientist for this observatory. A large telescope with a singular lens holds a grand view on the new gold and silver Saturn and Earth's Saturn. The Orion constellation connects the observatory to Alnilam, and a large blue supergiant star entwines a brightness amongst Alnitak and Mintaka. The power of three expands along the celestial equator," he said.

"Cassiel wears a blue robe over his large shoulders," Osahar began to explain. "Cassiel has a primary card: VII-Chariot. He travels in space and is the supremacy for the Tree of Life. Gabrielle and Michael have a closeness to Cassiel in spirit; their mind and body center with him to join the Tree of Life. Saffron and Efren build up a strength and connect to the Tree of Life with two Neptune. This helps Gabrielle and Michael to overcome many hardships through Cassiel's spirit. His time in power reigns over all portals, two suns and two moons bring him a higher force. Cassiel is a Godly leader who can only remove the protectors of the universe who have gone astray. His spirit sits by the Creator, Samuel, and Galasus, and rules the gold and silver Saturn and Earth's Saturn. Josh and Blake wear his amulet. Cassiel protects the young men. Ben, your sons' mindsets are one with the Creator; this should make you happy."

Ben was feeling very upbeat after hearing this. "Thank you," he replied. "To understand my sons have a connection to such a Godly leader is incredible."

Bing reached back. "Splendid news, Ben. Team China will always be ready because we are the watchful eyes over your sons and are honored to do so."

The representatives from the other countries showed their respect by clapping and the noise echoed around them.

An upsurge of a cosmic flame led Australia to show up on The Golden Door.

"Hello, Ben, teams, and Osahar. Jacob Jones here from Australia. Our singular lens connects a lustrous view with the gray Uranus and Earth's Uranus. We tie in with the Orion constellation and it balances with Sigma Orionis. Sigma Orionis lingers as a multiple star system, it fuels an open cluster in the universe. There's a brilliance to this connection, and we here at the observatory find it exciting," he said.

Osahar had more to add. "Raguelle is a female protector who adorns herself with a black cloak. Her channeling card is forceful: The Queen of Swords. She sculpted a blade that is jeweled and jagged; a fiery sword holds a deep silver flame. She is an insightful woman who can also be bad-tempered. Raguelle upholds a title as the highest female celestial warrior in the paradises. Her spirit connects with the throne. As an elite warrior, she watches over Gabrielle and Moon-Star. Gabrielle's spiritual brightness is present and at her command for an army. Raguelle will step into battle in stages; her time in power reigns over the gray Uranus and Earth's Uranus."

Scientists studied the changing universe with fresh eyes and waited patiently for Osahar to continue.

Chapter Eighteen
Supernatural Strength Primary & Channeling Cards

Nineteen stars brightened across the universe and took the shape of pentacles—the pattern symbolized the power for destiny. Osahar continued to introduce leaders from the paradises. The Golden Door shifted; spirited particles introduced Mexico.

"Hello, from Mexico's observatory. I am Juan Beltre. Our telescope has a special lens that reveals a slice of the new blue Neptune and Earth's Neptune. It partners with Betelgeuse, a reddish star which exists as a semiregular variable star in the constellation of Orion. It connected with two ghostly figures in the earlier stages of our expedition. This could be the reason this magnificent star is dimming at a rapid pace," Juan concluded.

"They are spiritual pagans who bear a supernatural force," Osahar said. "Six blank tapestries await their victory or failure in the Coliseum on planet Eugleston, which rests deep inside the spiraling Triangulum galaxy. Saffron and Efren both remain superior defenders on the planet. Saffron wears a decorated ivory cloak over her shoulders. Her channeling card is the Queen of Pentacles," he said as he took pride in the pagan's appearance.

"The clever use of her magic makes her a successful leader and her speed as a warrior seats her on a crystal throne in the paradises. Efren's cloak is black, and he is as effective a leader and warrior. His channeling card is the King of Pentacles. Efren's loyalty and wisdom to the paradises placed him on a crystal throne in the paradises. Together Saffron and Efren will work with the new planet's water using the blue Neptune and Earth's Neptune. Saffron and Efren connect with Cassiel's Tree of Life.

"Ariel gifted Saffron and Efren with native spirit animals. These animals bear a Godlike protection for Gabrielle, Michael, Sun-Star, and Moon-Star. Saffron is now a Guardian to Gabrielle, as Efren is to Michael. They're both sanctioned by a pledge to protect Moon-Star and Sun-Star, along with their followers on the new planet."

An image of a sun and moon brightened The Golden Door. Two glittering scepters were raised alongside two crowns and two thrones, and a golden Tablet came into view. The scene was striking. Two leaders came out in plain sight—Queen Moon-Star and King Sun-Star.

Osahar stood in front of her image. "There are two royal cards that belong to the Creator and power the Royals with a spiritual and supernatural connection. This is the Queen of the new planet," Osahar said and bowed his head gracefully. "Queen Moon-Star has a primary card: XVIII-Moon, and a channeling card: The Queen of Wands. The sun shines in her heart, it acquaints her with King Sun-Star. Her wand rests on a throne buried in vines and grapes. She holds two scepters."

Osahar paced over to face Sun-Star. "This is the King of the new planet," Osahar said and nodded his head to the King respectfully. "King Sun-Star has a primary card: XIX-Sun and a channeling card: The King of Wands. The moon brightens his heart, it acquaints him with Queen Moon-Star. His wand too rests on a throne buried in vines and grapes."

With a rapid movement, a spiraling galaxy spanned across The Golden Door. Osahar continued to Sariel's introduction.

"I will move forward with Sariel. Draped over his shoulders is a decorated black robe, he is another noble warrior in the paradises. His primary card: XIII-Death. He contributes to the spirit of death as it flows throughout the universe. Sariel finds a way to see through the dark spirits; he arranges a path for the angelic beings. He is a leader for a celestial army and supports Michael and Gabrielle so they can reach their supremacy. Gabrielle, Michael, Sun-Star, Moon-Star, and their spiritual armies have fixed symbols on their shields from Sariel. He is an exceptional warrior when it comes to defensive techniques. Sariel bears the responsibility to safeguard all living beings. When Michael and Gabrielle call to him, he will appear to aid them. Michael will serve with an all-male noble army, alongside Efren, as Gabrielle will serve with an all-female noble army, alongside of Saffron."

"These Godly leaders, Guardians, and spirit animals in the realms are incredible," Ben said. "Now I can see how Michael and Gabrielle would have many concerns." He shook his head and knew this journey will only get more complicated.

"Dark entities are on the new planet; we are not familiar as to where they are or their movement," warned Osahar.

This stirred Ben, as what he saw in front of him was another twist on the planet. He couldn't quite grasp what to say, but he considered his words. "Please continue," he said and rubbed his face.

Spirited winds encompassed The Golden Door, and swirls of animated dust swung into place and showed England.

"Hello, from England's observatory. I am Angela Jones. Our telescope has a special lens; it shows a spectacular view of the new white Venus and Earths Venus, and a joining with Bellatrix. To the west, the supergiant Betelgeuse and Bellatrix together mix a superior ingredient in the Universe," she said.

"Here is Anaelle who wears a white robe and her channeling card is the Queen of Cups," Osahar said. "Her heart stays warm and she increases in her brightness when she orbits closer to Mercury. She rules the white Venus and you only need one breath of her air from her. She can put a new life into those in need. Anaelle carries with her an extensive duty, and she is a great friend in the paradises."

He nodded and continued.

"Anaelle has a secret oath to watch over Mira. Venus is the second planet from the sun and spins in the opposite direction. Anaelle has a brilliant radiance around her; she will change a person's emotion in relationship to death."

When Osahar bowed in sadness, Ben realized Anaelle was necessary for Mira.

"Mira's orders must obey a Royal ruler's dark star. When she reaches near death, Mira will call upon Anaelle."

"How are you and Mira connected?" Ben asked.

"I cannot explain the bond I have with Mira; you will learn in time, Ben. Mira's attachment is with The Golden Door, and at no point must we interfere."

Ben stared at him; he sensed a terrible ending in Osahar's future. Ben, Osahar, and the scientists took a well-deserved break.

Chapter Nineteen
XVI-Tower Samuel Raiphualas II

A galactic wind entered the pyramid, a streak of black lightning struck the ground, and Austria was lit up on The Golden Door.

Osahar clasped his hands and faced the door.

"Hello, from Austria. I am Adalard Dorn, and the leading scientist for this observatory. Our telescope has a superior lens and makes us the notable eyes of the new gold Mars and Earth's Mars. This fits together with Saiph. In the constellation of Orion, Saiph intermingles with fifty-four of the brightest stars. The gold Mars and Earth's Mars link to The Golden Door," he said.

"Metatron allowed an entrance and exit for internal movements through The Golden Door," Osahar said. "He brought Mira and me through this portal. Galasus holds my card, I will know what card (II) High Priestess honored me with soon. But it is unknown to me if Mira has a card."

Flames fanned up and down The Golden Door, and black lightning hit the ground once again. Osahar was now ready to reveal the Royal from planet Eugleston who had become the villain.

"His primary card is dark: XVI-Tower. There's an image of a male silhouette at the top left corner of The Golden Door," he said and pointed. "The Creator placed his Majesty's, Samuel Raiphualas II, bright star on this door. But his dark star surfaced before his billion-year epoch and soon took over. There was a shocking change that took place in the universe, where relationships and trust fell apart. His Majesty's dark star is now out of control," he added.

Osahar saw this news intrigued the scientists.

"Now I know why the prominent leaders in the paradises have called upon a high chain of command," Ben said.

Ben wondered if this gathering of Gods would be enough to hold back the Royal ruler. He had doubts and worried for the safety of his sons and his colleagues on Varco-XVI.

Osahar told them more. "The prophecy for the alternative world has changed, and it's because of the Royal ruler's unforeseen transformation," he said. "His Majesty received several secret cards from the Creator. These cards belong to the tapestries belonging to the fallen inside the theater on the planet Eugleston. Unknown entities will unfold from the tapestries and move forward to become known in time."

A double star flashed across The Golden Door. Osahar looked away and recognized who this belonged to and concentrated on continuing to forewarn the scientists of the good and evil on The Golden Door.

"His Majesty's cosmic strength pulls in a ghostly slice from two of the mightiest elements in the universe. Hydrogen and helium are the intense energies that encompass him, and thus many rebellions will take place in the universe." Osahar dropped his head and sighed audibly.

He looked up at a brightness on The Golden Door. "A bitterness assembles inside the cosmos; his Majesty will pass as much suffering onto humanity as he can and work his way to destroy all who rebelled against him. Adorned over his shoulders remains a black cloak. Samuel's bright star reversed, now an essence inside of him switched him to become a dark celestial warrior. He rules two Mars and connects with Pluto. He controls an abundance of stardust, creating an atomic weapon inside Orion, where he can draw in individuals and annihilate them. On the west side of Varco-XVI, a monumental tomb awaits his command. This is where two dark spirits are close to resurrection. Samuel governs dark figures on the planet and contained them on a bronze and silver gate. He has now released these dark spirits; this signifies war."

He turned to Ben who was watching emotions playing across his team's faces. "Gabrielle, Michael, Saffron, and Efren accept these images, Ben. When Gabrielle and Michael opened their gates to the new planet, the spirited images vanished, and most turned to serve the dark star, Samuel. They are no longer human as we understand the concept, but are much more in tune with the universe and have a deeper connection with its roots. The Creator shields your sons from the deep emissions on the planet, and the secondary measures are Cassiel's amulets that protect your sons. Josh and Blake remain human in all aspects."

Ben shook his head. "My leading scientists crossed over from being human, and my sons didn't. I'm counting on Gabrielle and Michael to stop these dangerous spirits, and I want them back on Earth along with my sons. What you have explained so far tells us Gabrielle and Michael have a cosmic embodiment, so can they eventually come back to Earth as human?" he asked.

"In time this will be made clear to me but what I can identify now is they have the courage, the weaponry, and the aids to overturn this evil threat. I believe they can stop these dangerous spirits and withstand these battles."

Featherlike beams of light flared up and brightened the surroundings; an arc of cosmic dust flew from side to side. The interior edge of the pyramid captured Ben's attention. He walked toward the interior west wall, looking at myriad images swirling in a cloud of dust. Tension in his neck muscles caused him to roll his shoulders. He turned to face Osahar. "I have one more question. Do you understand this deep-seated imagery that is etched into the inner and outer surface of this pyramid?" he asked.

Flashing lights drifted over the pyramid; glowing images were fixed on the spirited walls.

"The interior and exterior part of this pyramid connect with a metaphysical order," he replied. "On this pyramid made of bronze and silver, stately Gods near their mission, they serve as a sanctified existence on Earth. The Golden Door conceals a great man in a white cloak. They received his message. Individuals in living form will bring their blissful spirits to justify the prophecy. They will carry out their purpose to protect humankind and cross over to Varco-XVI."

Ben realized a power would rise off the pyramid. These celestial beings on the inner and outer limits put him somewhat at ease.

"Our attachment continues with Saiph, the new gold Mars and Earth's Mars," Adalard Dorn continued from Austria. "We will show an energy flowing towards The Golden Door and we will warn you immediately."

Austria was on red alert. "Thank you, Adalard," Ben said.

"Additional information will also turn up," Osahar said. "Let's move forward with what the Creator has arranged with Galasus in the paradises."

"Thank you for your help, Osahar," Ben said. He appeared pleased with his description. "And for sharing this valuable knowledge with everybody associated with Project Solar Escape. My sons, Gabrielle, and Michael need our help. They survive on Varco-XVI, where dark spirits dwell inside a war zone. A Godly ruler has gone rogue, and we now understand his intentions." He looked troubled at the overwhelming evidence of a spiritual and supernatural battle about to take place and shook his head.

Sylvie Gionet

Osahar turned and saw Mira came out of the darkness; he moved back into the darkness with her while Ben was preparing to address his teams.

Facing the monitors, aware of how tired he felt, Ben strained his voice to speak in a positive tone. "Project Solar Escape has given us the confidence to move forward with our Guardian. Osahar, introduced us to a supreme reign in the paradises. Now that we are familiar with their good intentions, let us respect our obligation as scientists to help Gabrielle and Michael, and my sons." Ben and the rest of the countries involved in the project would do their utmost to help rid Earth and the new planet of these dark forces.

Chapter Twenty
A Special Gift from Moon-Star

Gabrielle needed rest; after meeting the two mesmerizing creatures in the castle chamber, she had a continual feeling of being unbalanced. She had collapsed onto her bed.

A soothing breeze came along with Saffron when she approached Gabrielle's large bed.

"Lady Gabrielle, it's time to get up," she whispered.

"Thank you, Saffron, for taking care of me, I guess fatigue got the best of me. Strange wouldn't you say?"

"Yes, my Lady, I will be sure to keep a close watch if you continue to look fatigued."

Gabrielle yawned and raised her arms to stretch, then she stepped out of her bed. She walked forward to check on Moon-Star and gave her a slight nudge.

"I'm feeling a lot better, Moon-Star," she said. "Let us go soak in a nice warm bath. Later we can get ready for our celebration."

Moon-Star threw back the blankets and jumped out of the bed. "I do need a bath, and I plan on enjoying the festivities this evening," she said quickly and wiped her glazed eyes with her palms.

"My Lady, there are towels, face cloths, and suitable clothing organized on a table for you and Queen Moon-Star."

"Thank you, Saffron."

Radiant sunshine glimmered through the acacia windows and a sun streak glossed the sculpted marble floors. Mixed bouquets of flowers filled the surrounding spaces and the fragrance put Gabrielle in a good mood. She undressed and walked down a spiral staircase. A large in-ground tub rippled with daisies floating on top of the water, and perfumed oils lingered over the surface, making it peaceful. The heated water eased Gabrielle's body and mind; she relaxed, closed her eyes, and drew in a heavy breath. Pleasant aromas brought her a calmness.

Moon-Star undressed and followed her mother into the tub. She sat down and closed her eyes. A few minutes later she opened them, peeked over at Gabrielle and noticed she was relaxing. But Moon-Star struggled to relax.

"My Lady." Saffron offered Gabrielle a large towel who took it as she got out of the tub, closely followed by Moon-Star who wrapped one around her too.

"Mother, you seem refreshed; I guess it's time to go eat—I sure am hungry."

"Yes, let's enjoy dinner and our last night here."

After they got dressed, and brushed their hair and teeth, Saffron passed an item to Moon-Star.

Moon-Star's eyes glistened as she hid an item in her palm. She was glad Saffron gave it to her before their dinner. Trying to conceal her excitement, she stood tall. She was now ready to hand this special gift to her mother. But her hands trembled. She inhaled, composed herself, and approached Gabrielle.

"One minute, Mother, I have something for you," she said with a huge smile.

Gabrielle turned and saw how Moon-Star was radiating happiness. "Yes, what could you have for me?" she asked.

Moon-Star raised her hand and opened it to show Gabrielle the pearl which had been a gift from Raguelle.

"The craftswomen weaved the pearl to latch on top of a white leather braided armband. Bronze and silver chains surround the edges. The fine chains lace across the radiant pearl," she said, and gazed into Gabrielle's eyes.

A stream of cosmic dust filled with particles from space, spun around the exquisite white pearl.

Gabrielle smiled at Moon-Star. "How exquisite," she expressed. "Moon-Star, thank you. I love this bracelet, and I cherish you." She flung her arms around her and held on tight. This moment brought out Moon-Star's moonlit ability and the room began to brighten.

"Please fasten this superb bracelet on my wrist." She wiped tears of happiness from her eyes.

Moon-Star weaved the bracelet around her wrist and fastened it tight.

Gabrielle observed her thoughtful daughter as she wiggled her wrist to make sure the bracelet was nice and comfortable to wear.

"There, it's not too tight, or loose, it's perfect." Moon-Star stared at Gabrielle.

"How did you get this pearl from me? It was safely tucked away in my pouch."

She chuckled and came back with, "Oh, Mother, I got it last night when you went to sleep."

"Our craftswomen are a special gift to us. I will have to thank them," Gabrielle said. She admired her eye-catching bracelet.

Moon-Star turned to thank Saffron for her help.

"You're welcome, my Queen, it was indeed a pleasant surprise for Lady Gabrielle," Saffron said and nodded. "Now, shall we?"

"You bet, Saffron, we're hungry," Moon-Star said.

As they strode through a lengthy hallway, they knew a grand room filled with food and music was ahead.

"Well, you two did this without my knowledge," Gabrielle said. "What a nice surprise. Thank you, Saffron, for supporting your Queen and arranging this."

Saffron leaned over and tapped Gabrielle's shoulder. "Our Queen suggested shielding your pearl, Lady Gabrielle. I fulfilled her wishes."

"Well, my thoughtful daughter, I can't wait for more of your surprises."

Moon-Star was overjoyed and now in a great mood due to her mother's reaction.

***

Valda, Vance, and the High Priestess had organized a grand celebration in the castle. This was for their honored performance in simulated warfare. They were as ready as they could be to fight for their right to secure Varco-XVI. With a joyous mood, they continued to walk toward the primary room. What they found at the entrance brought them all smiles. A group of dancers was gathered at the bottom of the marble stairs, ready to entertain their audience. Gabrielle observed her lustrous spirit animals, attendants, and noble army feasting and enjoying the celebration. Attendants packed their tables with steaming trays filled with pheasant, beef, and lamb. Large wicker baskets overflowed with colorful fruit, and decorated plates sat alongside piled high with fresh steaming vegetables. Gabrielle detected the aroma of fresh bread. Chalices arranged together with clay containers were filled to the brim with white and red wine. A long, decorated table stood alone in the distance; Gabrielle spotted a choice of sweets.

"Look over there, Moon-Star. They loaded a large table with a variety of desserts," she pointed out.

Moon-Star's eyes brightened. A grin widened across her face. She licked her lips and reacted. "How tempting. I need an assortment of those delicious desserts. I can taste them now," she said.

"Let's go, you keep a keen eye on those delicious sweets, we can eat plenty after dinner." Gabrielle smiled and took her hand.

They looked beyond the polished floor to where mosaic marble glimmered in the light. Attendants had organized seating for Lady Gabrielle and Queen Moon-Star. Valda and Vance sat at the far side of the room and stayed quiet.

Saffron glanced at Gabrielle with vigilant eyes and continued across the room to join their followers. She pulled out a high-backed chair and sat in front of a large timber table; alongside was the High Priestess. Saffron watched the attendants filling their chalices with wine.

As they sat, nearby Saffron and company, Moon-Star glanced at her mother. "Are you feeling better, Mother?" she asked.

"I am fine, why do you ask?"

"I am worried for you. Your actions have changed; why are you so fatigued and I don't feel that way?" she said awkwardly.

"Please relax," she said and patted her hand. "Let us be thankful for this last evening here in the castle. I promise we will both be okay. This weariness I experienced should be temporary. Remember, I am human with a celestial essence overpowering me, so I must adjust to something. I feel great."

Moon-Star smiled but was not sure about that. Something was still odd.

The scent of fresh baked bread filled the open room with a pleasant aroma. Gabrielle inhaled deeply and closed her eyes for a few seconds; her senses were sharp.

A small group of musicians arranged themselves on a circular surface and turned to face the main table. The women plucked large harps and pressed their feet on wooden pedals. A soft stimulating melody streamed across the room.

Gabrielle gazed at the captivating scene. Bulky candelabras towered with burning decorative candles, and alongside them drips of hot wax formed unusual shapes. Mystifying silhouettes became outlined on the castle walls. Appealing decorations throughout the room generated an amiable frame of mind for Gabrielle and Moon-Star. Attendants placed sizable plates of food on a decorated table. Pheasant, lamb, beef, bread, and vegetables were loaded onto Gabrielle and Moon-Star's plates. "Let's dig in, Moon-Star," Gabrielle suggested.

"This food is amazing, and we have our favorite. Warm bread with whipped butter."

As Gabrielle was eating, she focused on the surroundings and didn't acknowledge Moon-Star's comment. She looked at the sculpted acacia windows draped by splendid ivory silk curtains. A refreshing breeze blew through and feathered the veils.

She gazed at Moon-Star. "How is your dinner?" she eventually asked.

"Splendid, the pheasant melts in my mouth, it's so tasty. It is now my favorite dish!"

Undetected by anyone, turbulent winds blew large white clouds into the room. Two entwined spiraling galaxies hid a figure and this Deity floated in and lingered in mystical vapors. Her presence remained concealed from all those around her.

Valda, Vance, and the High Priestess had set up a superb feast and entertainment. Dancers twirled their myriad batons and as the harps played louder, the large audience was swept up in the music and dance. Gabrielle became entranced with the artists and a sudden thought took hold of her. One she could not quite grasp.

Slipping her hand over Moon-Star's, she gave her a squeeze. "My dear, I need to dance," she said.

She glanced quickly at her mother. "Go ahead, dance away. I am overjoyed you're better," she said. Moon-Star stuffed her mouth with bread. She swallowed and added, "This bread is delicious. I think a good rest, a warm bath, and hot food is what we needed."

Moon-Star's relaxed tone indicated she believed her mother had recovered, and she was back to her normal self.

135

"Yes. I am in a great mood."

"There's room in my belly for those mouthwatering desserts over there. How about you?" she asked.

"Yes, I have room," she replied. "I'm surprised you managed to save enough room after eating all that bread," she pointed out. "Make us a plate with a variety of those delicious desserts, I'll have more than a few later."

Moon-Star stared over at the dessert table. She stood and pushed her chair aside and headed right for the appealing desserts.

Gabrielle got up and watched the dancers and her focus was drawn to a prominent circle in the center of the marble surface. Performers circled Lady Gabrielle as she strode towards it. A wave of batons shifted a stream of satin here and there. Silk dresses brushed alongside her face and frame and the dance now involved her. A mist was flowing toward Gabrielle. It encased her in a sphere which shielded her. Flames ignited the circle she was on and as vapors rose in front of her, fiery dust took a shape. Two hands reached out and a woman grabbed Gabrielle's arms and drew her in tight. This woman kept Gabrielle in her sights and Gabrielle was unable to move or look away. Gabrielle stared into her glassy green eyes; her long dark hair floated inside vaporous trails. A rainbow-colored cloak of brightness camouflaged her and Gabrielle from everybody in the room. The crowd could only see a mirrored image of Gabrielle dancing.

The circle rotated with a blazing inferno, the woman pressed her fiery lips upon Gabrielle's, and she extracted a portion of her essence. Gabrielle was fixed into place. The circle spun faster as the woman entangled Gabrielle in her arms and bright stardust sparked rainbow colors everywhere. A sudden push sent Gabrielle away. Her body went limp, and she fell to the floor. The dancers stopped and drifted apart. This woman raised her rainbow cloak and pushed it aside whereupon she fled to the east side castle window. Then she turned to glare at the High Priestess who did not detect her. But Saffron did.

Saffron stood up and hit the table with one hand and pointed with the other and raised her voice. "A woman camouflages herself." She pointed to the east window. "She's hovering over the edge of the windowsill."

This alerted the spirit animals and the army. The spirit animals dashed over to Lady Gabrielle and the army toward the window with their swords in hand to find this woman.

Trickery bewildered Saffron and the High Priestess. They had to find the source of Gabrielle's perplexing interference.

Saffron and the High Priestess got a glimpse of a curious image. Moon beams coursed across a large acacia window and outlined a silhouette in the flowing curtains. The High Priestess sent a surge of lightning bolts toward the image, but she slipped away.

Valda and Vance jumped up and received a message through their psyche from Saffron and left the room.

Moon-Star heard the commotion and dropped her arranged plate of desserts on the floor, and they splattered everywhere. She ran to Gabrielle and dropped to her knees. Both arms reached under her mother's body. Moon-Star pulled her into her arms, stared up, and pleaded with the paradises' leaders.

"Help her, help my mother, please come," she said in a trembling tone.

Metatron heard Moon-Star's cry as he was tuned in to safeguarding the selected essences on The Golden Door.

Moon-Star's help came quickly. Raguelle and Metatron arrived and faced Saffron.

Saffron reacted with no hesitation. "The forces of evil are present. It's greater than imagined; there's trickery in play," she said and thought about how this woman came to Gabrielle without notice.

He leaned toward Moon-Star and said forcefully, "My Queen, let me take Lady Gabrielle to her room."

One knee went to the floor. He stretched both arms under to get hold of her. He braced her listless body and paced through the castle with her in his arms. Saffron pushed open the wooden door and Metatron went inside the room. He placed Gabrielle on an enormous bed and positioned her head on a pillow. Gabrielle's eyes were still closed.

Saffron turned to Moon-Star and discovered she was in a panic, pacing the floor. She knew Moon-Star was frantic about her mother. Saffron reached over to Moon-Star. "Touch your mother, draw in a moonlit strength, my Queen."

"Yes, Saffron, I will," she replied.

Moon-Star stared at the acacia-framed window; a superb moon arrived in her view. Her glossy wet eyes shut, and her natural ability prompted a part of her moon. The bright moon rays sent out a quick outpouring and routed a spirited moon beam straight to Gabrielle.

Gabrielle's eyes opened and she took in the scene. "Hello, what is going on here?" she asked and caught her breath.

"Mother, you scared me."

"What happened?"

Saffron's darkened eyes glared at Raguelle.

Raguelle sensed Gabrielle's mind was unstable and was unsure how this happened. She hoped Saffron and the High Priestess could resolve this weakness before she went into battle. This confusion with Gabrielle caused her to turn the other way and leave the room. She disappeared in a flash.

Moon-Star was confused about the events.

"Your mood seemed great, you went on the dance floor and started dancing." She wiped her tears with her palms. "Something happened and the next thing the army and spirit animals found you lying across the floor."

Gabrielle reached out and held Moon-Star's arm. She drew her closer, gazed into her eyes and realized how much these strange transformations were affecting her. "Moon-Star, compose yourself," Gabrielle said. "Dancing brought a vision of change to me. I can't recall anything else. I am not sure why I acted this way. Did anyone else feel this weak?" she asked.

"No, this weakness you are experiencing is only within you," she replied.

"We will leave this castle in the early morning. Saffron and the High Priestess will sort this out."

Saffron's raven flew in the room and landed on her shoulder; she went outside to give instructions to the army. Spirit animals moved into the room. Moon-Star's owl flew in and remained on the windowsill. The white hawk circled in and landed on the tip of the bed. Spirit bear and the fox went to Gabrielle. They rested by her bed. Spirit wolf entered the room. A quick leap settled the large wolf at the end of the bed, her eyes fixed on Gabrielle. Soldiers safeguarded the castle entrance and patrolled in front of the door.

Saffron returned and continued to check on Gabrielle. She sat beside the bed and her pentacles lit up and sent a light to circle Gabrielle and Moon-Star for the evening.

Metatron left the room to meet with the High Priestess. "What developed with Lady Gabrielle?" he asked.

"A woman was cloaked inside a moon beam. I saw her silhouette when she uncovered herself by the east side of the castle's acacia window," she replied.

"What did this woman need from Lady Gabrielle?" Metatron asked.

"I am uncertain what took place, I did not see anything unusual with Lady Gabrielle," the High Priestess said and frowned. "A block in our mindset shielded us from her presence. Saffron eventually noticed this woman's existence and saw her flash a rainbow cloak."

"I will uncover what I can, High Priestess," Metatron said and left.

***

Metatron stepped into a gateway. When he opened it, a glinting pyramid appeared. He strode into a spiraling tunnel and it closed. He was going out after the woman who turned up at the castle since her appearance had not been noticed until she entranced Lady Gabrielle. Bronze and silver lightning flashed in front of him when he reached the higher realms. He discovered a female silhouette outlined near the throne, but the Creator then instructed Metatron not to obstruct this Deity. Metatron nodded and left with the understanding that this involvement brought no danger to Lady Gabrielle.

He returned to the castle and called for Saffron and the High Priestess. They both left the room to greet Metatron.

"This visit was a secret meeting sanctioned by the Creator. She dealt no harm to Lady Gabrielle. The purpose of this visit is something I cannot interfere with, so please keep this in mind. Lady Gabrielle and Queen Moon-Star must not learn who this woman is; we need to keep a close eye on Lady Gabrielle."

The High Priestess faced Metatron. "A secret it will be; Lady Gabrielle and Queen Moon-Star will not learn of this meet. Saffron and I will take care of them. It seems much is evolving around Lady Gabrielle, and I unveiled a modest transformation when she completed simulated warfare. I will look again into my crystal ball, as there must be a clue as to what is leading to her confusion. But I haven't found anything yet."

Metatron bowed to the High Priestess. She pulled back from the confusion, so she could go somewhere private to investigate her crystal ball.

"Thank you for your prompt attention to Lady Gabrielle's wellbeing, Metatron," Saffron said. "Valda and Vance have stayed clear of this confusion; rightfully so that they do not use their magic. I sent them a message through my psyche and asked them to remain in their chambers until we find out what has happened with Lady Gabrielle."

His duty to protect ensured that he had to know of Lady Gabrielle's encounter. His sense of responsibility along with that of the High Priestess and Saffron remained unbroken. He nodded and disappeared.

Saffron meditated around this trickery. Gabrielle had changed in the last couple of days. She reentered the room and a quick glance over at Moon-Star showed her distress due to these transformations. But something else besides what had just happened obviously still troubled Lady Gabrielle. Beside the bed, a high-backed chair offered a place for Saffron to rest.

Moon-Star tucked Gabrielle in and relaxed beside her. Torches and candles flickered a silhouette along the castle walls, and a pleasant aroma wafted in via a breeze that fluttered through the silk and satin curtains.

Gabrielle fell into a realistic dream that she was in combat. She tossed and turned on the bed. Moon-Star woke up and detected something was wrong. She reached over and alerted Saffron.

"Why is my mother tossing and swinging her arms? She is acting so strange, Saffron, what's going on?"

Saffron leaned in and saw the circling light she had placed with her pentacles stayed secure, there was no breach. But she detected Gabrielle's mindset was looking for something. What was this trickery, she thought? An interference continued to rest inside Gabrielle's mind, even when she was asleep.

Moon-Star and Saffron both shook Gabrielle to wake her.

Gabrielle's eyes were wide open. "What's wrong now?" she asked.

"You were hurling your arms from side to side, and your voice echoed around the room as you made strange noises. What's wrong with you?"

Gabrielle took a deep breath. "I believe I took part in a battle, it's just a dream." She stared at Moon-Star and had a look of confusion on her face.

Moon-Star peered into her mother's glossy eyes. "Saffron and I are here for you, please relax."

Moon-Star hugged her. Gabrielle gazed at the ceiling but could not remember what had just taken place in her dream. Something was blocking her thoughts and decisions; she could not tell Saffron what was happening as most of her experiences had vanished and she couldn't remember them.

Something was also blocking Saffron and the High Priestess from these developments.

***

Morning arrived, and Gabrielle wanted to leave behind the castle and get on their path. Saffron had their army prepared and arranged for the spirit animals, along with their companions, to be ready for another long journey. Gabrielle met up with Valda and Vance and said her goodbyes, but they both seemed rather strange to her. They bowed to her and then to their Queen and turned and walked back toward the castle. She gripped the reins and swung her horse and raised her arm to signal. "Move forward," she said. The sizeable crowd moved on with the supplies and rode into the sunrise.

Moon-Star examined Gabrielle; she discovered her mother was uneasy.

Gabrielle faced an unsettled Queen. She reached over and tapped her hand. "We will be fine, my Moon-Star," she said.

"You bet we will."

Horses trotted along the path set in front of them.

The High Priestess found two blocks in Gabrielle's mindset, but could not resolve this disorder. She would have to go further into her crystal ball and Gabrielle's psyche to discover what anomalies had power over Lady Gabrielle.

A signal tapped into Saffron's mindset; the High Priestess had sent her a telepathic message.

When I searched for clues in my crystal ball, it was then I detected two blocks in Lady Gabrielle's mindset. One is impenetrable, but the other almost allowed me to see it. I believe this one is trying to sabotage her ability to succeed in her reign, so let us hope we can recover control for Lady Gabrielle. When we reach our destined place of rest, let us look further into her psyche and try to find out what is distracting her. We must keep a close watch on her.

Saffron nodded and continued to ride up alongside Gabrielle and Moon-Star.

Chapter Twenty-One
The Carefully Selected

Back at the pyramid, Osahar and Mira stayed out of the way in a dark corner. But a sudden change on the door caused them to move up front. She turned to Ben to account for it. "There's a foretelling the west bears evil, and a dark cloud will appear on Varco-XVI. The prophecy on the western side has identified dark spirits, and the conflict for survival has just become real."

A dark haze loomed over the door, which then advanced toward the northern and southern side. With each unknown development, this one had Ben alarmed by this new phase.

The teams paid close attention to the changes, and Ben realized the battle was beginning. He bowed his head.

Osahar stood beside Ben and continued. "These prophecies are now beginning. Your sons go on as the selected ones, as do Gabrielle and Michael. I may not interfere. Spiritual guidance carries a paranormal change for them; Gabrielle and Michael will go to battle."

Ben had no other choice but to accept the inevitable. He faced the live cameras and expressed to his colleagues, "My fellow countries, no one is now to interfere with the actions taking place on Varco-XVI. Let's stay focused on Earth."

Mira's wistful eyes peered into Osahar's. "Please tell Ben," she said.

Osahar reacted when she sparked him with a surge of her cosmic energy. Her shockwave was declining. The variable star's life was coming closer to its end. He leaned in and pressed his lips against her cheek and took a hard breath. But he knew he had to eventually let her go, so he turned away and faced Ben. But he could not tell Ben about Mira's departure yet, so Osahar went on, "I understand Gabrielle and Michael's stability; their drive can overturn the dark spirits. Josh and Blake have a celestial leader in Cassiel and will be protected."

Sandra chimed in with an urgent warning. "Ben, there's a shimmering star that has just appeared on The Golden Door."

Ben opened his mind to this peculiar anomaly, but another high alert in the form of Austria came through. "Adalard here. The Orion constellation now erupts with an extraordinary flow of energy, and a signal is coming out from the pyramid. Saiph flashed a transmission toward the golden Mars, again to Earth's Mars."

The teams in the pyramid fell silent, as they watched a wraithlike cloud mix on The Golden Door.

"Upheavals in the universe means someone is searching for something and its clues are on this inexplicable pyramid. The cryptic Golden Door remains a far-reaching mystery. We are now in a different phase. This transmission goes everywhere, and a heavenly power generates a precise change within both solar systems. This set-up continues to unveil a blend of eerie vapors on The Golden Door. Swirls of astral dust direct a message right here," Ben said and concentrated on Osahar. "I hope you can explain this sudden movement in the universe?"

But at the command center, another sudden ping from Austria once more grabbed his attention.

"Adalard here again. Saiph is flickering inside a dust storm. There's a flow of starry waves around it, and it appears broken in the middle. It's moving straight to the gold Mars with intervals of rising black lightning. There is an interruption in the connection. But we can see a path of brightness carrying something. In manifestation, I'd suggest it's an astral shockwave detaching two ghostly figures. Earth's Mars communicates with the pyramid."

Huge solar flares sparked over the pyramid's inner and outer surface. The Golden Door drifted in a rise and fall motion, and a cascade of lively vapors rippled over this magnificent wonder.

This left the scientists speculating what this unknown phenomenon was. Standing back at a distance, Ben crossed his arms. There was a major force striking The Golden Door, coming in at lightning speed and in silence.

"Look at this," Ben said. "The gold Mars mixes in a cloud cosmic dust from Saiph, now it's routing to Earth's Mars and straight down to the pyramid."

Ben stepped back and gripped a chair when he felt a rumbling going through the pyramid. Black lightning struck the exterior, and an unexpected arrival plunged in through The Golden Door. Two soldiers stepped out on the tails of billowing stardust. Blistering flames rooted a celestial imprint on The Golden Door.

A striking adult woman in an ivory hooded cloak stood before them, but she was only an imprint of a painted image to what would develop further on the door. Next to her, inside a gaseous cloud, stood an equally striking adult male; he too was a painted imprint of what would develop further on the door. He displayed a dark hooded cloak. They were both attired in radiant black armor, along with jeweled breastplates which were fastened to their chests. Solar flares sparked and lit up their gems, making them resemble stars. Both soldiers gripped peculiar black shields, and along their port side were black scabbards. They both embraced crafted swords, and a glistening bronze and silver rope coiled around their black leather grips. Their painted images on the door were awaiting their human spirits.

Ben glared at these two distinct soldiers, and tried to fathom who they might be.

The lunar outburst continued and dark clouds gathered in a circular motion. Chariots of gold and ethereal horses surfaced, with sparkling jeweled spears arranged by their side.

These characters, drawn out of a universe, had Ben concerned.

"Now what? Are these two soldiers assembling for warfare on Earth? This is a painting on the door with gaseous clouds hovering around two soldiers." He glanced over at Osahar and waited for an answer.

"They mirror these details as they're settling into place." His eyes flickered. "A release will result with the next lunar eclipse. These soldiers will have a life form. Temperance entered a new cycle with her hourglass, providing me time to figure out their purpose."

Osahar comprehended that Samuel had set up a game plan inside the pyramid. He placed two of his weapons on The Golden Door as a painted copy. However, he was not ready to share this information with Ben.

"Who are these two soldiers? Why did they come to Earth, and where did they come from?"

"I don't know these two figures. They're just symbols." He was as unclear as Ben was as to who they were.

"These new anomalies on The Golden Door look mesmerizing as painted images. So, what you're saying is we have to watch these soldiers because they will come to life?" He was attempting to assess the situation

145

before it became a hazard. He glanced at his teams who were all looking on in puzzlement.

Sandra wandered over and tried to ease the tension around the room by announcing that there was sustenance available for the shift change.

Ben sighed and said, "Food and drink will be welcome as I need to refuel. This has been an extraordinary day."

They both turned their heads to see a sudden flash sweeping across The Golden Door as a curve of white lightning. White clouds surrounded another unexplained phenomenon in the form of a new image. It was a grand temple appearing on The Golden Door, over a wave of water spraying up from the intensities of a dark sea. Rippling water shot up and submerged the temple, whereupon it disappeared. What was coming to Earth and what was going to Varco-XVI? The scientists handed over for the shift change; Ben needed some rest. He left the pyramid, but not without giving instructions. The scientists would get hold of him if any other strange activity occurred.

Chapter Twenty-Two
An Unknown Planet

Ben and his team left their tents after they had breakfast and cleaned up. They returned to their posts in the pyramid.

It was a fresh day, and everything was going as planned until The Golden Door rumbled. Black lightning struck the Temperance. She turned over the hourglass and released the sands of time to continue toward a new phase. An unexpected flare up caught the attention of the scientists. They watched a violet flame spiraling from side to side inside the hourglass.

Ben's mind was racing through possibilities. The events transpiring around him were making it difficult for him to think. He turned to Mira and Osahar who had entered the pyramid and pointed out, "These forces appearing as images on The Golden Door continue to be troubling." He ran his hand through his thick, dark hair. "An interesting day approaches. Temperance shows there will be a change in events." He walked to the monitor to receive a call.

Adlet from Turkey had pinged the command center. "The constellation of Orion powers a transmission," he said in a hurried voice. "It shows an intense form of space dust from Alnitak, and it points to the pyramid. Certainly an impressive view, Ben. The illuminations stay fragmented, it follows a particular direction and bounces off into the distance."

Osahar glared over at Mira and picked up a misleading signal. It led to a false Queen, but the Alnitak connection led to the real Pharaoh. The chamber she directed a prominent lead to carried her stardust. It was from Alpha Draconis which steered to a shaft inside the pyramid next to the King. The real Queen actually aligned with Sirius and Beta Ursa Minor. He studied her movement, but he had to stay silent, because she had no control over her psyche. When Samuel placed a command within her stardust, it overwhelmed her.

Mira had prepared a Queen from the underworld.

Samuel gave a spiral of neutrinos to Ramiel. His tapestry unfolded in the Coliseum and theater and he went to his Majesty.

"You must enact a sequence of steps to have the rank of a Royal when you raise my Queen. She will be a force alongside of my dark star," Samuel commanded.

Ramiel acknowledged his request. When she was ready, he would take her to the west side tomb alongside the intensity of Venus and give her Samuel's left-hand neutrinos. Samuel's dark star would rank her as a Royal.

Andricia from the South African observatory then paged the command center. "The Orion Nebula has sent a force of an infinite brightness toward the Bakoni Ruins. An alien world entered the exosphere. A new planet now absorbs ultraviolet emissions from the sun."

Scientists view a mirrored image of a man on The Golden Door. The XX-Judgment card cast a shadow on XI-Justice Ramiel. But the High Priestess had given him the power of a double-sided card, and one side was joined with Galasus who had the right-hand neutrinos. His tapestries awakened and fluttered in the great Coliseum and the theater. Ramiel remained as an unseen force in the paradises.

"Pluto eclipsed this planet. It includes a weird intensity, and a glare rests upon the Bakoni Ruins. Many rays point skyward. They're headed in a path to you. An outbreak of solar winds pushes a terrestrial alignment towards Earth. Ben, verification from an unspecified source states Planet X approaches Earth," Andricia said.

Jimmy Black, one of Ben's scientists in Egypt, piped up. "Planet X has an elite force on it, as was noted in ancient scripture it shows a return to Earth. They will destroy us and set up a superior tribal group."

Ben waved his arm at Jimmy dismissively and ignored him. His attention remained on what was now taking place. He crossed his arms. "It turns out to be a proper orbit around Earth. Pluto secures this world. We must follow the gravitational tug for debris. Let us hope Planet X didn't drag in comets, or asteroids, or change our orbit and disrupt the magnetic field."

South Africa's Andricia came back. "Planet X is a lone object; Pluto is stable and positioned in the solar system."

"Stacks of secret plans and people spread across this Golden Door. I hope this doesn't include more ill-omened images. Let us have faith Planet X approaches us in solidarity. The Golden Door requires a different focus. Teams, plan a sharp lookout for Planet X, and learn how it moves in the solar system," he requested. "Planet X passes Earth every thirty-six hundred years; this world has now entered our solar system."

A team of scientists set up specialized equipment to explore the distant world; Planet X hovered behind Pluto and stayed in the Earth's exosphere. The scientists marveled at what they were currently seeing and studying. Pluto's heart was overshadowed, and it spun and unveiled the mysterious planet—a multihued orb interweaved inside an ethereal web.

Osahar watched Ben and his associates. He had more information and stood ready to announce a fresh change. Ben walked to him.

"Planet X is Nibiru," Osahar began. "We will swear an oath to protect this world too. Their celestial influence will shine upon us and your world's defense for paranormal activity. This world's soldiers must commit their focus to receive a paranormal vitality, this will enhance them. This rule carries a wisdom and will give the soldiers a specific strength to contend with the nefarious spirits. Written scriptures show, those who appear and cast a shadow on Pluto's rooted heart, will be an immeasurable force. Their connection to humans comes to us in peace. We must be ready to connect with a high-spirited force in the universe."

Ben stared over at him. "What? You're saying our world forces here on Earth will join in ghostlike warfare with a connection from Nibiru?" he asked and walked over to a separate monitor to talk with the military. "We have received forewarning and must set a high alert; Osahar will explain." Armed forces from many countries could now pick up the message on this new progress.

Osahar faced the monitor and was ready to communicate with top military officers from around the world. "I will give you the decrees from a high-spirited force, and these will connect the military establishments dealing with the paranormal activity to Nibiru. Your supplies will come soon."

Some of the officials stood nodding but they all watched Osahar as he continued. "These weapons have a specific military purpose. Instructions from Highborn Leader Galasus will show up on The Golden Door."

"Do you know when this will happen, Osahar?"

"These specialty weapons and rules will materialize soon."

Military establishments set up for the highest red alert. They were now aware that planet Earth would be under attack. Generals from around the world communicated to arrange specialty companies to pick up these orders and weapons from off The Golden Door. The presidents and prime ministers were now briefed from around the world. They understood Earth and a new planet would be under attack. Ben was familiar with this pyramid, and he knew things were about to become unstable.

"Teams and countries, we must stay calm. Osahar will prepare us for this involvement. Everybody, a coded red alert is in place. I have faith we will be ready for this line of attack," Ben advised.

South Africa reported in. "Nine monumental stones have sprung up one by one in the Bakoni Ruins. Each stone has a sequence of illustrations. We can see hieroglyphics glowing on the surface. Our team is busy examining these impressions through high-powered binoculars and telescopes. These stones appear as painted images in the Ruins. They are spectacular."

"These painted images set their place," Osahar replied.

The pyramid sparked with an intense force, and bronze and silver lightning weaved through the inner and outer surface. Everyone backed away from The Golden Door. The pyramid vibrated. Once again, an uneasiness settled over everybody. A dynamic force fell upon The Great Golden Door, and an intense outburst of cosmic rays passed through an intense energy. Images captured a light through a raging movement from Planet X. Now in view were nine colossal painted stones. Seven wrought-iron gates formed beside the stones and awaited direction from Samuel. Above each gate was a silver plate. A blurred message emerged in bronze writing. This was for the High Priestess to interpret. She would be the one to unlock the seven iron gates. The High Priestess' mindset would shift and operate for the bright and dark side of a prophecy. The Creator directed her path.

Ben looked at these magnificent painted stones and gates illustrated on The Golden Door. "Do these stones and gates have something to do with Nibiru?" he asked.

"These stones are a part of Earth's network and ruled by the Imperial Council. Cryptic images surround this pyramid, they will vanish when awakened. These gates will open soon."

Nibiru mystified Ben. "So, Nibiru floats above us, and again Pluto teases us with a new mystery. This planet is on our side, right?" Ben asked in an unsettled voice. He did not want to dwell on the worst-case scenario, he just wanted answers.

"Nibiru will contribute a power to many mighty warriors on Earth," he replied. "More warriors will move up to Varco-XVI. Your militaries will merge with an elite dominance," he said.

"This Golden Door has a darkness; we need a powerful offensive to lead our armed forces. Thank you, Osahar," Ben added. But Ben was worried, he had a hard time concealing his emotional state, and he saw his teams were on the edge. "We are all committed to one's ability to meet the heavens' expectations. There is a huge chance for success here," Ben said. "I will continue to try to make sense of these high intensity areas on The Golden Door."

Scientists feared what their destiny might be. They assumed Varco-XVI existed for humans to colonize. But those theories were now thrown aside. Godly leaders were arranging a paranormal campaign on Earth. An uneasiness gripped the scientists. What would the aftermath be?

Ben had not spoken to Gabrielle or Michael's family members as to what had taken place.

He advised the team. "Please will one of you set up a flight plan, and bring Michael and Gabrielle's family here."

Likewise, he made his wife aware of what was happening and she agreed to be on her way. Sandra contacted Emmanuel, and later Zadkiel, and explained the circumstances. They both understood the urgency and were prepared to travel to Egypt.

But Sandra told Zadkiel something peculiar along with the instructions to come to Egypt. Zadkiel then called a separate contact—a person of importance.

The Golden Door erupted in light and guided solar flares to be attached to the seven gates in the Bakoni Ruins. Spiraling stardust arranged itself on the luminous surface and revealed a mysterious vase. The scientists could see ghostly soldiers swirling inside a mystical flame on the vase. Samuel's left hand ascended and set a rule upon this cryptic vase. An ethereal power developed, and his mercenaries he called upon in the theater's tapestries would now serve a false Queen.

Osahar watched Mira interfere with the vase, she sent numinous flares to suspend the progress. He knew Samuel was waiting to unravel a hostile order.

The scientists gazed at The Golden Door in fascination; they watched nine mysterious stones gain patterned murals in the Bakoni Ruins.

A sudden gust of wind streamed through the pyramid. A woman in a mirrored image appeared at the first of seven gates. Draped over her shoulders was a black hooded cloak. Orion interlocked a movement around this woman.

Ramiel was a man who worked on both sides of a divination and would raise her from the underworld. He would give rise to a threatening force on Varco-XVI with two Venus.

Placed on the north side was an eerie castle, situated alongside was a pyramid. Two Mars orbiting above the pyramid struck the apparition with streaked black lightning; this would power the false Queen's night star with an irrepressible force. The Great Golden Door now displayed her items of importance. An eight-pointed star symbol symbolized a rosette, two lionesses associated with two Venus surfaced. Emblems became etched on her right and left wrist. Her left emblem was a dark star connected to Samuel. Her right emblem was a bright star connected to the Galasus. A special gift awaited her arrival; Emissaries operated alongside of the Creator and Galasus. The great seers honored her right symbol with a polished luster. Her bright morning star would deliver her freedom from strife during the day.

Observatories in Egypt and South Africa both contacted Ben urgently over the video cams in the pyramid. They were both studying an extraordinary feature floating in space, but Ben already knew of this.

Andricia reported, "Can you find an Egyptian Solar Calendar on The Golden Door because we have these solar images right in our faces? Adam's Calendar includes a celestial alignment pointing south, it shows us a great Pharaoh will have an afterlife. I thought Blake and Josh reported a great Pharaoh and Queen will take an afterlife?"

"Meissa flashed the same image," Ammon reported from Egypt.

The world scientists could see a mysterious placement appearing on The Golden Door. Ben became tense, and he wrung his hands. He could not place his finger on exactly what was happening.

Turkey sent a red alert and Adlet chimed in. "Orion awakens with fiery plumes; we detect this eruption is far reaching. Alnitak aims a structured alignment of the universe's strength to the pyramid. Alnitak and Alpha Draconis are flashing a light which might be an alert; guided strikes are advancing to two chambers inside the pyramid."

"Marco here, Ben. There's a great brightness within Orion, it stirs up vapors towards the Nile Delta. Eruptions of gaseous clouds soar in from the Belt of Orion. A structured alignment unveils a galactic shaft of murky clouds; this movement is on a course to the pyramid."

Everyone followed new movements on The Golden Door as a colossal new tomb materialized on the surface.

Intense jets streaming in from the universe reflected extraterrestrial dust across The Golden Door. It struck the arrival of two spirits and encased them in two chambers. The impressions on The Golden Door awakened inside the spectral clouds. In the impressions they could see spirited winds elevating a black granite sarcophagus upon The Golden Door. The Nile rippled up with an overflowing of water. It hit the two pyramids, and they disappeared in a billow of dust. Vulture's wings expanded and they readied for departure. Amulets shone and revolved around a bronze chariot; flails and a headrest thrust out. Inside a cosmic explosion, transcendent horses awakened. Scarabs piled up on the surface, two sphinxes stood tall, two Egyptian Ankhs showed a symbol of life after death. Orion raised two obelisks to position themselves alongside a black granite sarcophagus. The Golden Door brightened; a beam of light broadcasted a signal. The Pharaoh and the surrounding objects vanished inside a deep pulling vapor. Gravitational waves sent a Pharaoh to the south side of Varco-XVI, along with items of interest.

Osahar's mind drifted into the realms, and he now knew who this important Pharaoh was. He would explain the need for his departure to Ben soon. He was aware of a false Queen, as she soared up in a universal energy and it was from the wrong chamber in the pyramid. There was a sudden vibration rippling the terrain in the pyramid. He watched Samuel take hold of the false Queen's essence on The Golden Door. Then he realized the real Queen remained on The Golden Door and the purple planet's silver gate. Silver dust entered Osahar's eyes and showed him the existent Queen's replacement had exchanged her life for her gifted and cherished sister.

Behind locked gates, Samuel's ominous spirit had tricked this special Queen. A secure grip kept her inside a raging pulsar. Uncontrollable forces made her noble soldiers kneel to him. Samuel's strength oppressed the Queen's sister, so he could keep her captive in the underworld. The false Queen was now being ruled by Royal Ruler Samuel Raiphualas II. She was now his dark Queen. Her left wrist showed the marking of a dark star, a splendid star remained on her right. Seven wrought-iron gates had a passageway which was visible at the Bakoni Ruins and on The Great Golden Door.

Several broadcasts made the scientists scramble to make sense of the events transpiring.

A great Pharaoh reached the bronze gate on Varco-XVI. Metatron positioned himself alongside the Pharaoh in spirit. The silver Queen remained on The Golden Door. This worried Ben.

Mira had stopped the rightful Queen's movement on the door and thus completed an order. Her flamboyant shockwave still revolved around her body. She had now raised an identical silhouette of the false Queen from the underworld. His order positioned her to be on the west side of Varco-XVI to organize turmoil. Her devotees were from the fallen dark spirits on the tapestries in the theater, which would rise from the dead.

Ramiel stood at the mercy of Samuel, his dark tapestry unfolded. He encased a thunder from the celestial realms, and he would support the terror. Ramiel was the Lord of forbidden dark souls hidden inside the tapestries. His star-crossed time in power would reinforce the false Queen in the west side's monumental tomb and set her on a mission. Two Venus would then move her to the east side where she would face Blake and Josh.

Ben faced the webcams. He was ready to report this revelation to the countries.

"My colleagues, it was in the earlier stages of our breakthroughs that the Creator placed many features on this Golden Door. But we still have sight of a silver Queen, as she remains on this door. This Pharaoh went to Varco-XVI. I hope this will be a friendly meeting. In Blake and Josh's message to me, they said a great Pharaoh and Queen would have an afterlife. But their predictions are not taking place here." He glanced over at Osahar and Mira and asked, "This mirrored woman who stands in front of us, is she a false Queen?"

"You will learn in time who these individuals are. This new assembly awaits a release."

Ben looked dazed. He stepped over to his colleagues. "What do you make of this?" he asked.

They look at him with confused stares, but Sandra reacted. "We're not sure, we know as much as you."

Flashes from a far off celestial shockwave moved through the pyramid, and golden beams spread across The Golden Door. Luminous vapors traveled to a notable warrior: Metatron. Now at his awareness was a specific message. Metatron would guide the High Priestess to regulate a psyche, and later he would greet the great Pharaoh on the bronze gate. The High Priestess would then be able to unlock the secrets of the false Queen from the underworld.

Chapter Twenty-Three
The Awakening of III Empress

Osahar's duty was to protect humans on Earth. Inside the pyramid, he was sharing his knowledge about Royal Ruler Samuel Raiphualas II in order to investigate what trouble he was causing. Samuel had, in the meantime, gained a large number of supporters on Varco-XVI; they could be found on all four corners of the planet. The Emissaries spotted many dark spirits stationed along the planet's vast landscape and reported on his movements to Galasus. This news came by way of his Ace of Pentacles in his palm. He would read the messages and inspect the dark campaigns developing on Varco-XVI. His Ace of Pentacles was like a compass where he could view the different points.

There was a minor earthquake near the northwestern desert in Egypt. Nighttime arrived, and a shift change had a different group of scientists keeping a sharp-eyed view scanning The Golden Door. A quietness stilled the scientists; something was untangling in the universe. They watched the Orion constellation swell inside an infinite deepness. Blackened vapors swelled and shifted in the Veil Nebula. A large supernova remnant materialized on The Golden Door. You could see the stellar nurseries brimming with radiant new stars; an assembly of soaring arms pushed forth an enormous bubble. Osahar warned the scientists to expect something big, and what they saw was a silhouette trailing in on a shockwave packed with fading stars. An outline of a woman became clear on The Golden Door.

Osahar expected this approach by Samuel, and now he could explore the door to learn more of this woman. This was a courageous woman, who has ancient scrolls archived in the dark and bright room and two tapestries hidden on planet Eugleston. Samuel opened a dark scroll; this was how he forced her to form an allegiance with him. He worked his rule and triumphed over a double star Queen. Samuel was ready to move in his darkness. Now he would have power over her night star. But he knew he took no authority over her day star, so he backed away from the essence of her bright star as it faded. Her bright star shone on the ancient scroll in the bright room, which is where Galasus noticed it. Her two tapestries became known and would now serve on a two-sided prophecy.

Anger thundered through Osahar as he saw this prophecy would bring this higher power to an afterlife: she was a double star Queen.

Her startling features had the scientists taking notes of her presence. She developed into the frame of a winged woman with webbed feet. A spectral mist then shaped her into a mortal. The last phase for this Queen Samuel kept in the underworld would be awakened by the High Priestess.

"Brace yourselves for the entrance of an exalted man," Osahar said.

A brightness led to Metatron gliding off The Golden Door. His sapphire eyes sparkled, and his muscular physique grabbed Sandra's attention. She fixated on this distinguished warrior and examined him. Metatron nodded. He glanced over at Sandra and noticed her beauty. Sandra picked up a fire within his eyes and sensed an excitement. She was entranced by Metatron's presence. A chill arose and swept through her poised body. She touched her arms and gripped them. Metatron raised his left arm and turned to face The Golden Door. He was ready to introduce the scientists to the Creator's celestial leader from the heavens. Taking place in the universe was a merger of spectral vapors and it led to an opening. He showed them a flame of influence, a spiral of cosmic dust delivered by the High Priestess in spirit.

Sudden outbursts of silver lightning glided over an apparition. Brisk winds nudged the High Priestess to fill the essence. She stepped off The Golden Door and looked magnificent in her ritual silk and satin embroidered gown. Her eyes were lit with a hue of emerald green, a cosmic breeze whirled her long blonde hair from side to side.

Metatron reached out to introduce the High Priestess and showed her where the planned ritual would be finalized on The Golden Door. He stayed by her side in silence.

Meanwhile, Samuel was ready to engage with his new Queen. He directed a flash of black lightning to resound the Orion Nebula. A flurry of ghostly vapors moved in a panorama. His hand reached out. He raised one of the many cards he had received from the High Priestess. The Eight of Pentacles whirled in to set up the Rosette Nebula. Two Mars streamed in a surge of black lightning and struck the rosette. The rosette fastened to his Queen's dark star. Dynamic outpourings moved in a swelling of plasma. Her mystical body absorbed a protected balance of shock-heated winds. A signal directed her to move forward. Mira raised her arms and gave power to The Golden Door. She surrendered a part of her shockwave to the Rosette Nebula. Cosmic dust showed a burst of liveliness to a Queen who was ready to move up from the underworld.

The universe changed and showed the scientists the Orion Nebula would support the Rosette Nebula to set up a captive in wait in the underworld. Her dark star balanced inside a rosette; the illumination of her star pointed to a predetermined agreement with Samuel.

The Rosette Nebula unleashed an astronomical change, and a gravitational shockwave rippled on The Golden Door. Samuel's spirit absorbed the widespread stardust drifting along the door. He felt a hunger for his efforts and a passion entered his body. She was what he wished for. Various particles weaved cosmic rays through The Golden Door. This showed the High Priestess it was time to face Mira. The High Priestess understood Mira's potential and accepted a mysterious attachment.

"I will begin with the prophecy," the High Priestess said as she went into motion.

With both arms lifted, a selection of ethereal cards expelled from her palms. Seven gates in the Bakoni Ruins mirrored a copy on The Golden Door and met a portion of her cards. Then she enclosed them with a lightning charge. Her arms lowered as she approached The Golden Door to study each one.

Confined as one inside a helix were nine stars. They pushed forward and brightened in front of the High Priestess. This signified a placement would take place. "Nine massive stones have risen in the South African Bakoni Ruins. I will return and arrange my Divine cards upon these stones. This will show you the Imperial Council's Emissaries who work as a leadership in the paradises and here on Earth at a Space Agency." She nodded at her work so far.

Ben looked around him in the pyramid but saw no one new was around. The teams sat on the edge of their chairs. Sandra stood with crossed arms and gazed at both Metatron and the High Priestess. She admired Metatron, but when she gazed over at her, she was spellbound by the High Priestess. She wondered if they could involve her with this honorable man. Her thoughts of Michael slid aside.

Black lightning unveiled a windstorm, and it whistled through the pyramid. The coarse sands whipped around their ankles. Samuel sent an order for the High Priestess to continue.

"I will now interpret the Divine cards on this Golden Door. I will open the seven gates in the Bakoni Ruins from here and raise an entity from the underworld."

Samuel hurled a card in a flurry of vapors. It reached The Golden Door and spiraled through a black flame.

The High Priestess gasped for air. "I am here to operate with the Creator, the Godly rulers, and the Emissaries in the paradises. My calling is to make you aware of the heaven's hierarchy," she said. "This first card is a primary card from his Majesty, III-Empress." She reached to The Golden Door and removed the card. "This is her awakening," the High Priestess said.

The rising of two radiant stars streamed across The Golden Door to a long-awaited awakening.

"Now you will see how the prophecy must serve Samuel; he will operate with a woman of his choice. This is a sacrifice selected by Royal Ruler Samuel Raiphualas II. He craves her and wants to have this woman for eternity; a cosmic wakening currently alters her consciousness. She will support her Majesty's plan and meet his darkness."

Brisk winds whirled and branched out a white tapestry and a black tapestry. The High Priestess placed it on The Golden Door.

"Look at these tapestries," the High Priestess said. The tapestries ignited in a flame. "The white is a fondness for her life. She has a brilliant spiritual star on this tapestry, and it is inside the great Coliseum on planet Eugleston. The black tapestry is on the opposite side of the planet in the theater, it serves as a readiness for a dark nebulous star. This predetermined divination presents a supernatural order, yin & yang, and this weight involves a human balance. The universe aligns with a bright star, this will increase her spiritual power. The dark star offers a supernatural order, she will set up paths of destruction. III-Empress card combines with the universe, a coming alive for Samuel brings a turnabout of her awareness. His dark star serves as an awakening for an Armageddon against creation and the rule of Varco-XVI and Earth."

As the awakening came to a halt, the universe ignited with the Rosette Nebula. An outpouring of brightness drifted across The Golden Door. Streaming dust led to a flash. The gates unlocked, and the Rosette Nebula whirled in an inferno and left the door. A powerful turbulence opened the gates, it produced a violent squall and poured out a murky veil.

Ben and the scientists observed a woman ascending out of the vapors and watched her step into a paranormal essence. She lifted her head and opened her eyes. In full view, was a striking woman, with long blonde hair and piercing caerulean eyes. She was tall and wearing a black hooded cloak, and she was a vision of beauty. She met the second gate.

The Golden Door rumbled with a flare; energy spread through an ethereal entrance. The range reached a gloominess; it turned out to be overwhelming. Black lightning bolts flashed and encircled Samuel. This allowed the scientists to see a remarkable clearness of Samuel. They backed up and bumped into each other and fled from the door.

Samuel awakened and stared at the woman he desired, she stood in a mirrored image on the door. His spiritual being set alight a radiance from his bright star, then he replaced his judgement with his dark star.

He sent the High Priestess another card. "The second card is XVI Tower. Royal Ruler Samuel Raiphualas II is a successor of the universe."

A glow surrounded The Golden Door, a tower appeared to be in an inferno. Samuel's control over two Mars allowed it to hover above the pyramid; black lightning continuously struck the tower.

"What this card tells me is that Royal Ruler Samuel Raiphualas II wants victory. Stress and tension develop in this card. This card carries determination, a passage to Varco-XVI will bring forth an upset. This is a powerful card and it will push forward with a need to become triumphant. A bright star turned dark thirsts for vengeance and now we find a mired love. His Majesty took an extraordinary double-sided woman from the ancient scrolls, and she is now at his mercy. He needs to wipe out her bright star—by doing this he will own her dark star for eternity."

Samuel's voice resounded with an order. "Distract the powerful pagans on Varco-XVI, bring me the blood of one," he commanded.

Ben and the scientists become startled by the dark spirit's voice. Feeling distinctly worried, they all moved further away from The Golden Door and kept their distance.

III-Empress passed through the mirrored gate on The Golden Door.

She reached for a card on the door from Samuel. "The third card: The Seven of Pentacles; trickery," the High Priestess clarified.

"Beware of this card as it offers trickery upon many. The paradises have six swords, and they're in authoritative hands. With the seven of Pentacles in your command, Empress, you must take away one sword. The sixth sword in the celestial domain, a spiritual sword. Double-edged steel can contribute to much havoc. A sword from the heaven's hierarchy defends Gabrielle, so brace yourself. Deception and betrayal are in this card. Two swords will stay in the ground as a reminder. An illusion will illuminate a person who is keeping a secret. Seven pentacles will be traumatic. It will serve as a dishonorable act."

Samuel fueled his neutrinos, and a burst across The Golden Door passed his unnerving voice in private, whereupon it reached III-Empress' consciousness. *"If you do not destroy Gabrielle and Michael, weaken them. I have superior beings waiting for their human essence. Find the golden Tablet. My need for you grows deeper, you will be mine."*

III-Empress nodded and passed through the gate. She bent forward and reached for her sword, deep-seated with seven pentacles. Her firm grip caused a sound that echoed as she set it in her scabbard.

The room darkened. The fourth card was the Ten of Cups hovering on The Golden Door. Glistening, sparkling, and shining, it was a message from Galasus.

Celestial rays rippled over the door and suspended this moment in time from Samuel.

The High Priestess used her psyche to relay Galasus' message. The Queen of the underworld's dark star moved out of her vision. It coiled inside a stillness where her radiant star illuminated.

"This card carries a sinister side with the yearning for a love with one not destined. Troublesome times are ahead, III-Empress. This card bears a senseless suffering. Your dark star's movement will arrange extreme obstacles on a magnificent new planet, Varco-XVI. A reminder that this card, when upright, can give you a freedom for your brilliant star. The Ten of Cups will bring a happiness for the dark or bright side; this card gives you an enlightenment to either an upright position or the reversed. Only one side will show the light, so choose a belief in this conflict," the High Priestess said and saw III-Empress acknowledged the message.

The scientists watched a dark star unveil in front of them—the enlightenment by Galasus. This reminder of her two celestial stars would aid her awareness in time.

III-Empress walked through the gate and put on the armor that appeared in front of her. There was a leading light showing the next card for the High Priestess.

"These two cards are joined and stay alongside of the Creator. The fifth card: Queen of Wands: XVIII-Moon: Queen Moon-Star. Ruler of Varco-XVI. She is a noble woman, proud, caring, and successful. She expects a Queen's throne—one adorned with fiery emblems of lions. Her moon is bright, and the sun shines by her side. There is a new symbol deep-rooted on her right wrist. She bears a forceful celestial vitality; it comes from the heart of the heavens. She is accompanied by a scepter expounding a noble power."

The Golden Door vibrated; Samuel sent out another directive. "I command your dark star," he said in a vibrating tone. "You will meet this so-called Queen. Cause her misery, destroy her," he decreed.

The Queen of the underworld's dark star learned what her plan was toward Moon-Star.

III-Empress went through the gate.

"These two cards are joined; and stay alongside of the Creator. The Sixth card: King of Wands: XIX-Sun: King Sun-Star. Ruler of Varco-XVI." The High Priestess nodded and continued.

"He's a noble man, proud, steadfast, successful, and compassionate. He is a man of great strength. A glorious robe embroidered with grapes drapes over his broad shoulders. There are vines climbing up a throne to be seen on it and it is etched with crystalline leaves. A new symbol is on his left wrist. Influential forces carry him a greatness, he draws this force in from the heart

162

of the heavens. His fire burns awaiting a glorious scepter, so he can rule alongside of his eye-catching Queen."

The Golden Door rumbled and Samuel's motivation came by way of a bloodlust. He was impatient, and a vengeance was now overpowering him. Samuel called for III-Empress. "Bring him seduction, bitterness, and trickery; destroy Sun-Star."

Her dark star now knew of Sun-Star, she was to destroy him.
III-Empress stepped forward through the gate.

Samuel hurled a card to the High Priestess; it was the Eight of Pentacles. She reached out and took it off The Golden Door.

"The Seventh card: The Eight of Pentacles," she said. "His Majesty picked up eight pentacles. A clever escape gave him back his privileged power. The eighth pentacle is an eight-pointed star symbol—a rosette. When this transformation is over, the pentacles will change to dark coins. He can transform her two stars with the Rosette Nebula in the celestial realms, but only upon his victory."

Stardust set down from the universe and encircled a rosette on III-Empress' wrist. The Rosette Nebula built up her strength for Samuel's connection. An intense burst of light passed through her left wrist; the eighth pentacle planted by Samuel was complete. The pentacles converted to eight dark coins.

When she finished the awakening, the High Priestess conversed with her Majesty on The Golden Door. She went into her psyche. The room went into a deep silence when the High Priestess stepped forward to engage in a meditation with her Majesty.

Samuel related a signal to the High Priestess, so she would understand who this woman was. She accepted. The High Priestess picked up a piece of information from his bright star. This was when his mind was distracted in the earlier stages of creation, and he had no idea if he had done anything. He tried to tell Galasus, but he was often hard to find or too busy. His disorder in his mind led him to a double star, now a winged woman in the theater's tapestries. She had asked for an afterlife as a Queen's sister in the eighteenth dynasty. The Council granted her wish and put both her stars on tapestries; a white dove hovered above and stipulated a rule over her two stars in the

Coliseum. The High Priestess saw this woman and Samuel showed her one example of a great power he had for retrieval.

The High Priestess nodded; she was spellbound by Samuel throughout this incantation. He ordered her to direct the ultimate message to III-Empress. "You must defeat Gabrielle, Michael, Sun-Star, Moon-Star, Efren, Saffron, an elite army and followers. They must perish. To declare this honor in the paradises, you must claim two spiritual thrones, two crowns, two scepters, a golden Tablet, and Varco-XVI. You must gain the gems and expose the Creator's message on the golden Tablet. The Rosette Nebula will set off in the night sky. Your sinister star will fade during the day when Galasus' star brightens."

The High Priestess bowed when the sands in the Bakoni Ruins whirled and showed a human likeness of a new Queen from the underworld.

"Inanna, you are III-Empress and the Queen of the masterful forces from the underworld. Violence and a ruling power are now upon your dark star."

Samuel sent out a bolt of black lightning to Inanna. She gasped for air and was now a part of a dark line of attack. His chilling voice directed a vibration for everyone to hear.

"This result justifies your dark power, together we will rule the entire universe," he said.

The High Priestess stood in silence and bowed her head to his Majesty. Samuel became silent.

III-Empress walked through the last gate and picked up her vase. There was a mysterious ember stirring a far-reaching luster in the inner core of the vase. It was her mercenaries spinning inside and held in by stardust; a ghostly command developed to serve a false Queen. Before Inanna could leave, she had to meet the gatekeeper from the underworld.

Dax was half fish and half human. His channeling card was the Ace of Cups. It opened from his torso and sparked a light. The Ace of Cups flashed a ray of illuminating stars. They drifted here and there. He lifted his right arm and his voice resounded to fill the room. "The forsaken of the underworld captured by his Majesty cannot escape." He inquired, "Who drew you to the surface from the underworld?"

"A great Pharaoh called for me," she replied.

He studied the sky and saw Sirius glowing; the Creator then enlightened him. Inanna lifted her head. He stared at her glassy eyes and stepped aside. The gatekeeper signaled and permitted the Queen of the underworld a final exit. Dax glared over to follow her, and he became curious about this attachment because it was with Alpha Draconis and not Sirius. He withdrew in a spiraling of cosmic dust.

Osahar saw the seven gates Inanna walked through, and it granted the order for annihilation with her dark star. Galasus took over her brilliant star.

Samuel's eyes brightened on The Golden Door. He concealed her dark star with two Mars and a rosette where he plotted a course for extinction. The High Priestess stayed in meditation.

"I now know who this woman is," Osahar said. "The High Priestess performed and brought a woman from the underworld through the seven gates. She handed over the Sumerian goddess Inanna. Samuel drew her aside, then took her from her sister and committed her to the underworld. Her sister is the legitimate Queen whom I do not know," he said and had another vision. "The real Queen fell to her knees when his dark star seized her, so she could never look at her sister again. There's a silver gate, and The Golden Door shows a constraint of the real Queen's spiritual presence. Inanna's power will sweep beyond the planet and arrive at the celestial beings. We now establish her by two Godly rulers; her tapestries are high ranking on planet Eugleston. The real Queen will rest on this Golden Door in silence."

Osahar also understood that she had the righteous essence for love, fertility, and warfare. He saw Galasus had arranged a set of pearls around her neck and he protected them from anyone noticing them with her bright star. Inanna was one of the most influential creations in the paradises and she remained a Monarch in the spiritual realms. Two magnificent stars would now rise on Varco-XVI. Samuel could seize her dark star upon victory and burn out Galasus' glittering star. This would force her to embrace Samuel for eternity. He had a want for Inanna's love. His plan would secure her as a faithful dark Queen at his side.

Silence filled the room; the scientists could not believe what they had just seen. Ben realized this movement on The Golden Door was just the beginning.

"The Pharaoh on this Golden Door will now proceed to his destiny," the High Priestess said. She raised both of her arms to execute an intense outburst of dust clouds. A whirlwind entered the pyramid and encompassed The Golden Door. Streams of cosmic dust moved up and struck the bronze gate, a vitality awakened the Pharaoh. Mira delivered an enormous source of power through The Golden Door. She extended her shockwave to surge for assistance from Valda and Vance. Orders were to open a portal to receive Inanna. They were both mindful of the request. Samuel had changed their mindset to work at his rule to open a suitable portal for Inanna. Valda and Vance took the book of magic and spells and worked.

Cassiel detected an intrusion, but the council decreed him to look away from this portal. They opened a portal to pick up the Queen of the underworld. Valda and Vance's yin and yang were off balance. Yin the feminine energy black, Vance controlled. Yang, the masculine energy white, Valda controlled. In the distance a tornado materialized, The Golden Door absorbed the swirling dust. Ramiel's shielded spirit validated her awakening. Ramiel gripped Inanna's hand and soared her up through The Golden Door. He placed her in the west side tomb.

Metatron reached for the High Priestess' hand. He turned to glance at Sandra. She gasped for air as his intense stare grabbed her interest. He walked through The Golden Door and the doors closed. Sandra sat abruptly with her heart beating strongly. She needed to find a way to get Metatron back to her.

The Golden Door darkened. Samuel was impatient. Osahar picked up his signal for two Mars. He watched Samuel send a streak of black lightning to Ramiel. Osahar's guarded watch saw Ramiel had raised Inanna from the monumental tomb. An unrestricted power showed a gleam of auroras flowing with two Venus. Inanna stepped into an inferno.

"Two Venus carried her to the east where she will rise the next day," Osahar confirmed.

Ben was concerned. "What just took place?" he asked. "Who is this woman?"

Osahar turned to Ben and responded. "The prophecy is in place. Gabrielle and Michael converted in the spiritual realms and deepened into

166

mighty warriors. They both carry many fighting techniques. Celestial connections will serve them well. Their Guardians are strong, and alongside is a spiritual army filled with an abundance of the paradises' privileges." Osahar nodded to Ben.

"Will the dark star meet up with Blake and Josh?" he asked. He clasped his hands and was quite concerned about this mysterious woman.

"Your sons will be fine, Ben. I know this," Osahar replied.

Ben turned, relieved, knowing Blake and Josh would not face Inanna's dark star. The teams scrambled to get footage together in order to broadcast to the world's military what had just happened.

Chapter Twenty-Four
Sariel, Metatron, and the High Priestess

The High Priestess was on Earth inside the enigmatic pyramid where her spirit was at the mercy of two Royal rulers in the universe: Samuel and Galasus. Her Divine cards came alive, and were freed by the Creator. The Creator kept her mindset in silence to the events that had transpired.

There were signs that a major campaign was brewing on Varco-XVI. Metatron felt a change in the universe when he returned the High Priestess to the northern side of the planet.

Her sparkling eyes acknowledged Sariel in the distance.

He stepped over to her and gripped her hands. She paused for a moment and drew in the want Sariel carried for her. An emotional moment caused her to close her eyes. She enjoyed a gentle kiss on her cheek as his soft lips crossed alongside her face. He hugged her. "Please forgive me, Eleanora," he whispered.

Trickery had caused them to move away from each other and they had not seen each other in centuries.

She stared into his fiery eyes. "I need more time, Sariel," she expressed.

Sariel stayed genuine. He glanced at her and added, "Let me point out, Eleanora, that something altered our mindset. My fondness remains heartfelt, please let us amend our differences. The paradises sanctioned us to come together."

The High Priestess was overcome by disappointment. She understood the Creator had contributed to a bitterness between them. Their love had been forced to eventually stir anger between them. She considered his irresistible warmth but she had to shift to resentment.

Facing him, she stared into his fiery dark eyes. But her mood suddenly changed. "Someone misplaced your emotions. My obligations stand to oversee Lady Gabrielle and all that follow and so are yours," she said in a huff. "Keep focused on the prophecy. Remember the circumstances our Creator and Galasus have instructed us to work out. Your mind weakens for a craving you shouldn't allow," she said and backed away from him. "You touched upon our past emotions; we have no time to negotiate a relationship." She pointed to the universe. "The Creator placed the forces to sway with my Divine cards, they are present as a challenge; you know this, Sariel. Osahar classified several stealthy cards on The Golden Door, I am kept in silence to these. Certain cards allow me to follow early development and the closing stages. What I do for this prophecy stays under Galasus' master plan and stays unknown. I am sworn to secrecy to the Creator and Galasus," she said and turned to Metatron.

The High Priestess flapped her cloak in an unexpected movement. She turned to mount a spiritual white horse situated nearby and galloped off quickly. She wanted to get back to Gabrielle as fast as she could.

Metatron stepped forward. "Please be strong, Sariel, a tenderness in our hearts will impair our decisions," he said.

"I realize this, Metatron, but I thought she might accept," he said disheartened with Eleanora's reaction.

"Something drew my awareness to a woman on Earth. She fascinated me with her elegance. This attempt on us and maybe others intensifies as a reversal in power, and our focus would become unstable in this prophecy. The Creator allows this passion, so if we leave our passage to go after another, we will fail. These encounters will only consume us. I will look elsewhere and stay focused. Many dark creatures exist on this planet, and they will create diversions. Treachery has come into play and it comes from the dark side. Someone meddles with our open hearts; we must be careful, Sariel," Metatron said as he made him aware.

"Yes, there's an obligation to be cautious. We can't let our thoughts be occupied with these women," he said. Then he drew in a deep breath and continued, "Galasus' master plan needs an undivided focus."

"We can do this."

"Yes, we can. Eleanora exists as my destiny. I will align my mind, or I will fight with her throughout this campaign. I hope we don't meet up too soon," he said and shook his head.

"Forget about her. Remember the High Priestess could soften and change her mind about wanting you," he pointed out.

"Thank you, for trying to make me feel better. But I doubt Eleanora will approach me. She is holding on to vengeance and is tireless when it comes to something like this," Sariel said.

Sylvie Gionet

"You realize she won't give in to you, Sariel. And you know the High Priestess rules an esoteric magic, and the Creator suppresses a force inside of her. Right now, her occult magic has her standing alone, so she can focus on Lady Gabrielle and Queen Moon-Star," Metatron replied.

"She won't be for long. I will go after her when we finish fulfilling our sworn oaths. Now I realize, and so does she," Sariel said and lifted an eyebrow.

"Yes, those are our intended women, so let's be strong," Metatron responded.

Sariel and Metatron focused on the task at hand and reminded themselves that they would guide and protect Gabrielle, Moon-Star, Michael, and Sun-Star.

Chapter Twenty-Five
Josh and Blake Travel the Vast Landscapes

Varco-XVI was home to an extensive choice of unique plants and many species of animals. Brushwood, to some extent, obscured the terrain between the plant life. Fruit trees and edible plants and safe drinking water were easy to come across. Josh and Blake traveled for hours on the east side of the planet. A large army and a team of companions hauled buggies and carriages with supplies behind the horses. A glimmer of sunbeams came through the massive trees and brightened the area.

"This place looks good, Josh, let's set up camp here," Blake said in a weary voice.

"It sure does; we need to rest. I must stretch my legs," Josh said while he was rubbing both hands along his aching legs.

Blake and Josh stopped and alerted the followers to set up camp. Large trees muffled the sound of flowing water. They decided to look around a bit and moved past the trees. Sparkling water was cascading down a waterfall and flowing over mossy rocks then out into a wide river.

Blake dismounted, and Josh followed him. Blake placed his hand on Josh's shoulder and asked, "Are you okay?"

"Sure, I'll be fine, but both my legs feel cramped, a good stretch will do. How are you feeling?" Josh asked.

"I'm fine, it sure is nice here." They both looked around at the planet's splendor.

Blake nudged Josh. "Hey, there's a woman standing by those big rocks, can you see her?"

Josh turned and faced the woman. She had on a long black hooded cloak and when she drew back the hood, her loveliness was revealed to Blake and Josh. The tall female with blonde hair and flickering caerulean eyes then approached the weary men.

"Wow, is she a messenger, Blake? Was she brought here to aid us?" he asked and watched her for clues. He wondered if she had a weapon.

"I hope so, let's go see why she is here. This chance meeting must be okay because Cassiel isn't here," he said and looked around the area. They both stepped forward and approached the woman.

Behind a set of towering rocks was her horse and a luminous vase.

A sudden warmth spellbound Blake. Inanna stepped toward them both. Her hand reached forward to shake Josh's hand. Then she leaned in and took a firm grip on Blake's.

"Hello, I'm Inanna, congratulations on your expedition to build a new Kingdom," she said in a cheerful tone.

Inanna's intense look had transformed Blake and Josh's perception of her; she had persuaded them for the moment to envision her as a messenger.

Cassiel picked up on this transformation. Her brilliant star appeared and showed Cassiel where her starting point was on the planet. He was aware of her plans, but he knew he had to stay away. When she departed, their mindset would switch back to him.

"I will travel alongside you for a brief time," she informed them while flirtatiously flailing her cloak.

Inanna's eyes had a glint of fire and focused on Blake's. A sparkle could be seen on her wrist and lit up her brilliant star. She wandered around him; seductiveness oozing from her curvy body. Then a blinding jolt passed through Blake and a passion for Inanna overtook him. Galasus imbedded a seed in both. But not only was Blake feeling a rush of awareness for Inanna, so too was Inanna feeling something unexpected—an enticing wakefulness. She turned away quickly when warmth rushed through her and flushed her skin.

Blake and Josh had now met a Queen from the underworld currently exposing her bright star, but who was an evil Queen with no forgiveness when her night star ascended. A gripping force possessed her when she approached Blake. A yearning for him enhanced and overshadowed her dark star. Inanna preoccupied herself with his magnetism. It was dynamic and like nothing she had ever known. Blake's existence distracted her. But a lingering thought reminded her that she needed to leave to fulfill a foretelling not known to her bright star.

Blake glanced over at Josh. "Well. We have someone who wishes to follow us," he said, his eyes sparkling.

Josh examined Blake's face and discovered his eyes were lit up like fireworks. He responded, "Sure, nice to meet you Inanna. Please join us for supper; Blake and I are setting up camp here for the evening. Then we will continue our journey in the morning where we will ride further east. From what we understand, our destination is not too far."

Mixed thoughts flooded Inanna's mindset; Blake fascinated her and the connection she felt to him was intense.

She approached him and gazed into his bright blue eyes. "Blake, I have to go, but I will come back," she said in a timid voice. She caressed her arms and sensed a happiness flowing through her.

The universe surged out and attached a celestial orbit to Galasus. He stuck a triskelion to her right wrist with a piece of his bright star to Inanna's brilliant star.

She raised her hand and discovered a set of pearls around her neck. Stardust had molded a bond for her, and it carried in lust. Now she could engage with Blake's affection. The pearls were firm around her neck and were protected by her bright star.

As she watched him, her mood became pleasant. His eyes sparkled like lustrous stars. Inanna felt hypnotized in Blake's presence and she could not stop looking at him. Their emotional calmness blended. Blake pulled Inanna closer and took a steady grip upon her body. He leaned in and pressed his soft lips to hers. She was enjoying his kiss; a deep passion sunk in and warmed their hearts. Inanna's thoughts faded into sensations as she was wrapped in Blake's arms.

Josh stood to one side, rubbing his head. He was checking the vicinity and wondered if anybody else would join them. His brother was different around this new messenger, and this left him unsettled. So he paced around looking for Cassiel.

Inanna had now broken an agreement with Samuel; an embracement of her dark star was meant to sit at Samuel's sinister side. This pledge had freed her sister's predestined life from bondage with Samuel, but delivered the suffering to her. Now Inanna's passion experienced another. Blake was a charming man, who had unknowingly met a Queen from the underworld.

But Galasus let her bright star shine in front of Blake. An intense experience with Inanna led Blake to wonder if he could ever be a part of her life.

He released her; she gasped for air and stared into his glossy eyes. This encounter confused Inanna as to what she was doing. She turned and departed. She went in an unfamiliar direction but her brilliant star glistened through a pointer. This signal showed her she needed to assemble her army in the north soon. Inanna drifted away.

Josh stared over at Blake and raised his eyebrows. "Blake, how refreshing," he said sarcastically. "You got to greet a woman messenger with a kiss. I thought you two would never end. You scared her away."

A surge of light was noticeable in the distance. Cassiel entered their view and stepped towards them.

"You are both working out what's expected of you," he said. "Move forward from your camp in the dawn." Turning to Blake he added, "A fine action executed."

"What did I accomplish, Cassiel?" Blake asked, puzzled.

"You warded off a marked woman who belongs to two unmatched Royals in the universe. She is III-Empress, Inanna. Both royals each have control over one of her stars. Her dark star belongs to his Majesty Samuel. Her bright star belongs to Highborn Leader Galasus. He will work his rule within her bright star. Galasus will try to bring her freedom from a conflict that Samuel has placed upon her," he said and walked around them. "After you complete the magnificent Kingdom, she will aim to kill you both and all who follow." Cassiel saw Blake and Josh were confused about this new encounter. "But," he said and waved his hand, "you came upon her brilliant star; this is a pleasant part of her being. Her bright star is part of Galasus' master plan."

Josh threw his arms up in the air and huffed. "He kissed her, Cassiel. I thought they would never stop. We believed she was a messenger. I knew something wasn't right," he said and crossed his arms.

"She is not a messenger. Inanna has fallen in love with your brother. She accepted Blake and will come back for him."

Not thrilled with this outcome, Josh frowned. "Oh sure, it figures," he said in a strained voice. "You would have to fall in love with a woman who follows her dark side." He rubbed his face. "Wow, this is great, and now we know she occupies a twofold of stars that are just waiting to explode." Josh rubbed his arms. "Blake, what exactly did you accomplish?"

Cassiel moved in and answered. "No need to worry, Josh, her love is real and so is Blake's. There is a positive and negative view of this prophecy. Mindsets mean everything on this planet. You're both managed by the Great One. Inanna's psyche could not contain you indefinitely, only for a brief time. Our Highborn Leader, Galasus, allowed this," Cassiel said.

Blake had warded off the Queen from the underworld. What he had accomplished was to be able to make her brilliant star more prominent and stable. This left Inanna with an intense belief in him.

Inanna was currently sheltered behind the rocks as her mind was filled with a desire for Blake. This reaction to Blake was like nothing she had ever known. She had a passion for him that felt as if it could not be filled. Her bright star sparked on her wrist, and it triggered a thought on how and when she should leave. Then it began falling into place when she realized her two stars would work with a prophecy. Inanna understood she must not show her emotions for Blake when her night star ascended. She looked down at both her wrists and saw mystical symbols streaming stardust. She did not know how to interpret her dark star yet. But she thought this encounter might contribute to a dark view of Blake, and she would end him. Inanna became preoccupied with her intention, and realized she must find someone to block her emotions in her bright star. She was worried this could be beyond her powers.

"Inanna is the sufferer; she is a Godly figure on planet Eugleston. She spent some time in power and reigns over a dark and a bright tapestry. The tapestries were both awakened in the underworld," Cassiel said. "Samuel controls her night star. He permits her to enforce misery and death. But her day star works through Galasus; when risen it will sparkle with her kindness, Blake," Cassiel clarified.

Josh was not amused. "What are you trying to take care of?" he asked. "You assume you're courageous enough to cage her up when her night star rises. It will be hard work to try to take on a Queen from the underworld. She will probably execute us after we finish our mission," he said, and was looking for a reaction. "Blake, listen to me, we understand nothing about what this dark woman is prepared to do. Remember, we know nothing about this planet."

Blake

Blake did not know how to respond. He stared at Cassiel and he acknowledged him. "Just work out what your spirit seeks, Blake," Cassiel said. "You will discover her two sides in time."

Josh was tenser than before, as he was certain this would lead to death. "This is foolish to put Blake in harm's way," he expressed to Cassiel. "How could you do this to my brother?" Josh walked to Blake's side with a troubled expression on his face.

Cassiel extended an unyielding expression to Josh. "Blake will be fine," he replied with an impassive stare.

Josh struggled to comprehend the danger of Inanna's two stars.

"Okay, I will take care of you the best I can," Josh said in a tired tone. "There is a two-sided woman on this planet, and she realizes she has an opportunity with you," he said and shook his head. "This puts me on the edge. Let's ask the Creator for a mental boost to deal with her. Gabrielle and Michael will eventually face this woman and she will definitely unleash an evil force," Josh said.

Blake's stare was uncertain. "I will think of Gabrielle and Michael, Josh, with the hope that Inanna will meet them with a positive mindset." He stared at Josh and hoped he would understand.

Inanna was now behind an enormous mountain of jagged rocks. She understood what she needed to do now. She was to seek the golden Tablet. So, now she must go back before nightfall to accept another passionate kiss from Blake. This would set up a kiss to bond them as one, that might lead to his death.

Blake understood Cassiel supported Inanna's bright star. She added an unusual relationship to the prophecy.

Josh realized that Blake was too emotional to think clearly. He knew he needed to stand by his brother, to be of aid when Inanna materialized.

"I accept this new proposal, Cassiel," Josh said. "But how did a double star Queen take control of my brother?" This weighed heavily on his mind.

Cassiel ignored Josh and saw he accepted this new obligation. He glided away.

Cassiel's sudden departure and this alternative approach irritated him. Josh slapped his hands to his side and went on to the campsite with Blake where the army and companions had finished setting up.

Several followers had set up a large timber table with an appetizing meal of beef, lamb, bread, vegetables, fruit, and wine.

Two attendants walked quickly across the grounds to alert the brothers. "Time to eat," one attendant said.

As they walked over, Josh glared at Blake and saw his brother was obviously thinking about this woman. He swung his head and considered it too. *Why did this woman create a bond with my brother?*

Josh and Blake enjoyed a quiet dinner.

"I'm tired, it's been a long day, and an interesting one wouldn't you say?" Josh frowned as he asked this. "Let's follow through with this new connection, Blake." He stood and moved aside from the table. "It's time for me to clean up in the river, we can talk tomorrow. I assume the Lady of the day went away," he said and looked around the surrounding area.

Blake reached out his hand to shake his brother's. "Be strong, Josh, our solidarity as brothers will take us through this," he said with surety.

"For sure, let's stay focused, and remember Cassiel is by our side," he said and looked skyward.

"Good night."

Josh strolled over to the tumbling water of the waterfall and waded into the shallows of the pool at the bottom. The water swirled around his feet and over the edges of stones and large flourishing trees. Sudden worries of Gabrielle came to mind. *How can I get her in my arms? I hope, no, I believe she is safe.* A spray of refreshing water soaked his face. He disrobed and dove into the flowing water. Upon surfacing, Josh took a deep breath and felt his mood lifting. The brisk water and ambiance set him at ease. An attendant stood by the edge of the pool. Refreshed and dripping wet, Josh walked out of the rushing water. He wandered up into a clump of sand, where an attendant passed him a large towel. He covered himself.

"Thank you," he said to the attendant.

"You're welcome, I've arranged shaving gear and separate things for you," the attendant replied and pointed the way, then strolled away with a pile of his dirty laundry.

Josh cleaned up and shaved. When he finished, he walked along the landscape and sensed an uncertainty in the air. He hoped it would pass. He got back to his tent and, flipping the tent flap open, he spotted clean clothing spread out on the bed. The darkness drew nearer, Josh closed the tent flap and settled in for the night.

Blake had been sitting at the table staring upward to find how much daylight remained. Summer warmed the air, and the days were longer. He stretched his long legs out and moved away from the table. He also decided to take a stroll toward the river and when he reached it, he stripped off entirely. With arms overhead, he readied into a diving position and dove into the water. The air in his lungs forced him to the surface and he carried out a few strokes to get him further into the river. He turned over and floated effortlessly on top of the rippling water. As he gazed at the sky, his thoughts turned to consider a future with a woman from the underworld. Blake marveled . . . *was it even possible to keep Inanna's magnificent star? So she will sparkle for me?*

Some form of river creature jumped near him, spraying droplets of water all over his face. The sun was reflected in the spray and a rainbow appeared from one side of the river to the other. As he finished washing, he swam back to the shore and walked along the sandy ground. An attendant was standing by and placed a large towel in his hands. With a twist of the towel, he tucked it in around his lean waistline. He noticed the attendant had placed a basin on a table with a shaving kit and separate assorted items.

"Thank you," Blake said.

"You're welcome," he replied and wandered off with a pile of Blake's dirty laundry.

Soldiers and attendants had put the tents up at the lake's east end. Soldiers patrolled the territory, as they were aware a strange woman had entered the region.

Feeling refreshed, he was amazed at how he met this girl, and how she spread her passion through him. Her softness had showed a blush of her radiance that lit up her face. His cautious nature had him questioning. *Will I ever meet her dark star? I don't want my brother to face the danger I have brought upon us.*

He paced to the tent to rest for the night. Upon entering, he noticed the attendants had arranged clean clothing on the bed.

Suddenly, the silhouette of the rocks beside the tent molded into Inanna. She came out before the darkness fell and was watching the sky for a night star. But both of her motifs on her wrist evolved with little tugs of swirling stardust. This symbol showed there was little time. Inanna slipped into Blake's tent. He twisted around and confronted her. With both arms extended she rushed to him. She brushed her palms along his exposed chest. With a gentle tenderness, Inanna kissed his sturdy upper body everywhere. Both hands moved up to embrace a muscular torso. She stared into his entranced eyes. Then she pushed forward to place a kiss upon his awaiting lips. Blake pulled her curvy body closer. His desire for Inanna was overwhelming. He did not recognize what Inanna had succeeded in doing, and he didn't know she now possessed Blake's life. She had placed a brush of death upon her selected man.

Inanna backed up, but Blake had an urge to kiss her again. She knew embracing him again would give him an advantage over her brilliant star. They both blossomed with excitement. It rose to peaks of a powerful reaction for each other. Blake stood at the mercy of Inanna, he pressed forward and held her tightly. The intensity astounded them both.

"I am yours for eternity, Blake," she whispered softly in his ear.

He rubbed her arms. "You are mine until the end of time, Inanna."

Strong arms pulled her in. "I realize you are a dark star and a bright star. I will stay away from your night star, so come in the day," he said. "There is a Royal who is a dark star in the universe, and he is torturing you. We can work out his darkness. Highborn Leader Galasus is in control of your bright star," he said. "We will find a way." His eyes brightened at the thought. There might be hope for her.

"You are my genuine love sent to me from the paradises." She placed a finger on his lips. "My desires are real, my heart blossoms with a love in your presence, and it warms my essence. I have a choice; my bright side wants you. I know nothing of this darkness. When it falls upon me on this planet, then I will understand," she said sincerely.

Blake held Inanna tight. She faded into his muscular arms to hang onto his strength. The passion of kissing was nothing like they had ever experienced, and it was still rising. He was spellbound by Inanna when she took his seed. Blake lifted his hand to stroke her face and stared into her glistening eyes. As she turned away, he moved aside to get dressed.

Sparks entered her rosette, and a sudden movement in her wrist caused her to glance down at it. coiled on both wrists. Now a powerful feeling showed a dark star pulling closer. This Stardust movement allowed her to detect a satchel containing a tablet in the corner. A quick peek over her shoulder showed Blake still getting dressed.

"I must leave, it appears I have violated a rule," she said in a trembling voice.

Blake turned. "I will resolve this darkness in time," he said. "Our meeting is due to Galasus. Please remember, I carry your bright star in my heart." Inanna ran her hand along his smooth chest to touch where Blake's heart lay. She studied his eyes as he slid his hand over her heart. A radiant spark of light surfaced; the spiritual influence had joined them. They were as one on the bright side in the paradises.

"I will help you, I have faith we will be together again one day," he said and stared into her emotional eyes.

She brushed her lips along Blake's cheek, and turned to exit the tent. She took and hid the golden Tablet from Blake.

As her day star weakened, her dark strength was enhanced. A reminder warned her brilliant star to leave and ride fast to the north. Inanna mounted her horse and steered the reins to ride to a castle on the northern side of the planet. With a brilliant star and a dark star, the two sides gave her an opportunity to accept who she could love. Inanna chose Blake because Galasus made her aware through her bright star that his mindset was one with the Creator. Samuel alone could control Inanna's dark star. But Inanna needed to be careful. This passion she shared with Blake might be obvious to Samuel.

The High Priestess had contributed to an awakening in that she prepared a Queen from the underworld to walk through seven wrought-iron gates. A bright and dark star from the underworld had been raised. Galasus gave Planet X a channeling card, and it hid a secret within Inanna. The Eight of Cups reached her splendid pearls. When a solitary star rekindled, the Anunnaki people would power her freedom to the bright or dark side of the realms.

Chapter Twenty-Six
Gabrielle Reaches her Second Destination

After her chance meeting back at the castle, Gabrielle was unsure what was taking place within her mind. She left the castle in a rush as the gala had wreaked havoc on Moon-Star's emotional well-being. Apparently, she could not stop thinking about her mother's many mood changes.

They traveled alongside of their companions across a stunning landscape when Gabrielle pointed out a splendid sunset.

"The sun is casting a rose-colored beam through those clouds, Moon-Star; it's perfect," she said and leaned over her horse to get her attention.

Moon-Star smiled at her mother, then she focused on the sunlit clouds.

The last of the heat blew through the trees and sunbeams glistened on the leaves. The faint swooshing sound of leaves settling could be heard. Rays flashed and passed through a series of giant timbers. They watched the radiant sun fade out. And a lustrous full moon filled the night sky. It moved in and arrived at full view. The long journey had taken its toll on Gabrielle and she realized they must stop to set up camp. Ahead, she noticed a fog rising. It turned out to be a valley below them covering a small town.

Saffron raised her arm to stop everybody. "I will continue forward, my Lady." The army swung into position and continued to the front in search of any danger. Spirit birds spread their massive wings and soared into flight, gleaming eyes watchful of the perimeter. While the clever fox pushed to the front, spirit wolf and bear sat by Gabrielle and Moon-Star's side.

Saffron returned with good news.

"My Lady, this town is vacant, I detect no risk. We can rest here. Our infantry waits on patrol."

Moon-Star glanced over at her mother. "Okay, let's go."

"I will position our army and companions in the neighboring houses, later I will join you for dinner," Saffron said.

"This place is perfect," Gabrielle said as she leaned back on her horse. "We will see you soon, Saffron." Gabrielle and Moon-Star and a few others stayed to take in the view while the companions went on ahead to start setting up the camp.

The group then traveled on a dirt path and reached a picturesque village with a stunning view. There was a special world in front of them, and it was filled with similar features to Earth. A big moon brightened the night sky with radiant beams. Green grass had plenty of lit torches inserted at points to light their way. The ambient lighting edged the path together with multicolored flowers. Crafted fountains poured out water, beside were wells with buckets attached. Fire pits burned with anchored cauldrons on top. Gabrielle and company arrived at a large stone-built house partway covered in climbing ivies.

The High Priestess had led in a few companions to arrange dinner and set up a few bedrooms in the house. Gabrielle's sudden departure meant that they hadn't eaten before leaving as she was impatient to leave the castle. Her companions walked up to take their belongings off their horses and they all went inside. The High Priestess pointed in a direction. Gabrielle nodded and paced through a lengthy hallway. Moon-Star followed and found a room. She grasped a shiny brass handle and opened a sizeable wooden door. Shimmering moon beams misted over the acacia windows. Two large beds with fine linen and big fluffy pillows on top had been made up for them. They noticed two basins filled with water, and alongside an arrangement of toiletries and towels were available.

"Wonderful, let's get cleaned up," Gabrielle suggested. She walked over and opened a set of sculpted acacia windows. She took a deep breath when a gentle breeze arrived without a break. The ivory silk curtains fluttered alongside her face.

Moon-Star stared at Gabrielle wondering how her mother was dealing with what had happened. The spiritual animals in the dungeon made her worried that her mother was at risk. "Mother, you know you have two spiritual animals in a dungeon at the castle? A white dragon and a black cobra."

"I know, Saffron will enlighten me about them when the time comes," Gabrielle said. She recalled that Moon-Star had seen the dragon and the cobra.

The High Priestess walked out into the hallway. She called upon Gabrielle and Moon-Star, "My Lady and Queen, come into the kitchen."

Moon-Star hurried alongside her mother. "I'm hungry," she said.

"Yes, let's go eat," Gabrielle said and pointed the way to the kitchen.

Fresh bread and food cooking met the air and changed Gabrielle's mood. She now understood that their hasty departure without eating had weakened her. Notions of not being reliable set into her consciousness. As they entered the kitchen, she noticed attendants had arranged the chairs at a large timber table. Moon-Star pulled out a chair and worried if her mother was even hungry.

Saffron gripped a chair beside Gabrielle and joined them for an enjoyable late dinner.

"My Lady, our army and attendants have set up camp in a way to be ready to leave in the early morning."

"Excellent, thank you, Saffron."

The High Priestess analyzed Gabrielle. She seemed unsettled. So she left the kitchen to find a place where she could investigate her current frame of mind. Long branched out hallways led to a lit passage. Sconces affixed on the stone walls created a brightness leading to an open chamber. A towering stone fireplace was situated ahead. She lit a spiritual light on a pile of timber, a fire ignited. As she took in her surroundings, she noticed sturdy high-backed chairs and a large marble table surrounded by plush red velvet seats. More acacia windows with ivory silk curtains that fluttered were framing a view of the moon. Bulky candelabras shone on a polished surface, and she set ablaze many candles. Paranormal sanctions sent in a heavenly force to enclose her. An upsurge of fire tinted the bulky stone walls with reflections from the flames. She drew herself into a meditation and rubbed her crystal ball. Her vision grew, but Saffron then entered the well-lit room.

"You set up a charming ambiance, High Priestess. Let us set the mood with a warm drink, I'll be right back." Saffron flared her cloak to one side and exited the room. She went back to the kitchen to steep a pot of tea and considered Gabrielle and Moon-Star. *They might want to relax by the fireplace with a cup of tea too.*

But when she entered the kitchen, she met up with them leaving. Saffron met Gabrielle's weary eyes.

"Moon-Star and I need rest, say goodnight to the High Priestess for us. Thank her for arranging dinner." Her tired eyes were drooping.

"Good night, Saffron, we will see you in the morning," Moon-Star said.

Saffron acknowledged Gabrielle and Moon-Star, they both appeared fatigued. In view of Gabrielle's eyes, Saffron examined her for change. But she could not detect a weakness in her mindset. "As you wish," she replied. "Have a good sleep, we will be ready to leave at dawn, goodnight."

Feeling drained, Gabrielle and Moon-Star headed over to their room. As they entered, attendants continued to fill two large bathtubs with pails of water. They both decided to undress and have a bath before bed. Gabrielle set her head back against the rim and struggled to relax. Eventually, they both stepped out of their baths and got dressed. Moon-Star swept a brush through her long dark hair, and then Gabrielle leaned in and braided it. Moon-Star stretched both arms and yawned. Then she jumped into bed.

Several unlit candles lined the window ledge. There was a small candle lit in front of her, Gabrielle picked it up and lit another.

"Goodnight, Moon-Star."

Moon-Star felt secure squeezing one of her pillows; she sunk her head in one. "Goodnight, have a good sleep, Mother."

Gabrielle rested against the edge of her bed and brushed her hair. She realized they were both exhausted.

Moon-Star fell into a deep sleep.

Her knee sank into a spacious bed, and she positioned herself on the bed to stare at a blank ceiling. Still feeling restless, Gabrielle closed her eyes with a thought: this edginess will pass.

***

Inanna arrived at her destiny. A castle shone under a northern murky sky. Drawing on the reins, Inanna dismounted her black stallion and removed the encrypted vase off the saddle. The golden Tablet went under her arm, then she turned and stepped up a set of limestone stairs. Inanna felt a potent energy inside of her. Samuel had instructed her to go to a set of iron gates. She placed her items on the ground, and with both arms raised, pushed open the gates. When a flurry of air rushed through her hair, she realized that Samuel had unlocked her mindset to notice his dark star rising on her wrist. He was building up her leadership from inside a cryptic pyramid beside the castle. Pillars of star trails streamed in from the Rosette Nebula, and her dark star lined up. Cosmic rays routed a sorcerous dust through her body, to set up an awakening to interlock with Samuel's overwhelming power. She walked into the dreary castle and arranged her vase on the ground. She positioned the sack by a throne and pulled out the Tablet. Samuel's actions were guiding her rule now. Two Mars fed the cryptic pyramid with arcs of black lightning. Her rosette carried a steady flow from Samuel's energy. He was ready to give an order to her dark star—for a campaign on the north and south side of Varco-XVI.

***

Gabrielle fell asleep and started dreaming. A warning emerged and she woke up frightened. One of the small candles flickered by the acacia windows; a murkiness roiled on the stone walls. She slipped out of bed and went near the window to gaze through. She saw a peaceful town, no one was around. Gabrielle faced the entrance. Why was there no view of her army and spirit animals on patrol?

Trickery was in play, but those thoughts of no one being around drifted aside. She peeked out the window and looked to the south where she noticed the Tree of Life, and alongside was the Fountain of Enlightenment. She could see an apparition of a woman floating above a large rock; a glow erupted from her torso. Her eyes cast a featherlike wave straight to Gabrielle's psyche. This woman directed an enchantment upon her, to change her point of view so she would go outside. Gabrielle got dressed and made sure Moon-Star was asleep. She moved across the room quickly and left the house. Air rushed through her hair and Gabrielle walked over to meet this woman. But she was nowhere to be found. Intense winds surged up and surrounded her. Whispered words filled the air, but she could not make out what those words were saying. Her eyes became fixed on the Fountain of Enlightenment; a white clam shell materialized. She reached in and took it. Water dripped from her hand as she clutched the shell. It opened and a white papyrus rose from it; she rolled it open and viewed the black writing. Her eyes scanned the black print and she recited the words on the note out loud.

"An action requires your strength, Lady Gabrielle. This is in front of you. Find this before Moon-Star moves to her death. Your road is ahead, let your journey begin." Gabrielle glanced skyward and believed what she had achieved might get sabotaged, now she needed to protect Moon-Star.

185

Flames erupted and the papyrus caught on fire. She dropped it to the ground and watched the note fade. Her mind drifted as she looked around. Now she was in line to travel to a dark place. Gabrielle examined the night sky. Her consciousness understood that she must go alone, or her daughter might die.

She moved quickly back to the house knowing she must get ready for a quest to protect Moon-Star. Gabrielle's mindset unfurled her full armor and she tightened the clasps around her arms and body. Her magnificent sword glittered as she placed into a sheath on her loin belt. A quick check took her to find Moon-Star asleep, so she picked up her shield and exited the room and went out of the house.

She mounted her horse, sunk her boots into the stirrups and gripped on the reins tightly. Dark clouds seeped into the small town. Powerful lights beamed down and shone as a pathway. Gabrielle continued to gallop along a path she believed was leading to a purpose.

Saffron and the High Priestess were still enjoying a cup of tea by a lambent fireplace. Suddenly, the High Priestess' cards bolted upward and showed her something astounding.

Two cards fell into her view, they entangled inside a mist of roiling silver flames. XIII-Death and the Queen of Swords reached her. She accepted these cards and recited them.

Her sacred book opened and she placed the cards on top. "There's a stretch of blue tuscan teal dahlias. This essence will lead to a secret in time. Daisies are in her path. This exposes a betrayal of trust, a pearl put in her hand has control over her psyche. This celebrated pearl must stay with Lady Gabrielle." An alarm rang in her mind, and she stared over at Saffron.

"Raguelle gave Lady Gabrielle an exquisite pearl. This treasured stone is on her wrist," Saffron said.

The High Priestess studied the cards and read more in her book. "These messages show a distraction was placed upon Lord Michael when he was in simulated warfare. Raguelle reached his mindset through a guarded essence in the universe. She must return to the paradises. A restoration of her high spirits must expel an evil seed planted inside of her."

Cosmic dust sent an outburst to exit on both cards. Feathers of many colors directed a message to the High Priestess, glistening in its core, setting out a scene.

"This feather shows a turnaround in a destiny. I see a white and black tapestry in Gabrielle's path, this foretells a shift in her mindset. She does not understand what lies ahead. A patch of sunflowers in the distance shows a warning, an entity will seize her. This could end her life."

The High Priestess jumped up, faced Saffron, and advised her. "Alert the army and the spirit animals, use your inner powers. Gabrielle met an entity who put her on a path of danger. You must go to her now," she said in an alarmed voice.

Saffron dashed to her room to find Gabrielle was not in her bed. She saw Moon-Star remained safe and asleep. By raising both her arms she activated her magic. She sealed the windows with a flame and a blend of a fiery dust enlarged her eye-catching pentacles. Silver lightning streamed and delivered an order through her psyche. It reached the army. "Warfare is upon us."

Her mystical powers released the army and spirit animals from bondage—a dark incantation that had been placed upon them. Fear twisted in her gut. She thought about how this dark magic came through Gabrielle's pearl bracelet. The army and spirit animals rushed to the house. Saffron hurried outside.

"The battle begins," she said. Saffron raised her shield and gripped her sword by her side. "Celestial army, I need ten soldiers to follow me. Raven and hawk take flight. Spirit owl and fox secure our Queen. Spirit, wolf, and bear, be the driving force, and fight the dark spirits to their death." Female warriors fell out to Saffron's orders and arranged for combat.

She mounted her horse and followed a trail to find Gabrielle. They traveled at a fast pace. Then a vision appeared to her and it became uneasy in her thoughts. Now troubled, she knew Gabrielle was on route to a dark place and she was alone.

The High Priestess ran to Moon-Star's room and created a sphere around her. A dark power entered upon their psyche and cut the link to Gabrielle from them. Thoughts of how a restraint had fallen upon their army and spirit animals confused her. How this could have happened? She sat in a chair by the bedside to guard Moon-Star, then she moved into a deep meditation.

Outside, the warriors lined up and unfurled their armor to grip their bodies. Their hands reached for their loin belts and they drew their swords. Impenetrable shields were raised high and fastened to their arms. Women warriors set up a formation, they drew the bows and arrows off their backs and brought them in hand. Another line of the formation had jeweled spears fixed to hurl. The horses swept the ground with their hoofs and became restless, as they were ready to engage in warfare. In the remote sky, a sequence of spiraling galaxies progressed inward and plummeted down. When they arrived they flattened the soil. Upheavals in the universe propelled a deafening sound. Gravity pushed in a lethal ingredient: dark energy and it was freezing the ground. Shockwaves echoed a warning. Cosmic spiraling arms neared the small town, ominous veils spread out long-lasting sets of fiery and frozen trails. Murky clouds ejected a group of phantom horses, and dark warriors arose from the swirling clouds. They placed themselves on the backbones of vaporous mounts, and numerous horses treaded with a great effort into town. The High Priestess listened to the swords clanging and the shrieks that followed.

Moon-Star awoke, and when she got up, she noticed a sphere encircled her bed; it startled her. A quick glance over showed her mother was not in her bed. She scanned the table to see her sword and shield were gone. The noise outside the window got louder.

"Where is my mother?" she asked. "What's happening outside?" She tossed the blankets off and moved to the side of the bed. She stared at the High Priestess.

"Please, my Queen, calm down, bear with me. Saffron will be back soon, let us see what has become known."

Moon-Star gazed at the High Priestess with a flustered expression. This notion of her mother leaving her in the night kindled a panic.

Gabrielle's pearl swirled in a dark star's dust and created a false guidance which altered everybody's insight.

A deceitful passage had been placed in Gabrielle's dreams. This forced her to go into a realm of danger. Raguelle's mindset moved through a sphere in the cosmos, but she did not realize she had reached a maze followed by trickery; it took hold of her. This downfall contributed to the journey and became the alarming prime point for Samuel's bid to take over.

Gabrielle followed this predestined route and arrived in a field. She tugged on the reins and stopped her horse. She had reached her destination but her mindset was disoriented.

"Why am I here?" she said aloud.

***

Back at the castle. Inanna located the serpent keeper in the constellation of Serpens, Ophiuchus. Her signal to him showed her attachment to his Majesty and it was absent in the paradises. Ophiuchus obeyed the command and tilted the celestial equator, to give his Majesty an offensive to succeed with a poison. This power went straight to Inanna whereupon she, together with the pyramid, uncovered a monstrous silhouette in Serpens.

The galactic plane moved up in the Milky Way Galaxy, a widespread object cropped up in the northern Hemisphere. Gaseous clouds in the remote sky tossed out a set of spiraling arms, their bends creating a disquieting shape. The constellation of Orion veiled Ophiuchus' movement in the realms. Each segment of Serpens' eruption cast numerous immovable dust clouds. Shockwaves forced out a compelling pressure. An enormous tail moved in from the west. Serpens sculpted a cobra's head to face north. Sketchy paths dimmed the night sky and a ghostly figure wrapped a large frame inside a blend of vaporous clouds.

Gabrielle continued in silence. This trickery was still playing with Gabrielle's mind and would prove to interfere with her leadership. She noticed fields of sunflowers pop up with a tint of lively yellow. Being familiar with the smell of lingering incense burning, this opened a calming within her.

The Orion constellation demonstrated the setup of the betrayal, which drew a malevolence forth from the Serpens. On the ground, a shadowy oversized apparition slithered through a spectral cloud, and it spotted Gabrielle.

Her feisty horse bucked and lifted two front legs. She pushed heavily on the stirrups and pulled on the reins. Now Gabrielle understood that a serpent approached. There was a fiery gas cloud plummeting toward her, leading in an enormous serpent. She set up her impenetrable shield, but the serpent sensed a danger with this shield and veered away. Turning and twisting inside the gaseous clouds, the serpent sprung backward to retrace a route. It hid in the gaseous clouds, plotting an assault to pierce her with its venomous bite. Inanna issued an order to kill Gabrielle and bring her the grand sword she carried by her side.

The coiled snake inside a nebulous cloud was above her, and its vast shadow cast a silhouette across the land. She looked up to see the creature en route to her. Gabrielle became disoriented as she spun on her horse. It was out of control. Her spirited horse prompted her to defend herself, but she shifted to a position which left her open to attack. It was too late; she was now the victim of the viperous creature. Near enough to grab her in its powerful jaws, the white cobra arrived at her left shoulder.

"Moon-Star," she called out. The serpent bit her and forced her to the ground and squeezed her tight, attempting to leave her lifeless. Gabrielle became the victim, held by a viperous grip with no release. Now the serpent had time to inject a lethal venom.

Her talisman swung up and worked to overcome the serpent, and managed to disable the cobra. This action shocked the mammoth cobra into letting her go. A binding power vibrated through the terrain, causing the serpent to be unresponsive. Gabrielle's great sword remained by her side; the serpent did not recover it for Inanna. But it had succeeded in delivering a venomous bite and her seemingly lifeless body lay on the ground.

Seven jeweled cups appeared and floated above Gabrielle, then vanished.

Saffron's white raven and hawk led the way. Soldiers galloped alongside. Saffron raised both arms to shape a pentagram in the night sky. Black fire kindled a trail of silver lightning, firing a warning into the cosmos. Her psyche attached an alert to the pentagram, Gabrielle was in danger.

***

On the southern side of the planet, Efren received a remote signal from the universe. His opaque eyes scanned upward and he accepted a distress signal from Saffron. Her pentagram image settled upon him. Now he must go to her. Quick sparks flared out from his fingertips and formed a sphere around Michael and Sun-Star. Efren motioned for the army to be on high alert. He assigned the spirit animals to guard Michael and Sun-Star.

Sun-Star leaned on Michael and fell over. Michael grabbed him and panicked. He called over to Efren. "Where are you going?" he asked.

"I will tell you afterward, I must go to the northern side, my Lord."

Efren cast a mirrored pentagram and mounted his steed. He hurried through to reach the northern side.

Michael put Sun-Star on the ground and held him in his arms. He faced a darkened sky and called to the Creator. "Please go to Gabrielle, I know she is in danger. Support Efren, stand your ground with him." His hands trembled as he held onto Sun-Star. Efren's rapid departure confused him and Sun-Star being on the ground filled him with doubt. *Is this the end?* His throat clenched and his chest tightened with fear.

To be continued…

About the Author

The Guardians of the Sun-Star and Moon-Star: The Battle Begins, is Sylvie's second novel in heroic fiction. Inspired by creation, humankind assisted in turning the pages in the cosmos. Follow her into book three, as it brings plenty of adventures in the spiritual and supernatural world.

Sylvie's fascinations draw her into the cosmos and the ancient texts on the spiritual and supernatural. Her love of learning keeps her actively exploring the many facets of life's possibilities.

A Halloween Adventure with Jack and Ony Lantern is her most recently published book and her first children's book.

Author Sylvie L. Gionet

Made in the USA
Columbia, SC
15 July 2021

41892656R00114